THE
MARKED
CHILDREN

For Gert Visser
Another time, a different place.

CHAPTER 1

Silence. The forest is filled with it. Shallow breathing, accompanied by the rhythmic thudding of my shoes against the gravel, however, breaks the silence. The world sounds different when no one is awake. It's as if nature only reveals its true form when no one is watching. Only to those who are patient enough to seek it out.

My pace suddenly changes as I shift onto the road surface. Small droplets of dew still cling to the pavement, causing me to adjust my stride. The roads are absent of vehicles, and no light escapes the windows of the buildings I pass, forcing me to rely on stray road lamps to light the way. It is on days like these that I can almost make out a faint humming sound in the air surrounding me. Maybe the Earth emits it when all is silent, or perhaps the barely audible vibrations are always present, just not noticeable. Sometimes, on particularly cloudy mornings, I need to cover my ears if it gets too loud.

Turning a corner, I witness the Sun embrace the dark sky with its warm touch, causing the stars along with the veil of the universe to fade away. Then, as if all the brightly lit colours on a single canvas melted together only to roll off and drop into the ever-stretching abyss, the stratosphere is flawlessly laced with a mirage of gleaming colours. A melting horizon.

Every morning, I start my day with a jog in the woods. In a world that is persistently changing, to me, this seems to be the only constant. Living just a few blocks away, it's hardly a hassle to make the trip. I swear, this is one of the only reasons I get up in the mornings. That, and my mom and little brother. We live in a small, isolated house close to the edge of the forest. I wouldn't label us as poor or anything, but we definitely aren't rich either. We're getting by, which is more than most people can say, so I'm not complaining.

A few years after Carter was born, we sold our old home and moved across the country. I don't remember much from that time—only that my parents always seemed to be in a hurry. Most of our possessions were left behind, as they didn't fit in the moving van, or would have been of little use if they had. This included old photo albums, childhood toys and most of Mom's artwork.

Our current home isn't exactly next in line for the Most Charming House on the Block award. Compared to the rest of the neighbourhood, the old, rickety structure seems outmoded to say the least. Dad called this place a "fixer upper". He was supposed to change the locks, paint the walls, replace the roof, and so on. The final wedge of our picket fence was hardly knocked into the ground when he disappeared.

It happened on a Friday afternoon when I was waiting for him to pick me up from school. He never did. As the hours passed, so did hundreds of cars, each one sparking a bit of hope when I spotted the faint blur in the distance. But none of them stopped for me.

I try not to think about it too much, but I can say this, though: *You grow up a lot faster when reality strikes you at a young age.*

As I follow the trail, our property gradually becomes visible in the distance. The familiar grey tiled roof is infested with sunken patches of rotten wood that have absorbed the moisture of frequent rainfall. The unkempt garden grows wild and has even begun to climb the walls, creeping beneath the peeling white paint and covering the multitude of leakage stains. The forest has been sneaking closer over the years, steadily swallowing our house whole.

I leap over the hardwood fence and stride across the lawn. The brick pathway that leads to the front door is barely visible underneath the strain of dying weeds. I bend down and shove them aside out of habit, knowing very well that they'll be back within the next week.

I reach the porch and push my weight against the stubborn front door. It swings open with a familiar creak. As a general rule, the door tends to be unlocked in the mornings. This is partly because our house has no keys. Each door can only be opened and closed from the inside, using a twist-lock mechanism. This wasn't always the case, but Dad insisted that we replace the old locks, as it was a safer alternative. After all, keys can't be stolen or forged if they don't exist.

I close the door behind me, locking it shut. The cold outside air disappears behind the sturdy hardwood surface.

I slowly edge through the living room, trying to limit the amount of noise the old floorboards release underneath my weight. The house branches out to the kitchen, where the wooden flooring meets ceramic tiles. I walk over to the counter and grab hold of the kettle, placing it in the sink. Twisting the stubborn tap open, I push the kettle beneath the stream of water, filling it to the brim. The old, metal pipes groan beneath my feet, sending tremors through the floor and into the cupboards.

I grab a rattling cup and add a teaspoon of ground coffee, as well as brown sugar for good measure. The boiled water turns the mixture a steamy black, but a dash of milk brings it back to a cloudy brown. I stir the cup of coffee before bringing it closer to my lips. The warm liquid slides down my throat and fills me with fleeting content.

"Morning, John," a warm voice utters behind me. I place the cup in the sink before turning around. A creamy nightgown drapes over her timid figure, and her frizzled hair flows down her shoulders in waves. She inspects the cup in the sink, then turns her gaze back to me. I outgrew her long ago and look down at her with a protective gaze.

"Sorry Mom, did I wake you?"

"Not at all," she replies with a reassuring embrace. "I woke up before you left."

She slowly combs her fingers through my dark, wet hair. "I had the strangest dream… I keep having them."

"What about?" I ask, intrigued.

"Oh, it's nothing really."

Mom tightly grasps my shoulders and leads me down the narrow hallway. The small windows cast dim beams of light onto the paintings hanging from the opposite wall. Each surface is framed and marked with colourful traces of abstract imagery. Mom tends to paint when her thoughts are troubling her. She'll spend days before the same canvas, carefully covering one stroke of paint with the next. By the time she declares a project finished, the house is usually littered with empty paint canisters, along with the lingering smell of oils and solvents.

We continue down the dusky corridor and past her latest piece. This one isn't finished yet but seems to be entirely different from her previous work. The painting's edges are coated with a rusty tint, forming an artificial border. White specks of stars graze the darkness that engulfs the painting—all but for a large, orange circle in the centre. Whenever I walk past this wall, I find my attention being drawn to it.

"Go and wake Carter. He never budges if I try," she whispers.

I nod and quietly slip through his bedroom door. Although the exterior of our house is dilapidated, indoors it's clean and comfortable. Mom made sure of this. In the farthest corner of the room, a tiny figure lies entwined in fine sheets of white linen. I sit down on the edge of the bed and gently stroke his head with the back of my hand.

"Carter, you need to get ready for school."

He turns his back to me and whines in protest.

"We can't miss the bus again," I urge. "Mom's just going to make us walk."

"I don't want to go," his muffled voice protests from under the bedding. As I run my cold fingers through his soft hair, golden strands fall down the side of his neck, revealing a dark mark near the top of his spine. A bruise.

I immediately snap out of my tranquil state of mind.

"Carter, what happened here?" I press slightly on the swollen wound, but he responds by jolting away in pain.

"I'm up!" he declares, throwing the covers to the ground and leaping out of bed.

"Did somebody do this to you?" I demand.

He slides out of my grip and heads for the doorway. I quickly lurch to my feet and block his path. The difference between our ages is accentuated as I tower over him. For a brief moment, we just exchange stares.

"I don't want Mom to know," he whispers.

"I won't tell her," I lie.

His gaze falls to the ground. "Someone is picking on me."

Rage shoots through my veins. "Who is it?"

"You won't know him."

"I'll find out."

"No, promise you won't!" Carter pleads. "If he finds out I told someone, he'll do it again."

I hesitate, giving the matter some thought. His eyes follow mine as I examine the severity of the mark. It looks as if someone tried to choke him.

"Okay," I concede. "But if he does it again, I'm stepping in. Now get ready for school."

"Thanks, John." He quickly wraps his slender arms around me, then disappears around the corner.

I follow him out of the room and get ready for school. Searing thoughts fill my mind until the bus arrives. Five minutes late, as usual. As we board the rusty yellow behemoth, the smell of aging polyester seats overwhelms my senses. Carter takes the single seat next to the driver as he does every morning, and excitedly begins to tell her about his weekend. I slowly stroll down the aisle, scanning the rows for familiar faces. I might be a senior, but I prefer keeping to myself. Not everyone needs to know who I am.

Reaching the back of the bus, I finally slump down next to a window and sink into my seat. Before I can tuck my bag underneath the chair in front of me, two eager faces greet me with playful punches.

"What's up, John?" the fiery red-haired boy says. "You joining us tonight?"

I groan in response. Once Sam has his mind set on something, he rarely let's go.

"Come on," he pleads. "You never want to go out anymore."

"Yeah," Daniel chimes in, while drawing another worm on his condensed window. "*The Fourth Kind* is premiering tonight. You should come."

I shrug. "I'll try, but you know I can't stay out too late."

"That's the spirit!" Sam says, swinging his freckled arm around my neck and locking me in a tight chokehold. "Daniel already bought tickets so it's too late to back out now."

I pry his fingers off my neck, shoving his arm away. "I'm not in the mood right now."

He shrugs and averts his attention to Daniel's window, which is now filled with monstrous-looking worms. "Worms don't have teeth," he remarks.

"This one does," Daniel replies.

Without a second thought, Sam leans over and fogs up the glass with a breath of warm air. Wiping away the moisture with an outstretched finger, he draws two little legs sticking out from one of the creature's gaping mouths. Daniel closely inspects the half-eaten human, then grins, impressed by his friend's contribution.

I shift my gaze to my own window and stare out at the rushing scenery. Horns blare as moving vehicles slow down and fall into traffic. The Sun hides behind a blanket of clouds, allowing the birds to go unnoticed in the mist as they peck away at crumbs on the sidewalk. The morning seems overcast with a shadow of uncertainty.

My train of thought leads me back to Carter. He's grown quiet and is looking up at the sky as if noticing the same thing. Even from my seat at the back of the bus, I can make out the darkness of the bruise on his neck. I'm supposed to be protecting him, but I think I'm failing.

* * *

School went like it always does. Mindlessly moving from one class to the next, avoiding forced social interaction and aimlessly jotting down notes I'll likely never read again. I spent most of our lunchtime behind the sports benches, keeping an eye on Carter.

He prefers to play with the younger kids instead of sitting with boys his own age. This has been an ongoing issue since Dad disappeared, and it's clear that Carter is clinging to a sense of security he lost a long time ago. Younger children are familiar territory. They're predictable. At his age, Carter doesn't yet understand the gravity of his choices. Children can also be cruel, and from what I've witnessed this morning, the target has already been painted on his back. I've lectured him on many occasions regarding his choice of friends, but he refuses to listen. Besides, the younger kids seem more willing to share their food with him. Sometimes, Mom forgets to pack our lunches for school. At least, she pretends to. She doesn't have the heart to tell us what we already know.

When the bell finally releases its signature siren of three consecutive rings, I wait outside for a few more minutes before making my way through the dark and empty hallways. Power failures aren't that uncommon around here. In fact, it would be unusual if they didn't occur at least once a month. They seem to go hand in hand with bad weather, but classes continue regardless.

With a strenuous tug, the rusty hinges of my locker grate open and a crumpled piece of paper falls out along with my scruffy gym bag. I heave the heavy bag over my shoulder and slam the locker shut with a clatter. Bending over, I flatten the paper out on to the floor. Realising what it is,

I reluctantly fold the movie ticket into a little square and tuck it into my shirt pocket.

My muddy soles tap against the floor as I saunter into the changing room. Every few steps, a missing tile sends a dull thud echoing down the rows of empty bathroom stalls. At the sink, I wet my hands and wipe my face. Using the sleeve of my oversized school blazer—the one Mom insisted I would grow into by the end of 10th grade—I dry my face and peer into the mirror.

My father's blue eyes stare back at me through the dark. Approachable, yet vigilant, like a slate of thin ice that can crack at any given moment. My jaw is more prominent than his, but not yet covered with his signature morning stubble. What I lack in facial hair, I make up for in wild, black locks that graze across my ears and stick to my forehead in uncombed clumps. Pale skin accustomed to the cold air blends in with my neatly ironed white shirt.

I'm told that I have my mother's smile. It's true, most likely. We don't smile anymore, so I wouldn't know.

CHAPTER 2

I didn't go home after school today. The local news station sent out an emergency announcement, warning of an approaching storm. The weather forecasters predict gale-force winds to hit the area within the next week. Apparently, it will be the worst we've experienced in years.

By the time I was getting up to leave my last lecture of the day, dark clouds covered the skies in sheets of pleated grey. Instead of taking the bus back home, I began to make my way across town on foot.

Bill's Tool Shed is a two-storey hardware store that sells everything from hammer drills to padlocks and hasps. From afar, the yellow building stands out like a sore thumb. My father helped paint the roof back in the day, doing it in nothing but a pair of khaki shorts and an old tank top. Every time we walked past the shop, he would lift his shirt and show me the vertical tan lines that stretched down his shoulder blades. He'd do it with a proud smile, as if the second-degree burns hadn't taken an agonising month to heal.

Besides, he was just happy to help out a friend, and Bill was one of his best. They grew up together in this small town, but parted ways after high school. Bill remained behind and built his business from the ground up, while Dad moved far away and created a new life for himself with

Mom. She soon gave birth to me, and Carter followed three years later. Things were going very well, until they suddenly moved back to their hometown, bought a remote house and locked the doors shut.

A metal bell announces my arrival as I step through the door of Bill's Tool Shed. I have to stop myself from jumping back out when I spot the large crowd. Half the town arrived before me, clearly with the same plan in mind. Unrest fills the narrow aisles as agitated citizens prepare for the approaching storm.

I brush past the impatient customers and curiously glance down the different aisles as I head for the back. Window shutters and roof clips are in high demand, and the flashlights have already been emptied from the shelves. Those who couldn't find what they came for are compromising by scouring the store for other equipment. I leap into the nearest passageway as a lady in overalls rushes past me with an oversized pruning saw. She must be planning on trimming back the trees near her home. That, or she's about to cut a human in half. Assuming the worst, I sneak past the shelves of cat litter and wedge myself between two boys who are fighting over the last *Astro Boy* figurine. A bunch of parents have left their children unsupervised in the toys section, turning it into a war zone.

I grab the figurine and hold it above their heads. "I'll tear it in half if you don't stop fighting."

"No, don't!" the younger of the two cries.

The older boy yanks the doll away from me and sniggers. He doesn't really care about the children's toy and doesn't bother to fake an interest in its safety. He's only trying to elicit a reaction from the younger one. I peel the plastic toy from his fingers and hand it back to the sniffing child, whose eyes are welling up with tears.

The bully squeals at me. "Hey, that's mine!"

"No, it isn't," I growl at him.

I take a gander down the long aisle and spot the older kids looking at the latest poster of *The Fourth Kind*. It seems this one simply got bored doing that and made his way into the children's section to traumatise some easier targets. I glare at him until he shrugs and ambles away to the comic book section.

The little boy lightens up and inspects the *Astro Boy* figurine for any marks or imperfections. He doesn't seem to notice when I leave him behind, heading farther into the stuffy store. I've almost reached the back when I spot the familiar grey head of hair sticking out from amongst a crowd of rowdy customers. Bill has always looked much older than his real age. The stress of running the only hardware store in town has not been kind to him. Right now, he's cornered against the building's single generator. It keeps the top floor's electricity running when the power cuts off, making it the perfect contraption for an approaching storm.

Exasperated, Bill explains to the customers around him that the rusty generator is not for sale. A man in a tailored suit steps forward, clearly not deterred. He offers a set price for the machine, which instigates a bidding war. Numbers fly through the air, each one bigger than the previous. It quickly reaches a point where the prices are so ridiculously high that I'm convinced they're making it up as they're going along.

"Bill!" I shout into the crowd. The flustered man turns around, his unkempt hair sticking to his head. I speak loudly so that everyone, including the old lady in the front, can hear me clearly.

"What are you doing trying to sell the generator? That mouldy, old machine broke weeks ago!"

Bill's mouth opens as he begins to contest this, but a quick glimpse of my face closes it shut again. A smirk appears instead, and he feigns ignorance. "Did it now, John? That's a shame," he shakes his head.

"Yes!" I shout at him. "And you almost sold it to one of our customers!"

The crowd has now turned to me, waiting in anticipation. I scratch my head while pretending to be deep in thought. "They'd be much better off with those rechargeable batteries in aisle seven."

One of the women gives a faint shriek and disappears around the corner. The rest of the crowd disperses, running after her. Only the suited man remains behind, still not convinced.

"It doesn't sound broken," he grunts. "I could hear it churning from the other side of the store."

"Of course," I nod convincingly. "It's loud *because* it's broken. Do you want your home to sound like the inside of a machine gun?"

A boy emerges next to the man and tugs on his white cuffs. A frown stretches across my forehead when I recognise the *Astro Boy* figurine in the bully's sweaty palms. "Daddy, I need batteries for my new toy!"

The man scowls at him, but his nerves get the better of him. There won't be batteries left if he wastes any more time talking to us. He walks off in a huff, pulling the whining child alongside him. The two of them disappear down the aisle, leaving only Bill and me behind.

My father's old friend steps away from the vibrating generator and releases a long sigh of relief. The generator does in fact work—but it only lights up the main floor, and struggles to reach the ill-lit storage section. He raises an eyebrow, as if to ask if I'm heading downstairs. I nod, to which he responds by exclaiming, "Thank you, John."

Bill has always been a quiet man. He tends to choose his words carefully, as if they're a limited resource that should only be used after careful consideration. His self-contained nature reminds me a lot of my father. Perhaps that's why I keep on coming back.

He straightens his jacket and heads out to address the unruly crowd. I grab onto the railings and feel my way down the stairs. The ground floor acts as a warehouse, filled with supplies that are either not needed or are sought after so often that Bill buys them in excess. I spend most of my time down here, taking count of stock or organising the deliveries. Most people would call it a lonely job, but I requested it specifically.

I've been helping around the shop ever since I was old enough to make the trip on my own. Down here, I can get lost in my thoughts. More than that—I can indulge in them. I don't have to explain to anyone why I am silent, or fear that I might come across as rude or distant. More importantly, I don't have to hide the fact that I'm still trying to puzzle out my father's disappearance, three years later.

I sigh loudly, and the warehouse sighs back at me. Sound travels quick and far through this dark, hollow chamber. Each step I take is amplified, and every thought I grapple with feels palpable. With immense difficulty, I visualise the face of my father. His personality follows, along with the clothes he wore on that day. As I take note of the stock on the metal railings, I play the events over in my head like a fragmented recording.

Dad was acting strange before his disappearance. More than usual. I didn't notice it at the time, but vague memories have a way of solidifying themselves after tragedy strikes. I remember asking if he was coming down with a cold. The weather was calm and inviting, but Dad was wearing a thick, black jacket indoors. He would get upset if someone commented about it—but that didn't stop Mom from asking. Dad finally admitted that he felt a bit odd, and then informed us that he was going on a hike to clear his head.

This wasn't the unusual part. The mountain range that borders the woods was one of his favourite spots to explore. What's unusual is the fact that he never came back. The police found his phone at the bottom of a hill, its screen shattered. They sent out a search party but couldn't find a trace of him other than his car in the parking lot. By the week's end, I knew they were not searching for my dad anymore, but a body.

Bill was the one who repaired my father's phone. The chip was still intact, allowing us to access his call log and messages. To my mother's relief, we found nothing out of the ordinary. Dad wasn't running away with some mysterious woman downtown, and he wasn't receiving threatening calls from loan sharks either. There was one oddity, though. According to his phone record, three calls went out to my mother that day. Yet, she never received any of them. Her phone didn't even ring.

I went through her phone myself but found nothing. My dad's satellite phone doesn't rely on cell towers like traditional phones. It's able to pick up a signal from anywhere in the world, so a bad connection is rarely to blame. Unless all the satellites disappeared from orbit that day, there had to be a different reason for his phone malfunctioning. A more sinister one.

Now, I walk over to the dusty corner where the roof tiles are stacked. The concrete tiles were the first to sell out during the winter sale, and their metal counterparts followed shortly thereafter. These clay tiles are all that remain, but they've been sitting here for a while now.

I pick up a black tile and weigh it in my hands. It's not as heavy as the other brands but will be much easier to transport. Clay also absorbs less water than concrete, making it less of a burden on the house beneath it. I carefully place the tile back on the heap and take a step closer to inspect the product. If I work fast enough, I might be able to rebuild our roof in time for the approaching storm.

I spend the rest of the afternoon with my clipboard in hand, checking on the latest deliveries. The noise of impatient feet against the wooden floorboards above my head quiets down as the afternoon ticks away. Eventually, I deem it safe to go back upstairs and check on the remaining customers. I return to an empty store, barring the plants and fertilizer section that's been left untouched. Bill sits behind the counter with his head in his hands, exhausted.

"I was meaning to ask," I start, embarrassed. "Could I take this week's payment in the form of roof tiles?" He looks up at me with a confused expression. Then realisation crosses his brow. My father helped Bill with his shop's roof many years ago. Now, the time has come to return the favour. The roles have switched, but not for the better.

"Of course, John," he says, concerned. "Take all the tiles you need."

"Thank you, Bill," I say with sincere gratitude. "I'll borrow a bike from someone and collect them in trips—"

"Don't be silly," he interrupts me. "We'll pack the delivery van tomorrow morning and get them on your house before the storm hits."

I nod my head. I want to thank him again, but I know it's not necessary. "I better get going," I say instead.

As I turn around to head for the door, Bill stops me. He seems to be having an internal conversation with himself, weighing if he should ask me something or not. "Do you still hear that ringing sound in the mornings?" he hazards the question.

"Sometimes," I admit.

I don't tell him that the noise has been present a lot these days. Or that I started covering my ears out of habit when I entered the forest because it follows me around like a swarm of bees. I never hear these sounds when I'm around other people.

Bill looks at me strangely, choosing his words very carefully. "Your father complained of the same thing."

CHAPTER 3

Mom quietly studies my plate of food from across the dinner table. Still untouched, the meaty broth has long ago gone cold. I lower a spoon into the clouded liquid and stir its contents with a repetitive circular motion. This doesn't make it look any more appealing. Frustrated, I knock the spoon away from the ceramic edge and watch it sink out of sight.

After leaving Bill's Tool Shed, I made my way home on foot. I would have accepted a ride if someone was willing to offer one. The darkness of night arrived before I did, and the smell of brewing meats and spices escaped the house in alluring wafts. I instantly recognised the aroma of a traditional family dish and could hardly retain my excitement.

I greet Mom at the door, but she doesn't match my eagerness. I think this is strange but take my seat at the table without asking questions. Mom quietly lays the table and finishes slicing up the roasted garlic bread before serving me a large portion of broth. I breathe in the aroma of steamy tomato and roasted onion but keep my composure and wait for the others to take their seats. I lose my appetite the moment Carter enters the room.

At first, he tries to hide it, choosing the seat on my left instead of the one he normally takes to my right. Mom doesn't question this and serves him his meal before help-ing herself. She has already seen the mark, and likely had a heated discussion about it with Carter before I arrived. They both walk around on eggshells to avoid the topic.

Instead of reaching for the salt myself, I ask Carter to pass it along. Sitting halfway between the two of us, it's a little closer to him than it is to me. This makes for a convenient excuse to steal his attention. When he doesn't respond, I raise my voice, repeating the request. Defeated, he sighs and reaches reluctantly for the saltshaker. He turns to face me, his left eye swollen shut.

My eyes widen. I warned Carter that I would intervene if it happened a second time. He knew I wouldn't just sit by and watch someone hurt him like this. That's why he chose to hide it. At least, he tried to. How many bruises have gone unnoticed until now?

Sitting at the table, time slows down as I consider what must be done. When the salt reaches me, his fingers acci-dentally graze mine. My attention shifts from Carter's black eye to his reddened knuckles and hope flickers up inside me.

He fought back.

I look up and meet Mom's enquiring gaze. She's waiting for my reaction.

"I'm not very hungry," I confess.

Mom frowns. "You're not coming down with something, are you?"

I force a bite out of the garlic bread, but the food has already soaked up most of the negative atmosphere and tastes spoilt. I quickly wash it down with a glass of tap water.

"I don't think so."

We eat in silence, none of us enjoying the well-prepared meal. The wind blows against the house, picking up speed as it turns the corners. Gusts of cold air break through the cracks in our roof, whistling to announce their unwanted arrival.

"A storm is brewing," I say, not just referring to the thoughts in my head.

I excuse myself from the table and wander into the living room. Our fireplace howls every time the breeze rushes through the chimney. I chopped down an old pine tree last weekend but didn't think we'd need the wood for at least another month. I pick a few bulky logs and place them in the dusty hearth. It's better to be prepared for the worst.

I push some dry grass beneath the wood and light it with a match. As the smoke turns darker and trails away, a welcome warmth begins to spread through the room. I brush off my hands and re-join my family at the table. Still sitting in silence, Mom finally buckles under the pressure.

"You know, your father was absolutely covered in scars," she says out of the blue.

I raise my eyebrow. "Scars?"

"He didn't like talking about them," she admits. "If I didn't know any better, I'd say your dad purposely burned himself on that damn roof, helping Bill."

My eyes linger on the fourth, empty chair at the head of the table. It's been three years since someone occupied that seat. Perhaps my young mind has forgotten the details of my father's appearance. I don't remember him having any scars. They must have been hidden beneath the sunburns that turned his skin a golden brown. But why would he hide them from us?

Mom stares at her bowl of broth, deep in thought. "Your father loved you two very much. He would gladly have given his life to keep you safe."

Carter suddenly stands, shoving his half-eaten meal away. He looks teary-eyed. "Can I be excused?"

"First finish your meal," Mom says gently.

"I lost my bloody appetite."

"Language!" Mom yells. "What would your father say?"

"I don't know, what would he say?" Carter snaps back at her.

"Carter don't," I warn him.

"In fact, why don't you tell me where he is, so I can ask him?" Carter yells.

Mom begins to utter something, but then she stops herself. Carter doesn't believe that Dad lost his footing in the mountains or was attacked by some malevolent stranger. He doesn't spend most of his time in a dark warehouse theorising about what happened that day. In his mind, the answer is simple. Our father left us behind for a better life.

I stare daggers at Carter. He was ten when it happened and has no right to pretend like he knows the man better than I did. He rushes out of the kitchen and disappears down the hallway, slamming his door shut. Mom stares at the fire, watching as the flames begin to shrink. I jump up from my chair and throw more logs into the hearth, keeping the fire from dying out.

"I talked to Bill today," I shout at Mom from the living room. "He agreed to give me the materials I need to repair our roof."

"We can't afford that," Mom gasps. "We'll just use the bucket when the water starts dripping on the carpet again."

I walk back to my chair and move it closer to Mom, so I can hold her hands in mine. "I'll help him with deliveries in the mornings. Until the tiles are paid off."

Mom looks upset. "But that's when you go running?"

"That's why this job is perfect," I reassure her with a wink. "I can run the route while delivering parcels. It won't even feel like work."

"You barely have any time for yourself these days," she says.

"That's not true," I insist. "Just this morning, Sam and Daniel invited me to watch a movie with them."

Her face lights up. "You should go."

I flinch and immediately regret telling her. "Didn't you want me to help around the house tonight? I can wash the dishes while you finish that painting?"

"No, I want you to go. You deserve some time for yourself."

I sigh. "Are you sure you'll be okay?"

She gently grasps my arm. "You grew up far too quickly, John. I know you want to protect us, but I need you to act like a kid for once."

I close my eyes and lean into her. I'll never be a kid again, but I can at least pretend to be. I help clean the table and wash the dishes. After stacking everything in the drying

I wave my bloody hand in front of Sam's face, hoping it will snap him out of his trance. When it doesn't grab his attention, I try the same with Daniel. He doesn't flinch.

I can't take it anymore. I jump up from my seat and push my way through the aisle, stumbling over outstretched legs along the way. Hurriedly striding past glaring eyes, I burst out the back door and into the foyer.

The man behind the front desk doesn't seem affected by the noise. He remains aloof, analysing me silently as I approach. Stopping in front of the register, I rest my weight on the desk and groan.

"Please call an ambulance," I utter between strained breaths. My voice escapes my mouth in muffled bursts of air. The man remains unbothered by my troubled appearance. The noise is even louder in the foyer, drowning out my call for assistance. He can't hear me.

"Look here, I need help!" I scream at the top of my lungs. My hands leave red stains on the wooden desk as I lift them into the air. Like a statue, I straighten my arms before me and point my palms towards him, hoping he will realise what's happening. With a careful squint, his eyes betray the slightest hint of understanding. And then the man does something unthinkable. He grins.

I stare at him in shock. Stumbling backwards, I dart out of the theatre and down the steps leading to the main road. Thunderous clouds now cover the night sky, casting ominous shadows over the empty streets below. Hoping that the noise will subside, I run down the nearest alley. I dash around corners as the brick walls lean toward me, threatening to collapse and bury me underneath their weight. I jump over piles of trash scattered over the concrete and dodge a stray dog that rushes past me with his tail between his legs.

The noise is now louder than ever before, growing stronger with each pulsating drone. That's when I suddenly have a horrifying realisation. I can't get away from the noise, because it's not coming from an outside source. It's coming from inside my head.

I feel dizzy as throbbing pain envelops me. I reach the end of the narrow passage and collapse onto my side. Warm liquid seeps down my back and my entire body spasms in agony. The pressure inside my head builds until I'm on the verge of passing out. I can't hear anything anymore. Only a monotonous, screeching pitch.

My vision fades like an unfocused camera lens, barely allowing me to make out the approaching figures in the distance. Static vibrations emanate from the cold surface beneath me. I frantically gasp for air as a paralyzing numbness swallows my body, leaving me unable to move. Then, a blinding light engulfs me… and everything goes dark.

CHAPTER 4

When I was young, my dad would occasionally let me jog alongside him during the silent winter mornings. Even though he was a lot faster than I was, he would maintain a slow, steady pace, always staying by my side. When the Sun eventually rose and we neared the end of the forest, he would sprint ahead, knowing that I could find my own way back.

One morning, my foot got caught in some straggled tree roots, causing me to lose my balance and spiral into a trench. The overwhelming pain of my fractured ankle left me motionless. I remained sprawled out next to the edge of the road for fifteen minutes before my father came rushing back, finding me wedged between the rocks and gravel.

After his disappearance, I began to jog on my own. I did this compulsively, never missing a day. I would pretend that my dad was with me, but that he had simply run ahead. I kept telling myself that if something went wrong, I could just call out to him and he'd come rushing back. Yet no matter how fast I ran, I would never be able to catch up with him.

Warmth seeps into my muscles as I force my legs to push harder. Faster. Cool air brushes against my dampened face and the ground beneath my feet becomes a blur. Adrenaline rushes through my veins. I've never felt so alive.

Yesterday feels like a distant dream. I must have fallen asleep in my room after having dinner with Mom and Carter. Nothing I experienced at the theatre could have been real, since I safely woke this morning under the crisp covers of my bed. I was even wearing the same clothes, but I couldn't find a single drop of blood on me.

The house comes into view as I near our driveway. The sun falls differently on the roof today. It has a strange, new glow to it. When I reach the cracked pavement leading to the front door, I am suddenly struck by a strange feeling, like I'm about to enter someone else's house.

I shrug it off and close my fingers around the cold, brass knob, turning it clockwise until the movement abruptly stops. Gripping it tighter, I twist it again with a hard jerk, but it doesn't budge. It's locked. I always leave the door unlocked when I go running. It should still have been like that—unless someone locked it from the inside.

I begin to circle the house. The weeds have taken over the garden and pull at my shorts as I pass through them. At the back, I find an open window leading to the kitchen. I keep telling Mom to close it at night, but she still tends to forget. I carefully hoist myself up the ledge and climb into the dusky room. With a slight thud, I land on my feet. Before proceeding to the living room, I make sure to close and lock the window behind me.

The house is eerily silent. I wander down the hallway and past Carter's room, but almost slip when I step in a large puddle of red liquid on the floor. I suck in a breath of cold air, and slowly let it out. The unlit corner in the hallway creates a daunting sight. I kneel down and carefully inch closer to the puddle. It takes me a few moments to realise what I'm looking at.

The dried paint creeps up the wall, where it eventually meets Mom's latest painting—and consumes it. At least half a can of paint was emptied in the process. She must have added layer upon layer until there was nothing left.

Circular swirls dominate the centre of the painting in a whirlpool of fiery red. The trees that once surrounded the circle have disappeared beneath violent smudges, creating clouds of shadows. The artificial border could not contain her emotions, allowing them to spill over its edges and leak onto the floor.

I pull myself away from the painting and move towards the end of the hallway. As I enter my room, I'm alarmed to see someone sitting on my bed. The person doesn't notice me at first and continues to inspect the ruffled covers.

"Hello?" I whisper hesitantly into the darkness. The figure jolts in response.

"John!" Mom's voice erupts from the other side of the room. She jumps up and rushes towards me, embracing me tightly.

"Where have you been? We've been looking everywhere for you."

"I just went on my morning run," I explain. "Sorry if I took longer than usual, the forest was so inviting today." I notice by the growing wetness on my shirt that she's crying.

"What's wrong?" I ask softly, pulling her closer.

"I thought something terrible happened to you," she sniffs.

"Why would you think that?" I probe hesitantly.

"I walked past your room this morning and noticed that your covers were thrown off," she explains. "I found blood on your pillow."

I begin to feel uneasy. Strange memories from the night before come rushing back. Memories that are far too vivid to be dismissed as dreams.

"Mom," I speak slowly and clearly, gently pushing her away. "I don't understand what you're trying to tell me. What's going on?"

She looks up, analysing me uncertainly. Her eyes are red and swollen. "John," she says with a cracked voice. "You've been missing for a week."

CHAPTER 5

I take a step back. My eyes remain pinned on the unsettled face that uttered those words.

"What do you mean I've been missing for a week?"

"You went out with your friends and never came back," she says in a hushed tone. Nobody saw you at school and the police couldn't find a trace of you."

A giant lump forms in my throat. "I... I can't remember anything. It feels like a dream."

"You're going to have to try," she insists.

I close my eyes and think back to the night it all happened. "I went to the theatre in town, because Sam and Daniel wanted to watch the midnight screening of *The Fourth Kind*," I slowly recall the events. "When the movie started, there was a loud noise that wouldn't go away. It kept getting worse, yet nobody else seemed to notice. It finally got so loud that my ears were bleeding, so I ran out of the theatre to get help."

This story seems to puzzle her. "No, that can't be true," she frowns, dismissing my version of the events. "The authorities questioned the employee who worked behind the register. He said the only movie that was showing that night was *Astro Boy*."

I grow nauseous. The room is spinning around me and I'm finding it increasingly difficult to concentrate.

"He's lying," my voice breaks. "Sam hates children's movies. He'd never watch it."

Mom looks at me worryingly. "Your friends confirmed his statement, John. They said you were acting strangely during the movie, insisting that you wanted to walk home on your own."

I lean back against the wall, defeated. My friends wouldn't lie. If anything, they'd go out of their way to protect me, knowing I'd do the same for them in a heartbeat.

"I should let the police know that you've returned," Mom breaks the silence. She insists on holding me again before leaving to make the phone call. Each hug lasts longer than the one before. It's like she is trying to grasp onto an image of me that has already begun to fade away.

As I stand in the empty room, I feel completely void of emotion. I don't know what to feel. The story I told is hardly believable. If anything, I should be relieved that it didn't happen. I would much rather lose my mind than bleed to death in an alleyway.

I think back to the screeching sound in the back of my head. It felt so real. I can still remember the start of the movie, as well as the man who smiled when I showed him my bloody hands. There was so much blood everywhere. A sudden thought strikes me.

I walk over to the left side of my bed and sure enough, an array of small, red droplets stains my pillow. A belated surge of panic finally kicks in. I'm not crazy. I hasten down the hallway and into the bathroom, locking it shut behind me.

When I near the mirror, I twist my neck sideways to peer into my ear. Using the tip of my finger, I scrape the outer canal for any traces of dried blood. I hold my hand up to my eyes and inspect the brown powder lodged beneath my nail. Expecting to find more remnants of it, I pull my shirt over my head and toss it to the ground. Returning my gaze to the mirror, I freeze in shock.

A giant, circular black mark is imprinted on the middle of my upper right arm. The symbol is roughly the size of my palm, yet its interior pattern is more complex than anything I've seen before. I feel like I'm looking into a dark hole that shows a world far beyond this one. Deep inside of it, two obsidian stones block the way to a door that leads elsewhere. The rest of the image is fractured, like glass that has cracked in a thousand places. It feels unnaturally cold against my skin.

I stare at my reflection in disbelief, periodically glancing down at my body in case the mirror might be deceiving me. But the identical mark is still on my raised arm, just the same. I try to rub it off with my fingers, desperately hoping that it will smear away. Several minutes later, a red rash covers my arm—but the mark is still there as if pressed into my skin.

"Carter, the bus is here!" Mom's voice knocks me out of my frantic trance.

"I'm coming, too!" I call back, trying to sound as mundane as I possibly can. I sprint down the hallway to my room and throw on yesterday's jacket in an attempt to hide the insidious symbol. I chuck a few books into a ripped bag and sling it over my shoulder as I head to the front door. I step out just in time to see the bus turning at the end of the street.

Dismayed, I drop the bag on the floor and kick it aside. It's only going to weigh me down. Before I can dash after the vehicle, Mom stops me at the door. I flinch, knowing she wouldn't let me go that easily.

"They're about you, John," she says.

"What is?" Her statement surprises me.

"A week ago, you asked me what my nightmares were about, and I'm telling you now. They're about you." She looks me in the eyes, and I can see that she's holding back a lot more than she's letting on. "I kept them from you, because I didn't want you to be afraid. I had the same dreams before your father…." her voice trails off.

I pull her closer and she holds on to me a few seconds longer than usual.

"I have to go, Mom," I whisper.

"I love you no matter what happens," she softly breathes into my ear. "Always remember that."

* * *

I take the shorter path that cuts through the forest. The trampled ferns and bushes weren't meant to form a trail, but that has never stopped me from using it as one. After all, this isn't the first time I've missed the bus.

44

When I reach the school grounds, I scan the area for Sam and Daniel. As I gather my breath, the clouds seem to mimic the movements of my heaving chest, growing in size as the wind fills my lungs. A storm is brewing, just as the weather forecasters predicted. A hard knock against my back sends me spinning around in a frenzy.

The red-haired boy smiles eagerly. "Dude, you're back!" Sam feigns another playful blow before calling out to Daniel, who reluctantly puts his game away and looks up at me.

"Oh hey, we thought you were dead," he says.

They seem oblivious to the situation. Do they even know what took place in the auditorium that night?

"Sam, what did you think of *The Fourth Kind*?" I watch him vigilantly.

"Never seen it," he shrugs. "Should have watched it instead of that other garbage."

"You mean *Astro Boy*?" I analyse him, sceptical.

"Yeah," he shakes his head. "Wasn't really to my liking."

I'm not the least bit satisfied with his answer. "What didn't you like about it?"

"To be honest, I zoned out after a few minutes," he shrugs again. "It wasn't really to my liking."

I cock my head to the side, watching him closely. Sam's behaviour is odd. I turn to Daniel and ask him what he thought of the movie. He gives the same coached reply as Sam, as if someone is holding a gun to his head.

"It wasn't really to my liking," he mumbles.

I watch the two of them carefully. Then I lose it.

"We didn't watch *Astro Boy*! You were both there with me! Did someone threaten you? Was it the man behind the register?"

Daniel turns around and takes out his game, continuing to play as if nothing happened. I feel like I'm losing my mind. How can I protect my family if I can't tell what's real anymore? I look at Sam, helpless, but his expression catches me off guard.

His face is frozen like it was in the theatre when the noise started. This time he seems to be fighting against it. Desperately. He stares past me as his eyes flutter and lip twitches. A stutter escapes his breath, but he fails to grab hold of any recognisable words. *What if Sam isn't lying on purpose? What if someone is trying to control what he's saying?*

"Sam, are you okay?" I speak slowly.

"If—" he stutters. "If, if, if."

I touch his shoulder, breaking him free of the invisible grasp.

"If you don't believe me, look at your ticket!" he shouts.

I pause. That's it. The only tangible proof there is. I remove my sweat-soaked jacket and slip my hand into its pocket. My fingers feel around in the darkness, searching for an answer. As my thumb grazes the crumpled paper, I snatch it into my hand and pull it out.

All three of us now stare at my fist, each as eager as the next to see what waits inside. I slowly breathe in then open my fingers, revealing the ticket.

B22: *The Fourth Kind*

CHAPTER 6

I can't breathe. I gasp for air, but little enters my lungs. Still too weak to open my eyes, I frantically start coughing. Panic ripples over me like a wave of scorching water as a burning sensation fills my throat and spreads to my chest. It feels as if someone is rubbing sandpaper against its inner chambers, slowly shredding me from the inside. I try to scream, but no sound escapes my throat.

My limbs are stiff and unwilling to commit to the simplest movements. The sensation of being buried alive is overwhelming, and my body is struggling to wake up. I've experienced sleep paralysis before, but this feels far more real.

I'm going to die, the thought strikes me suddenly. A fading image of Carter flashes to mind. What's going to happen to him if I don't return? It's not safe in town anymore. There are too many things that could harm him if given the chance. Carter will grow up thinking that I left him behind just like Dad did so many years ago.

I inhale a mouthful of air. I'd never leave him. With fierce desperation, I manage to open my eyes. Light from every direction pierces my skull, almost blinding me. I swiftly cover the top of my face and gaze with confusion at my surroundings.

I'm surrounded by sand stretching forward in every direction. With a strained manoeuvre, I take a handful and lift it up for inspection. It's not as heavy as sand. Opening my fingers ever so slightly, I allow the sand-like substance to slip through. The dusty soil leaves a rusty, orange tint on my skin. I wipe it off on my trousers and suddenly notice how much my hands are shaking.

A surge of adrenaline rushes through me. I need to get out of the Sun. *Now.* With new-found clarity, I allow my primal instincts to take over. Rolling over on all fours, I begin to crawl forward whilst forcing the dry, hot air through my trachea. Beads of sweat roll down my temples, dropping onto the ground before me where it instantly evaporates into the unforgiving atmosphere. Within seconds the sandy stretch comes to an abrupt end, met now by murky, wet terrain. I fall forward on my chest and breathe in the damp vapour. My shirt soaks up the mud, so it clings tightly to my skin. Dazed but determined, I gather all of my strength and push myself up. My legs threaten to buckle underneath the pressure. I steady myself by placing my hands on my knees. Scanning the environment, I finally realise just how strange my surroundings really are.

I'm standing on the edge of a circular patch of sand. The desert I envisaged appears to be nothing more than a small clearing. A flawless circle. My eyes follow the trail I forged, leading back to the middle where it abruptly ends about ten metres in. That means the circle should be around twenty metres in diameter. I scan the clearing for other markings, yet no footsteps enter or leave the area. It makes no sense. I couldn't have dropped from the sky.

Finishing my rotation, I shift my gaze back to the muddy surface that surrounds the sand patch. It stretches on for several feet, ultimately reaching a flourishing forest that envelops the entire circle. Alluring shadows fill the few holes and spaces that are not dense with blooming leaves and other flora. I've grown accustomed to the sounds from critters and birds following me through the forest back home, but this place is completely silent. I pat my sides until my hand finds a hard, flat object. Breathing a sigh of relief, I retrieve the phone from my pocket and watch the small screen light up. I quickly type a message to Mom.

I am lost in the forest. Send help.

I press send, but nothing happens. The phone is not picking up any signal.

I frown because that's not possible. Dad's satellite phone can pick up a signal from anywhere in the world. I hope the storm didn't damage it, or else I'm in real danger.

Unsure of what to do next, I contemplate the situation. I don't know where I am, nor how I got here. It would be pointless to start off in a random direction without knowing where I'd be heading. In this case, the best course of action would be to hug the nearest tree until help arrived.

On the other hand, remaining here in the blazing heat is not exactly an option, either. Water could be scarce in this area, and I'm in dire need of some. If I begin to move now, I might come across a familiar route before nightfall.

I glance back at the circle, then up at the sky. My eyes haven't adjusted yet, and the brightness forces me back to the shadows. Towering trees loom over me as I creep closer to the edge of the forest. The shade provides some comfort and calms my racing heart. I look at my phone a second time, inspecting the device for any cracks or dents. When I don't find any, I steady my breathing and begin to dial Mom's number. I can't let her hear the alarm in my voice.

A sharp snap erupts from the forest, bringing me back to my surroundings. I freeze, cocking my head in the direction of the noise. It sounded like a tree trunk being bent in half. I peer into the shadows, just beyond the first few bushes. I'm almost certain that something is staring back at me.

I realise that I've been holding my breath all this time. I exhale but instantly regret it. As if on cue, the forest starts to shake. A large snout emerges from the bushes, followed by an even larger body. Reflective scales cover the monstrous figure from head to tail, like something out of the prehistoric era. Claws the length of rulers dig into the ground as it steadily approaches. Only after several paces does its tail finally appear. The sooty tip is covered with needle-pointed spikes that stretch along its back and increases in size near its head. Stretched out, this animal easily doubles my length in size.

Am I dreaming right now? I stumble backwards, keeping my eyes fixed on the beast. My right leg tangles with the left, throwing me off balance—and I fall to the ground. The beast keeps moving forward, coming to an abrupt halt at my feet. Clearly not too concerned that its meal might outrun it, the creature's movements seem hampered and restrained.

It stares into the distance, as if not aware of my presence anymore. I remain on the ground, too stunned to move. It's time to wake up from this nightmare. None of this is real. Hovering over me, a long string of saliva leaks from its growling mouth and splashes onto my left knee.

"Aaaargh!" I bellow in pain as the exposed skin melts away. The beast looks down at me and hisses, fiercely raising the large flaps at the sides of its neck. Swiftly, like a whip, its tail lashes in my direction—but my reflexes kick in just in time, and I roll out of the way. It barely misses me and hits the ground instead. As the creature lifts its tail and prepares for another strike, I take the gap and leap away, sprinting into the opposite direction.

I quickly reach the other side of the circle and enter the forest. Glancing over my shoulder, I spot the beast scrambling to get closer. Avoiding loose rocks and fallen twigs, I try to concentrate by visualising a pathway ahead. I struggle to make my way through the dense foliage, pushing away branches and jumping over bushes. Given the beast's colossal size, it manoeuvres around the forest's obstacles with even greater difficulty.

Something in my peripheral vision keeps stealing my attention. Every so often, a thick, yellowish stick protrudes from the forest floor, partially covered by leaves and dirt. It fails to blend in with the surroundings and looks out of place. I turn my head fleetingly, trying to catch a better glimpse, but within seconds I almost run over a mangled bundle of red-stained sticks. Some of them are connected to each other, forming a larger structure. A sudden realisation hits me like a hard blow in the chest.

Those aren't sticks. They're bones.

The smell of decay wraps the area in wretched fumes that cannot be avoided. Entire missing limbs are scattered among the decomposing pieces of flesh that litter the ground. Shredded clothes cover some of the bodies, leaving bits and pieces of fractured skeletons exposed.

Something horrible happened here.

I have to stop myself from retching as I jump over the corpses. I struggle to look away from the nauseating scenery, but when I finally do, it's too late. The forest floor before me has vanished, leaving nothing but empty space up ahead. Unable to stop myself, I take the last step toward the cliff and launch myself over the edge.

CHAPTER 7

Weightless. They say if you ever find yourself underwater and aren't able to differentiate between up and down, you're supposed to blow out some air and see which way the bubbles go. Similarly, if you find yourself spiralling through the air to your likely demise, you should spit out some saliva and follow the same approach. Fortunately, I didn't have the luxury of time to conduct any such experiments of my own. If I had, I would be dead.

The drop turned out to be more of a ledge than a cliff, but the fall was enough to render me incapable of getting back up. My ribcage absorbed the impact and got damaged badly. If I were having trouble breathing before, then I am dying now. As I lie on my side, gasping for air, I see the creature leap off the ledge and land beside me.

I release a bloody sigh. If this is my fate, then who am I to fight it? Everything I've been through this past week has built up to this.

No. My whole life has built up to this.

Motionless, I gaze up at the beast. For what feels like an eternity, I stare into the pitch-black pupils of its bright, yellow eyes, watching as they expand and contract. We hold eye contact in this manner until I finally decide to close mine and wait for the inevitable.

Seconds turn into minutes, but nothing happens. Its breathing slows to a steady flow of warm air, until I can't feel it anymore. When I hear movement a few feet away, I cautiously open my eyes in time to see the creature staggering into the distance. Shell-shocked, I stay on the ground.

Like a bad hallucination, the beast disappears completely. I might have believed it to be all in my head, if not for the gash in my leg and the bitter taste of blood in my mouth. I gaze into the treetops above and allow the protruding rays of sunlight to fall upon me. The broad canopy blocks most of the Sun's heat, providing for a much cooler atmosphere.

A large bird-like creature flies past, momentarily visible through gaps in the leafy branches of the trees. Now I am almost certain that I'm losing my mind. The flying creature looked similar to a pterodactyl, if not bigger. I know it's impossible, because they are long extinct.

With stiff movements, I push myself off the ground. A sharp pain shoots through my side, and I buckle over. There's no point in going back to the circle of sand where I woke up. The better option would be to find a river or mountain peak. Then I might have a chance of finding a way back home.

As I make my way deeper into the forest, the world around me begins to change. It's as if someone flicked a switch, waking Mother Nature from her slumber. Various buzzing noises escalate all around me, along with a constant drone above my head. I don't have much time to ponder the origin of the sound, because a few steps later it hits me in the face.

A bundle of moving parts, about as big as my head, plummets to the ground. With both wings damaged, it flops around aimlessly amidst the rocks. I crouch down to inspect the bug, but its anatomy is unlike anything I ever encountered on my jogging route. It has eight legs like a spider, yet three body parts like an insect. Its immense size is also uncommon in these parts. I swear someone must have dropped me in the middle of the Amazon.

It's only now that I get a chance to examine the surrounding plant life. I don't recognise any of it. None of the flora is indigenous to my hometown. As I travel farther into the unknown, the seed of concern grows. *How far away from home am I?* This has to be an entirely different country.

I must have been knocked out for quite some time. Mom and Carter are probably extremely worried by now. I start to walk faster. I must find my way back as soon as possible. I must get to higher ground.

After an hour the forest starts to thin out, making it significantly easier to navigate. With fewer trees to provide shade, and no moisture in the air, my throat dries up again. I would give anything for a glass of water right about now. Normally I wouldn't risk it, but I'll even munch on some fruit or berries if I can find some.

A loud thud erupts in the distance, and the hair on my neck rises. Not again. It's coming back for me. Another sound bursts into existence, much closer this time. There is no time to think. *Run.*

Breathing becomes nearly impossible as I break into a sprint. The fall has bruised my chest, and my shallow breaths now escape as loud grunts. This is very bad. Any predator within a mile's radius will be able to hear me.

The more I realise how screwed I am, the more I hyperventilate and the louder my breathing becomes. If I weren't running for my life, I might appreciate the irony—but the taste of blood can spoil anyone's sense of humour.

The Sun's tormenting heat worsens, thrashing down from above. I begin to feel light-headed, and my vision becomes strained.

A girl appears before me.

I stop dead in my tracks. It feels as if my mind is playing tricks on me. Maybe she isn't real? For a moment, we stare at each other. My breathing is the only sound that fills the space between us. Standing an arm's length away from me, she looks surprisingly calm, yet alert. Another ear-splitting noise resonates just a few feet away. I leap forward and grab her by the shoulders.

"Y-you have to run," I stutter. "It's going to kill us!"

The girl continues to stare at me, not moving. She doesn't grasp the urgency of the situation. I try to move her along, but my knees feel weak. Everything spins out of control and my legs collapse underneath my weight. I roll onto my side, now breathing uncontrollably. Out of the corner of my eye, I see more feet moving closer.

Several hands clutch me from underneath and lift me off the ground. I bellow in pain when one of them applies pressure to my bruised ribcage. With tremendous effort, I strain my neck to see the people attached to these limbs.

Four strongly built guys carry me on their shoulders. They all look about my age, perhaps a few years younger.

"Where are you taking me?" I wheeze.

None of them make any effort to acknowledge my question. Irritated, I kick one of them in the back of the head. He cusses loudly.

"To the Adjustment Shack," one of them finally states.

"What?" I ask, hazily attempting to stay awake.

"Have you ever heard of altitude training?" he asks while balancing the weight of my lower body against his face. "It's when athletes train at a high altitude for several weeks, so they can adapt to the lack of oxygen in the air."

"Ugh huh," I lamely nod my head, barely able to follow what he's saying.

"Well, you have one day," he announces.

I feel like protesting this statement and am about to kick him in the head again, but my vision finally gives out. The last thing I remember is a small child shoving a flask full of water down my throat.

CHAPTER 8

"It looks so intense," a young boy whispers beside me.

"Keep quiet, Matt," an older voice hisses. "We don't know what we're dealing with."

"It still looks intense," he mutters back, clearly disheartened by the lack of enthusiasm.

With some effort I open my eyes and shift my vision to the people talking. Both are inspecting the black mark on my arm. I almost gasp when the boy looks up at me. Rubbing the sleep from my eyes, I steal a second glance at his face, but let out a sigh. It's not Carter.

The boy looks approximately ten years of age. He's almost as tall as Carter but looks frail for his height. The other one, a girl, is much older. She could easily be as old as me. Maybe even seventeen.

"You're awake!" she exclaims, and our eyes meet. Hers are blue. "What's your name, dropper?" she asks sternly.

"John," I answer with a raspy voice, my throat still sore.

She gestures to the boy. "This here is Matthew, and I'm Skylor."

I notice a vivid blue mark on her arm, similar to mine, but not quite the same pattern. Hers looks like an intricate web of neurons bursting with sparks of neon electricity.

The stagnating energy gives the illusion of being contained within the circular borders of the mark.

"You have one too!" I exclaim, amazed.

"We all do," she says matter-of-factly.

I shift my gaze to the little boy's arm. He too has a mark, bright white. I have so many questions, but my throbbing throat captivates my attention.

"Why can't I breathe properly?"

Skylor quickly responds. "The air here is quite different than what you are used to. Where the Earth has twenty-one percent oxygen and seventy-eight percent nitrogen, this atmosphere contains about fifteen to eighteen percent oxygen—or so we estimate. It's not enough to make you asphyxiate, but I'm sure you can feel its effects."

I hesitate for a moment. "What do you mean *this* atmosphere? We are on Earth."

Skylor and Matthew both frown.

"He doesn't know yet," Matthew whispers to her in a worried tone.

She pushes the boy behind her in an effort to silence him, but he emerges at her side like an excitable lapdog, determined to remain part of the conversation.

I exchange suspicious glances with them both, getting frustrated as the silence prolongs. "What don't I know yet?"

"John," Skylor explains. "You aren't where you think you are. This isn't Earth."

I keep staring at her, my expression unchanged. "Where am I?"

"On another planet," Matthew blurts out.

This pushes me over the limit, and my confusion turns to anger. *"Where am I?"*

"We don't know," Skylor replies calmly. "But at least you're not alone—there are many more like us, all trapped here."

"Trapped? *What's wrong with you?*" I'm not willing to indulge in any more childlike fantasies. Reality is shaken enough as it is. "Why would you lie to me?"

"We're telling the truth, John," she insists.

"No, no, no," I repeat, as if saying it enough will make it true. "Do you honestly expect me to believe that I'm on another planet?" I lift myself up from the platform and step onto the floor.

"I didn't want to believe it either," Matthew says with sadness filling his eyes, "but it really is true."

I can't bear any more of this. I haul myself away from them and bolt for the door. These children clearly have no intention of offering me any sort of direction. They'd much rather have me as a playmate than help me get back home.

When I step outside, the blazing sunlight almost blinds me. I'm now convinced that the accident after school gave me a concussion. The storm likely threw me across the sand clearing and knocked me unconscious. That would explain my sensitivity to light, as well as all the subsequent blackouts. Now that I think about it, the beast in the woods was clearly the result of a bad hallucination. The creature only appeared after I woke up and left when I was at my most disorientated. My injured knee could have been the result of a fall.

I cover my eyes and search for an escape route. The wooden cabin behind me isn't the only one in the near vicinity. Farther up the gradual slope of land, a much larger structure peers out from over the hill. The construction I woke up in didn't seem like it was meant to house people—it seemed like more of an impromptu halfway point, containing two make-shift beds and a shelf stacked with strange supplies. Both seem to have been built in haste, the other still incomplete and lacking materials.

The bristling sound of flowing water fills the air. My suspicions were right. Sooner or later, a river always leads you back to civilization. Though I'm not yet sure these kids can be called 'civilized'.

A group of teenagers emerge from the building up the path and gather around the entrance. I abandon any hope of reaching the river today. Instead, I turn in the opposite direction and spot a towering mountain peak in the distance. If children are roaming these parts of the forest, then society can't be far off. From a high enough altitude, I'll be able to spot any houses or people nearby. Not wasting a moment, I run straight for it.

As I'm leaving the area, I pass another group of children, all bearing red marks on their right arms. They linger around a dimly lit fireplace and watch as one of the older ones prepares a meal. One of them spots me and alerts the others. The tallest male emerges from the crowd, his clothes torn and caked in blood. Without even feigning an attempt to stop me from leaving, the group of children merely cease work on their various tasks, staring after me in silence. I can't quite put my finger on it, but something about their expressions seems off. If I didn't know any better, I'd say that they wanted me to run away.

When I reach the foot of the mountain, I hear people calling my name from far away. Skylor must have notified the rest of my plan to escape. I frantically start to scale the hill, but the climb proves to be difficult. Loose rocks and clumps of soil give way beneath my weight, causing me to slip and fall repeatedly. Brutish plants and trees cling to the surface of the steep incline, making it almost impossible to get around them. Changing my strategy, I try circling the ridge instead of climbing it. Using the roots of upturned trees, I pull myself from one plant to the next, quickly ascending away from the voices and eventually out of sight.

The darkness arrives sooner than I anticipated. Even if I somehow managed to get high enough, I still wouldn't be able to see the landscape below until morning. Using the last flicker of daylight to find my way through the brush, I steadily move up until I come across an opening in the side of the mountain.

I would never have thought that the sight of a cave could bring me such relief. A low roof, sealed walls and a relatively clean floor. Not only will I be protected from the outside elements, but my pursuers from earlier won't be able to find me too easily.

I carefully peek inside, making sure that no monstrous creatures reside within. Fortunately, there's hardly enough space for me, much less an imaginary mutant. I crawl in on my hands and knees and fall to the ground. Catching my breath, I enjoy a bit of momentary peace as the voices fade away and the day gives way to night.

Like a candle that has run out of wax, the remaining light flickers from existence, leaving me alone in an empty tomb high in the sky. I close my eyes as a light breeze blows against the mountain, winding its way into the cave that eagerly howls back in response. The floor beneath me cools down, stealing the last bit of warmth that radiates from my body.

For a fleeting moment, I become aware of an uncanny presence beside me. Behind closed eyelids, a dark figure turns visible, its movements slow and unsure. The shadow creeps closer until I feel its cold breath on the back of my neck. I suddenly recognise the distinct pinewood odour that used to cling to my father's raincoat. I instinctively inhale another breath, basking in the nostalgic scent.

He found me.

I stretch out my hands, expecting him to pull me into his protective grasp, but instead my arms flail through the air and hit the ground with a loud thud. Just like that, his presence is gone. I must have fallen asleep, because when I open my eyes, the encompassing darkness is replaced with a wave of scintillating light. The entire cave is illuminated with magnificent colours that pulsate off the walls and onto the surface of my body.

Confused but enthralled, I stay on my back. I've never seen the polar lights, but I imagine this is what an aurora would look like. When the wind wraps its icy fingers around my neck and the freezing floor begins to bite away at my exposed legs, I sit up straight. The colours are still pouring in from the outside world.

I crawl to the entrance of the cave and look up but refuse to believe my eyes. Among the lights above, celestial bodies flood the night sky in the forms of stars and constellations I did not know existed. Magnificent planets and brightly coloured balls of gas orbit alongside each other in spectral harmony.

I lean on the edge of the stone incline until a piercing light brightens the sky, causing the array of colours to disappear. Not only one, but several sources of light soon become visible, lighting up the entire landscape below. It looks like three suns are floating in the sky.

There is only one thing that I am certain of at this point. Those kids were right.

This isn't Earth.

CHAPTER 9

I'm still gazing out over the landscape several hours later. Sleep didn't come easily after my initial awakening. The unknown galaxy a footfall away from the cave entrance proved to be enough of a dream for one night. The constellations of stars have all withered away into the morning dusk, leaving behind a sky too bright to admire. Three suns follow each other in the direction I've labelled west.

There seems to be a rough, but definite distinction between the various terrains before me. One piece of land bears a forest of green as far as the eye can see. Several winged creatures roam those parts of the sky, taking turns to swoop down and perch on the highest treetops. In contrast, a barren desert terrain—void of any visible life—stretches to the far east. Just beyond the desert, a glimmer of water sparkles under the suns' beaming rays. It could, however, be a mirage.

I cannot shrug the feeling of an almost unquenchable thirst. I should be heading back to lower ground in search of that river. I place a knee on the cold cave floor and tie the laces on my running shoes into sturdy double knots. Only now do I notice something sticking to my left knee. Some sort of bandage, skilfully constructed out of leaves and other materials, encases my burned skin. The others must have tended to my wounds while I was still unconscious. I sigh. There's no point in running away from them. They seem to have been telling the truth after all. I make the decision to go back to the camp and hear what else they have to say. Who knows, they might even know of a way back home.

Beginning my descent down the steep mountainside, I try to maintain my focus on the same path I took to travel up. This quickly proves to be a lot more difficult than I thought. As the boulders turn to rocks and the trees shrink to ferns, the pathway becomes a slippery slope. I slide along the gravel and kick aside the bigger stones that block my path, shredding my clothes on the way down.

When I reach the base of the hill, I realise that I've made an error in judgement. There weren't nearly as many trees at the foot of the mountain yesterday. I peer up at the cloudless sky and back at my shadow, which stretches out in three different directions. Clearly on the wrong side of the mountain, I decide to retrace my steps on the ground instead.

Breathing comes easier this morning. I inhale the humid air while incomprehensible noises lure me along the narrow gorge. Exotic smells of foreign creatures linger about the woods. Time seems a vivid abstract in this place. With my every sensation entranced, minutes and hours become interchangeable. The woodland produces an inviting warmth that was absent before. Instead of searching for the camp, I feel compelled to head deeper into the forest's embrace.

Reaching lower plains, the trees give way to an opening where the soil turns dark and lacks the abundance of plant life I've grown accustomed to by now. Only one inhabitant sprouts in the centre of the clearing: a swollen plant with a stem thicker than my waist, stretching up into the sky like a lamppost. Its slime-coated body is topped by a bulbous, clam-shaped head. It's almost as if it has somehow managed to suck all life from the surrounding area. I don't make too much of the enlarged spectacle and hurry around it.

As I'm about to exit the glade, something soft bursts underneath the weight of my foot. This is followed by a cracking sound behind me, causing me to freeze. It felt like I stepped on an inflated balloon, popping it. Curious, I examine the ground around me, but spot nothing out of the ordinary. I proceed to walk forward—but a piercing scream stops me in my tracks.

"*Stop!*" the voice shouts, resonating from the opposite side of the field. "Do not move," it warns, urgency tainting every syllable.

I obey, expecting a bomb to go off if I don't. Slowly turning my head to the left, I'm surprised to see a svelte Indian girl with a spear tied to her back. Various shades of mud are smeared in diagonal streaks across her face, and her wild black hair covers her shoulders, making the girl barely distinguishable from the shadows.

She scans me thoroughly, making sure that I stay still, before bending down to examine the ground between us. Rising to her feet, she starts to jump towards me, carefully calculating each leap. She lurches forward with tremendous grace and precision, like a deer galloping through a crocodile-infested lake. When she reaches me, she comes to an abrupt halt. I suddenly recognise her. It's the girl from the forest: the first person to greet me on this strange new planet.

The green mark on her upper arm compels my gaze to move to her eyes, which are an even darker shade. I feel like I might pivot into them if she moves any closer. She firmly clasps her hands onto my shoulders and steps down on my left foot, pinning it to the ground. She pushes her face against mine and whispers in a hushed voice.

"You're stepping on a landmine."

"Sky will want to see you," she says.

"Does she have a blue mark?" I ask, embarrassed.

"Yes, she does."

"I think we already met," I admit shamefully. "She's the reason I ran away."

Aiesha grins, a gesture I didn't think she was capable of showing. "Sky has that effect on people. I'll take you back to her." She grabs hold of my arm and begins to lead me into a different direction. "My shift is over anyway."

CHAPTER 11

My bearings were completely off. Without Aiesha to guide me back to camp, I would never have made it. During our hike, she introduces me to some of the elements we pass along the way. In the nearby forest, the sources of food that can most easily be obtained are berries and fruit. However, I am to stay away from those—they're mostly poisonous.

On this planet the ground itself is toxic, but only to humans. The flora flourishes with the planet's toxic minerals coursing through them, yet the animals feed off the plants freely. It's clear that we don't belong here.

Upon our arrival at camp, Aiesha leads me to what I now know to be the Adjustment Shack. I enter quietly and come face to face with Skylor. This time, a different child accompanies her. The older boy is sitting on the platform I awoke on a day ago.

Skylor hears me approaching and looks up from her work. "Oh, I didn't think you would survive the night," she states casually. "I'm almost done here."

"Verdauungsstörungen," the boy moans, pointing to his stomach.

"Again?" Skylor turns back to him.

"Ja, nochmal."

"No, I mean why were we all brought to this place? I need to go back home. My mom is going to think I ran away or hurt myself trying."

For a second his gaze drops to the ground. He kicks some dirt around with his foot while considering my question. When he looks back up, I notice a change in his expression. "You should forget about her," he says.

"What?" I fail to hold back the crack in my voice.

He shrugs. "It's for the best."

My skin turns cold when I realise what he's implying. Jeremy doesn't think that I'll get to see her again. "You don't know that," I protest.

"You're right, I don't," he admits. "But I do know this. Whatever you did back on Earth, whatever your role was there, *they* decided that they'd rather have you here."

This thought strikes me much harder than something coming from a guy named Germ should. What was my role on Earth? And who is it that wanted me here instead?

"Don't let that get you down, Johnny," he interrupts my thoughts. "I'm here, too."

Johnny. I'm not too fond of the nickname, but I suspect he's grown too attached to it for me to correct him now.

We begin our expedition through the camp. All around, teenagers and children are hard at work. Whether they're carrying dried-out tree bark from the forest to the fire, or scavenging through heaps of worn-out clothing materials that litter the ground. Several knee-high piles, enough to clothe an entire classroom of children, cover the terrain around us.

I look down at my torn shirt and loose-fitting running shorts. I'm sure one of the piles has something that will fit me, but I'll be damned if I go anywhere near them. I have yet to see a naked child running around the camp, leaving me with an obvious question. Where did all these spare clothes come from? A dozen pairs of mismatched shoes are stacked next to each other in a sturdy wall of rubber and laces. Two toddler-sized sneakers have found their way to the top of the tower, appearing even more out of place than the rest. The small, red shoes have faded into a dusty grey under the suns' watchful gaze. Long since abandoned, the material has withered away to the point of being worthless. Stretching the fabric even a little will likely cause it to tear.

It becomes clear to me that there have not been any toddlers around these parts for a very long time. I cringe, because the answer to my question has now become quite evident.

Germ notices my fascination with the clothing, and quickly tries to divert my attention elsewhere. "You know," he says, "before I was taken, I was obsessed with researching cases involving children who vanished mysteriously." He picks up the pace, leading me away from the dead children's clothes. "When I first arrived here, these people were like celebrities to me!"

He turns to face me whilst doing a terrible job of walking backwards. "Give me a name, I bet you I can recall their case file."

"Aiesha," I respond a little too quickly.

He rubs his hands together. "Let's see. She was reported 'missing' in India two years ago. Maharashtra, to be exact.

Her village told the authorities that a demon took her. Surely you understand why that story grabbed my attention." He appears to be proud of himself. "Who's next?"

"I don't know anyone else," I shrug.

"Okay. If we're talking Elementals, then how about Skeith? You'll easily recognise him on account of his painted body—and other attributes," Germ chuckles. "He was one of the youngest shamans to walk alongside the Zulu tribes of Southern Africa. His people believed that he could talk to the gods and summon rain at will. One day he rose into the clouds and became part of a storm. This wasn't the concerning part, believe it or not. Apparently, he did it all the time." Germ turns back around, and strides forward excitedly. "The problem was that, on that day, he never came back down."

Germ leads me to a burrowed hole filled with glowing red coals. Large chunks of roasted meat rotate on long wooden skewers over the heat. A circle of logs and boulders surround the fire pit in a relaxed, bonfire fashion. He takes a seat on one of the steadier-looking logs and indicates for me to do the same. "This is the centre of our camp. We always leave a fire burning throughout the night, in case a new kid is dropped in the Clearing and needs to find their way here."

"The Clearing?" I ask.

"That big ring of sand you woke up in. It's probably the most dangerous place on the planet, yet we all arrive there, alone and unconscious. At some point I thought they were dropping us there to feed their alien pets or something. Too bad we got good at killing them."

I nod attentively. "So, all of you were abducted and brought to this planet?"

"Exactly," he confirms.

"So, what happens then? What if someone doesn't find their way to this camp?"

"Good question. The Elementals patrol the forest throughout the day and night. If someone gets lost, it's their job to find them."

I remember the bodies I stumbled upon when the beast was chasing me down. They all seemed to be scattered around the Clearing. "I saw many bones when I came here. Human bones."

Germ shrugs. "Sad really, not everyone actually makes it to safety. Might get lost if an Elemental doesn't spot you in time. Some children get mutilated by Reptants or end up eating poisonous fruit along the way. Not everyone is cut out for this. If you can't make it to the camp, you wouldn't last a day here anyway."

He reaches into the fire pit and grabs onto something that looks like an animal's leg. He twists the connecting bones at the joint until a loud snap erupts. The flesh peeking out from underneath the roasted skin is dark in colour. Germ bites off a piece and groans in delight. "We're in luck. They hardly ever catch a Rodback." He takes another bite then offers me the other piece. "You should really eat something."

He's right. My stomach is growling. Hesitantly, I take the blackened meat and thoroughly inspect it. Pieces of flesh stick to my fingers as I rotate the bone. Grease drips to the ground between my shoes.

Germ looks at me, anticipating my next move. "Try it," he encourages. "If we were on Earth right now, I'd tell you that it tasted out of this world." He laughs at his own joke, almost choking on the chunk of meat in his mouth.

I give in to the temptation and sceptically bring it closer to my lips. The crust smells burnt, like the meat my mom used to serve after my father disappeared. She'd forget our food in the oven until we could smell the smoke from our rooms. By the time we got to the kitchen, everything would be burnt to a crisp. We'd eat it anyway, to spare her feelings. If I could bear that, this shouldn't be too difficult. I close my eyes and take a big bite. Tangy juices flow from the meat as I begin to chew. It's a lot tougher than I expected it to be, and it takes me a while before I am able to swallow it all. I finally manage to take another bite. Then another. I quickly forget about the strange taste and concentrate instead on filling my stomach.

Suddenly, a little hand tugs at the back of my shirt, almost unnoticed. I twist around. It's the small boy from yesterday, Matthew. Hiding behind him is a little girl about half his age. I notice that she has a white mark as well.

The boy gathers his courage and says, "Hello John. We heard you came back and thought you might need some water." He takes a wooden bucket from the girl and puts it on the ground beside me. "Talaya fetched the water herself."

The girl's cheeks flush red at the mention of her name. "I was wondering if you could show her your mark? She really wants to see it."

I look at the two of them. Despite the hazardous sun-rays, both have extremely light complexions, topped with fair heads of hair. Their clothes seem especially ragged. Matthew's muddy shoes have torn along the edges, leaving several toes exposed. A pale, blue dress drapes around Talaya's tiny figure, with frayed patches along the bleached lace. The intricate stitching used to mend some of the holes in her garment leads me to believe that the dress was old and tattered before her abduction.

"Sure," I say, trying not to spit out any of the food stuffed in my mouth. I stand up, so they can have a clearer view. Both stare at my arm, mesmerized by the obsidian mark.

"See, I told you," Matthew says to Talaya.

They would have gazed longer, but a loud group of voices emerging from the forest snaps them out of their trance.

"We have to go," Matthew says quickly. "I'll fetch the bucket later." He grabs Talaya's hand before they run off into the bushes.

I gratefully lift the bucket and gulp down the cold liquid. It tastes different than the water back home. More pure. I almost finish the entire bucket before putting it down.

"They came here together," Germ says between chewing and muffled breaths. "We found them hiding in a tree two miles from the Clearing. The boy is ten and the girl is six. Before you ask, we aren't sure what white marks mean either. They're the youngest kids here, and the only ones who have them."

"That's horrible," I say. "They're so little."

"Agreed," he nods his head. "Their jobs are to stay at camp and water the plants. That way we can keep an eye on them."

Germ finishes his piece of meat and throws the bone into the fire pit. He clears his throat. "Okay. So basically, we all have marks. Don't know why, but some of the Blue kids speculate it might be a sort of tracking device. The colours aren't given out randomly either. When more kids started to appear, we noticed that groups who bore the same colours displayed similar traits and abilities. Are you getting all of this?"

"Yeah," I sputter with a mouth full of Rodback.

"Those with blue marks are called the Neuros. They generally display superior intelligence and other heightened cognitive abilities. That would be the main reason why Skylor runs this place. She's the smartest person here."

The noises from the forest grow louder, interrupting Germ's lecture. I peer over his head to see a male emerging from the trees, carrying a large object on his back. Following behind him are two girls and another boy. The entire group looks exceptionally strong and trained for peak performance. Even the girls seem intimidating enough to make a grown adult think twice before telling them off. As they near the fire, I see that their leader is hauling the corpse of some large creature.

They boast loudly about their successful hunt. "Did you see the way it stumbled when I shoved the knife through its gut?" one of the girls shouts. Her face is covered in splashes of stomach bile. "It never stood a chance!" the second guy comments, using his shirt to wipe the blood from the edge of his spear.

I notice that they all bear red marks on their upper arms. The colour of blood. Not the kind that flows out when you accidently prick your finger, but the dark crimson that seeps from a ruptured vein in the neck. The internal borders of the red markings connect like the arteries of a heart. Not unlike the organ, four distinct chambers are etched out within the symbol, each wall connecting in the centre.

Up close, it's clear that the male leading the group is much bigger than the rest of his entourage. As he moves, his mark seems to beat forcefully, as if it is no less vital than the heart pumping within his chest. He comes to a halt next to the fire pit and drops the limp corpse to the ground. Its fangs scrape the soil where the mangled body falls. Looking at the long tail and triangular ears of the beast, I'd say it is some sort of feline. Tufts of ashen grey fur sprout from its body, stained with several patches of clotted blood. The fluid leaking out of its mouth forms a growing puddle of maroon next to my feet.

I shudder, realising the true detriment of my situation. Having a hearty meal or a bucket of water at my side does not change the fact that I am surrounded by kilometres of fierce wilderness crawling with these creatures. I am practically defenceless out here in the open.

The overgrown teenager sternly folds his arms and looks at Germ. Black stubble has begun to sprout across his squared jaw line. He must recently have undergone a growth spurt, because his clothes are tightly spun against his skin, barely fitting his enlarged figure.

"All you ever do is eat, you emaciated splint," he gripes to Germ. "I hunted this Leaper for five hours, but you're probably going to eat it too!" The others laugh at his banter. He turns to me and sees my mark. I know he saw it, because his eyes widen, and his mouth gapes open. For a moment he seems taken aback, but then quickly masks it with arrogance. "Who the hell are you?" he grunts.

"I'm John," I respond casually.

He turns to Germ again. "What are you doing, Germ? Putting together some kind of a freak show?" His group laughs again, hanging onto his every word. They remind me of little remora fish waiting for a killer whale to catch its prey before swimming closer to suck the meat between its teeth.

"Well?" he says to me. "Are you enjoying your meal? Can I get you anything else? Perhaps a glass of warm milk?"

With my mind still fixated on the dead animal in front of me, I miss his obvious sarcasm and respond with, "That sounds great."

He lunges forward and pulls me closer by my shirt. "Don't think you can get cocky," he utters with contempt. "To me, you're just another pathetic mouth to feed." He lets go, dropping me back onto the log with a thud. He gives

Germ another glance and storms off. His entourage flashes derisive grins, then follows.

When they are well out of earshot, Germ sighs. "I'm sure you can guess what a red mark means. Rather a lewd bunch if you ask me."

"Who was that guy?" I ask, irritated at his blunt arrogance.

"The vehement douche? That would be Kyle. Back home, our local newspaper wrote an entire article on his disappearance. They found his car after it crashed on a freeway in Illinois. His body was never found, which made it look like he fled the scene. I wouldn't ask him about it, though." Germ laughs nervously. "Kyle doesn't like it when you ask questions." He releases a sharp exhale. "Perhaps that's why he despises me so much. Anyway, where were we?"

"The marks?" I prompt.

"Oh yeah. The Reds, also known as the Apex, value physical attributes above all. They look up to Kyle because of his strength—not his intellect, I assure you. Their job is to help where brute force is needed, but primarily they'll hunt for food and never let you forget it."

"What about the Greens?" I ask, still thinking about the girl from the forest.

"Ah, the Elementals. Extremely adventurous and know everything there is to know about nature's elements. Hard to see where the forest ends and they begin. They are the only ones who get to explore outside of camp. Or they're the only ones who keep returning from patrols, to put it another way."

I look down at my mark, now more perplexed than ever. Am I supposed to be good at something?

"Let's walk," Germ says. I take a last swig of water and chuck my bone into the fire before following him. As we walk past the Adjustment Shack, I spot the hidden body of water that lies behind it. Taking the form of a narrow stream, it remains the only source of water I have come across so far. The camp is mostly surrounded by woods, but at the farthest edges the plant growth meets a stark desert that stretches as far as the eye can see. Separating us from the vast wasteland is a great hill that leans towards the river. It's not as large as the mountain I scaled yesterday, but the tunnel-like cave stretching through it makes yesterday's shelter look like a dollhouse in comparison. We stop at the entrance.

"Welcome to the Cave," Germ declares.

About a dozen Blue Marks are scattered throughout the hollow hill. From their stern faces, they are concentrating, each busy fidgeting with bits and pieces of separate contraptions.

"I present to you the techno boys." He chuckles and points to the only girl working in the corner. "And Rusty. They deal with mechanics and technology. We don't find much scrap here, but when we do, they'll be able to find a use for it."

Rusty notices our presence and leaves her workstation. She approaches briskly, wiping her oily hands on a dirty rag. "Sup, Germ, did you bring me another Neuro?"

Before he can answer, she lifts up my arm and pauses. Her pierced nose tightly wrinkles up. "What exactly am I looking at?" she demands firmly.

"No idea, Elizabeth. Better ask him yourself."

She instinctively touches her red curls of wild hair. "You know, if any other Mark called me that, they would have been kissing the cave floor right about now."

Germ smiles proudly. "Yeah, I know."

Rusty flashes a quick smile back, but then it disappears. She turns away from him and thoroughly inspects me from head to toe. Only once she is certain that I don't have an extra leg or tentacle concealed on my body does she offer me a hand to shake. "Name's Rusty, in charge of mechanics and technology."

"I'm John," I nod. "I arrived here yesterday."

"Yesterday?" she asks, shocked. "Why haven't you followed the set-out protocol? New drops report here ASAP upon arrival, unless suspended in the Adjustment Shack."

"I didn't know I was suppo—"

She cuts me off. "Doesn't matter, batteries are most likely drained already."

"Sorry," I utter hastily, not knowing what I'm apologising for.

She rolls her eyes. "Are you carrying any technological devices on you? Phones, watches?"

I reach into my front pants pocket and pull out my phone. An excited glint appears across her face. "Is that a satellite phone?"

"Yeah, my dad used it for hiking in the mountains," I say proudly.

"Smart man. This type of technology will have tremendous value to us here. Can't wait to see what's on the inside."

"Wait," I hesitate. "What are you going to do with it?"

"We're going to open it up and scrap it for any valuable resources. Standard procedure."

I suddenly regret showing her my phone and feel a lump in my throat. What if I find a way out of here? Then I won't be able to contact my family. Or my father. I may not know his whereabouts or even if he has a phone, but he knows that we have his. And he has the number. A small part of me still hopes that he might call one day. I'm not prepared to give up my last hope.

"Sorry, I can't let you do that." I attempt to avoid her gaze, but her eyes find mine, nevertheless.

She looks offended. "You're not going to be able to use a phone here. You do realise that there aren't any satellites floating around in orbit?"

I slowly begin to back out of the Cave. "I know, but I'm going to hold on to it."

"You're going to have to change that mentality, or you won't last very long here!" I instantly feel guilty over my decision, but I'm simply not ready to part with my only lifeline home.

Germ jogs up behind me. "That Rusty is quite a girl, huh?" he says in admiration.

"Yeah," I humour him, but not enthusiastically enough.

He picks up on my tone and scans my face. "I wouldn't be bothered by her attitude if I were you," he says. "It usually comes with the mark. You either love it or you hate it."

As we stroll on, the setting suns create a red glow on the horizon. Back near the centre of camp, Germ leads me to a large bungalow made entirely of wood. He stops in front of the entrance. "Welcome to the Lodge," he announces. "This will be the end of your tour for today. We don't accept cards, cash, or cheques."

I step inside to see three long rows of beds, at least fifty in total.

"This is where we sleep," Germ says.

"Are you still building it?" I ask. "Where's the roof?"

"No need for one. It never rains."

"Where do the plants get their water?"

"How should I know? Underground currents? Ask a Green."

As we walk through the rows of beds, I notice that most are already taken. Clothing and other miscellaneous items are strewn over the surfaces.

"Those at the far end are reserved for Elementals only. They are placed farthest from the entrance so they can catch up on sleep without being disturbed." We stop where the beds begin to fill up with people. Green Marks lie stretched out on the sturdy mattresses, exhausted from scavenging through the forest. Germ points to an open bed, then flops down on a particularly messy one sprinkled with dirty rags, rotting fruit, and even something that looks like a piece of animal meat wrapped in crumpling leaves.

"You can sleep here, next to me," he whispers, trying not to wake the others. "We plebeians need to stick together."

I place the empty bucket I've been carrying at the foot of my bed. Tightly stacked blocks of wood form the base of the structure and laid on top are neatly fitted piles of leaves and tinder. Four vertical logs, one at each corner, serve as posts used to strap long strips of foliage across. This final layer of woven material raised above the soft cushioning forms the surface of the bed. I climb on top and lie down in the middle, cautious as not to accidentally dismantle a piece. The hammock stretches underneath my weight, allowing my body to sink into the cushioning atop the sturdy base.

Germ looks at me while chewing on a piece of yellow fruit. "The Elementals built the beds, and they know their stuff when it comes to the importance of a good night's sleep."

Exhausted, I allow my thoughts to drift until the sky is dark and the beds are full. My entire body aches and shifts uncomfortably against the foreign materials. I struggle to relax, knowing that I might never crawl back into the safety of my real bed at home.

Bright points of light appear across the heavens, as if someone pricked thousands of minute holes into the surface of a blanket, allowing beams of energy to burst through. I finally turn my back on Jeremy and drift off into a dreamless sleep.

CHAPTER 12

I'm not sure what woke me, but a rumble shoots through my stomach. I retrieve the bucket at the foot of the bed and gulp down the remaining water. This doesn't fill me. I wonder whether there might be any food left at the fireplace. Too restless to lie still, I sit at the edge of the bed and weigh my options.

I could try to sleep through the hunger and wait until morning to eat. Or I can venture to the fire on my own, in the middle of the night, on a nightmarish planet I didn't know existed until yesterday. My growling stomach gives me my answer. Out into the nightmarish planet it is.

I hoist myself up from the flora-entwined structure and slowly tread through the rows of beds. Luckily the night sky is bright enough to make it out of the Lodge without tripping into someone's bed. Outside, I spot the conveniently lit fire at the centre of the camp, still burning. Without hesitation, I begin to prowl toward it. The warm air wraps against my skin like a damp blanket. As I near the fire, various silhouettes become visible around its brightly lit aura. I stay just out of its reach and listen to their voices. Two Neuros, sitting opposite each other, are in the middle of a heated discussion. On the other side of the fire, balanced on a large, upturned boulder, an Elemental looks out over the camp. Camouflaged within the depths of the night, his quiet demeanour and carefully chosen position make him difficult to detect.

The blue-marked boy continues. "I'm just saying, more males are born during times of war and stress."

"Oh please," the girl fires back, "the Returning Soldier effect is hardly applicable to our situation."

"It certainly is!" he exclaims. "You seem to insist that all arguments need a literal basis, when mine is in fact a metaphorical one. How did we arrive in this new life? Have we not been born to a new planet? As the newest species in this ecosystem, we are a prime example of the chicken coming before the egg."

"I think you need to shove your metaphorical egg back where it came from," she suggests.

"Alright then, Rusty," he continues in his patronising tone, "explain to me why there are more males at this camp."

"I'm not denying that fact," she says, irritated. "I'm just saying that in order to prove your hypothesis, you would have to use both variables. Yes, more males are dropped at the Clearing every month, but you have failed to prove that we are in a time of stress. The Returning Soldier effect is thus irrelevant."

Dumbfounded, he looks around and proceeds to spread his arms out, pointing to his surroundings. "We are literally in Hell."

"I'm not," she responds casually, and cracks open a nut before popping it into her mouth. He doesn't respond to her answer. Instead, they both stop talking and turn to me.

I stare back at them. As they spoke, I drifted closer and am now standing between them and the fire. With none of us talking, the protracted silence starts to feel threatening.

"Is there any food left?" I finally ask.

"Help yourself," the guy shrugs.

Relieved, I turn around and inspect the fireplace. Between the glowing coals surrounding the flames, various pieces of meat are positioned on small flat rocks. I recognise some of the darker Rodback meat Germ introduced me to earlier. Reaching into the heat, I grab the smallest remaining chunk.

As I'm readying to leave the fireplace, I realise that it would come off as rude if I immediately retreated to the Lodge—assuming earthly social standards are still relevant here. I choose to sit down on the boulder closest to the Neuros. As I move past the fire, the light illuminates my mark.

"Oh," the boy remarks. "You're *him*." He stares at my arm critically, which makes me feel uneasy. He notices this but continues anyway. "When they spoke of a bloke with a black mark, I thought some strain of psychedelic mushrooms must have made its way into our food source." He leans closer to get a better view. "The symbolism is remarkable. What could it possibly mean?"

"Oh, cut it out, will you?" Rusty snaps at him.

"Well, as Plautus once said, seeing is believing." He finally averts his gaze from my arm and then introduces himself. "I'm Connor, and that there is Rusty."

"We've met," she declares derisively and rolls her eyes at me yet again.

"Where are you from?" I ask, taking note of the pinched tone in his voice.

"East Asia. Japan to be precise."

"And your name is Connor? That's a very English name."

"It's not my real name," he explains. "I changed it, seeing that no one here could pronounce it." He appears to be disappointed in his fellow Marks, as if the problem doesn't lie with their inability to pronounce his name, but rather with their lack of trying. "Regardless, welcome to Damnatus—it's Latin for the condemned."

"Or the damned," Rusty interjects. "I prefer that one."

I briskly swallow the meat I'm chewing on. "That's cool. Did you come up with it?"

"Me?" Connor asks, surprised. "No. Someone must have mentioned it one day, and it kind of stuck." He looks to the fire for guidance, then adds, "Nobody knows who named Earth, so it doesn't matter anyway."

As I'm about to finish my meal, Rusty decides to antagonise me. "Has anyone called you yet?" she asks sarcastically. I know she's referring to my satellite phone. When she says it out loud like that, it does sound ridiculous. I know it is.

"It's sentimental to me," I explain.

"It's imperative to our research," she replies.

"How so? What are you working on?"

"You wouldn't understand," Connor interrupts. "No offence, but you're not a Neuro." I try to brush aside his slight, but his words nudge at me anyway.

We sit in silence, half of us eating away and the other half staring up at the star riddled sky. I'm about to excuse myself when a deafening shriek bellows from afar. A long wail that pierces my thoughts and makes my insides churn. The others around the fire notice it too, but act like they didn't. I hold my breath as another disturbing scream follows.

"What the hell was that?" I sputter, wondering why everybody seems so at ease.

"It's a Shrieker," a rough voice emanates next to me. I narrow my eyes in search of the speaker. The Elemental looks down at me from his perch on the stone. During the conversation, he has shifted closer undetected, moving to another seat. How long has he been up there? He seems to enjoy my puzzled response.

"Nobody has ever seen one and lived to tell the tale," he says, "but we can visualise what it looks like based on the mutilated corpses it leaves behind."

I gulp, uneasy.

"Its tracks dig deep into the ground, carrying the weight of a full-grown elephant bull. Yet, it prowls with the ease of a leopard, never making a noise when hunting." He shakes his head. "Such a creature should not exist."

"You haven't told him the strangest part," Connor interjects. "Its appetite is insatiable, and if given the chance, the Shrieker will swallow a Rodback whole. Yet, when it comes to humans, it never finishes a meal. It does not like the taste."

"Why even go through the effort of killing us then?" I ask.

"Izilwane ezivela esihogweni," the Elemental utters in a strong African tongue, as if trying to warn me.

I hurriedly finish my meal and excuse myself. The rest stay behind, not fazed by the rest of the screams. I venture back to the Lodge and run inside. This time, when my head touches the hammock, I drift off almost immediately. As my surroundings fade into the night, another ominous cry clamours from afar.

Though this one sounds different. Fainter. Almost child-like.

CHAPTER 13

I awaken with a jolt, completely unaware of where I am. Panic sets over me until Aiesha's green eyes appear next to mine, and the memories come flooding back. Memories. If only they were nightmares. At least when I woke up, they would be gone. Aiesha raises her index finger to her lips, indicating that I should stay silent. She then points to the entrance and gestures for me to follow, before disappearing out of the Lodge.

For a few minutes, I allow myself the soothing delight of gazing up at the undisturbed void. Its scintillating surface breathes life into the morning dawn. *Things will get better*, I tell myself. *At least you're not alone anymore.*

To my left, Germ lies amongst his defective possessions, clutching onto them in his sleep. The bed next to him is empty, and devoid of any belongings. In the next one, two ruffled heads of hair stick out from beneath a large, yellow jacket. I recognise the light complexions of Matthew and Talaya. One of them must have crawled in with the other during the middle of the night. Matthew has retrieved the wooden bucket and lodged it underneath their bed.

I look over the rows of beds and survey the severity of our situation. Never before have I related to so many people at once. The Lodge is filled with children who were taken away from their homes and families. I wonder how long they've been here. Did any of them have a chance to say goodbye? Perhaps it's better if they didn't. A farewell is too final. It implies that there won't be a reunion.

Most of the kids look vulnerable and dejected, like lost toys lying around a shed, waiting to be found. But these aren't just any kids, I remind myself, for they are still alive. Ordinary children would be dead already. These unlucky few were chosen specifically for the attributes they possess. This bit of information continues to make me uneasy, because for some mysterious reason, I was chosen too.

After gathering my strength, I swing my legs to the side of the bed and place my feet against the dusty earthen floor. Without making any noise, I slip into my running shoes and haul myself up. Making my way down the narrow aisle, I scan the sleeping children as I pass by. Most look about twelve to sixteen years of age. Here and there an older kid appears, surrounded by the youngest of children. The smaller ones seem to gather around those who can provide protection. Kyle appears to be one of these targets. When I near the end of the building, I spot him sleeping in the middle of a group of Apex. Covering him is a large animal hide that conceals his entire body. I notice now that almost all of the Reds Marks have different kinds of skins for blankets, but none as big as Kyle's.

Aiesha is nowhere to be seen when I reach the entrance, so I decide to look for her at the campfire instead. Sure enough, she's already there, chewing on a particularly meaty rib. Her face is smeared black with the charcoal lying around the fireplace. Before I can utter a word, she covers her mouth with a finger again and indicates that I should take the seat next to her.

I quietly comply and break off a lengthy rib for myself. By the looks of it, we're both chewing on the carcass of the feline that Kyle killed yesterday. The creature they referred to as a Leaper. The meat has a lot more sinew than the Rodback and proves rather difficult to chew.

The weather-beaten log I'm sharing with Aiesha faces the forest, leaving the campsite to our backs. She seems so have chosen this position on purpose, and eyes the trees with an intent stare. I watch the trees sway in the light breeze, their gloomy branches brushing the air with an unyielding touch. The leaves rarely depart from their holds, preferring the shelter of wooden giants than that of the ground below.

I detect movement long before any sound reaches my ears. Squinting, I struggle to see through the misty air. One of the smaller-looking bushes is shoved aside and a shadowy figure emerges from the treeline. Hunched over, he silently makes his way towards us.

I look over at Aiesha to see if she's noticed this too, but her gaze is pointed in another direction, where two more figures have appeared. One of them stumbles across the field with a limp and slowly trails behind the other. All three are walking towards the fire, which serves as a beacon of light.

The boy from the bushes is the first to stop before us. His hair is matted with twigs and dirt. Glazed-over eyes peer at us, blinking far less than they should. His skin is painted brown, hidden beneath a thick layer of wet mud.

It looks like he's been trying to sleep on the forest floor, but with little success. Without exchanging any words, he kneels next to Aiesha and retrieves an item from a woven satchel. In his hand is a broken wristwatch. Aiesha frowns at it, clearly displeased. The glass panel has cracked open, and the dial has been crushed into unsalvageable pieces. One of the rubber straps is torn off, leaving behind nothing more than useless scrap. She takes it from him and reluctantly tosses it into the fire, feeding the starving flames.

With a downward nod, Aiesha dismisses the boy. Defeated, he pushes himself off the ground and wanders away. Before I can ask her what just happened, the next figure walks past us. The girl doesn't stop like the boy did. Awake and alert, she brushes away the grey dust that clings to her arms. Her hair is tied up in a high ponytail, drawing attention to the small, yellow dots that spiral around her eyes like blooming flowers. A green line is painted on the bridge of her nose, forming the stem.

She acknowledges Aiesha's presence with a lively salute and gestures to the injured party behind her.

"A Leaper pounced on him," she informs us, and paces away towards the river.

The last of the three forest dwellers edges towards us, his left leg barely touching the ground. He uses a broken branch as a makeshift crutch to support his weight. The camouflage has been smeared off his body in violent streaks, leaving behind exposed, bruised skin. A green mark is now visible on his arm, unlike the previous two who were covered in dirt.

A stark and pale expression meets us at the fire. The shivering boy looks down at the cleaned bones between my feet. "Ironic," he manages to force his blue lips into a grin. "Mommy Leaper didn't very much approve of your meal." He sighs and addresses Aiesha. "The Apex will kill just about anything that walks. Never mind the consequences."

Aiesha observes the remainder of the dark meat next to the fire. "I knew we'd pay dearly for this meal," she says. "Leapers aren't known for abandoning their offspring."

"The Apex took a cheap shot," he agrees. "They likely got their hands on the cub while the mother was hunting near the camp's border."

He turns to me again, tilting his head to the side while his gaze lingers over my mark. "Such ferocious, yet sensitive creatures," he muses aloud. "A Leaper's hearing is fine-tuned to detect the smallest of movements. It can distinguish the rustling of leaves from the quiver of a Whittleneck's wings, all while balancing its weight on pencil-thick branches."

Aiesha bends down and touches the edge of his left foot. He responds by tensing up and sucking in his breath. "They can't stand loud noises," he breathes out, straining his chest. "Luckily for us, the Shriekers are constantly circling our camp in the dead of night. Their cries keep the Leapers out of the area."

"Kept," Aiesha corrects him.

He scowls. "Too bad Kyle couldn't resist the trophy."

She carefully shifts her grip upwards and applies light pressure to the bones in his ankle. This time he doesn't respond to her touch. She nods, satisfied. She takes away his walking stick and forces him to walk four steps without it. He does this with gritted teeth, but manages it without assistance.

"It's just a bad sprain," Aiesha finally announces, and hands back his stick. "Skylor will be able to fix you up. Keep your leg elevated, and no shifts for the next two weeks."

"Two weeks?" he exclaims. "Just give me a good night's rest! I'll be ready again in the morning."

"I'm not done yet," she says, her expression unchanged. "You may return to night shifts in a month's time. Until then, you're only allowed out during the day."

"Bloody Apex," he mutters angrily.

"Go to the Adjustment Shack," Aiesha commands. "You look like death."

He finally gives in and thanks her for the aid. With a strenuous tread, he hobbles away, muttering more curses under his breath.

The first of the three suns lights up the plain in front of us. As if on cue, rows of indistinguishable faces, each camouflaged with different shades of mud and other elements, emerge from the forest. The rays of light now reflect the Green Marks treading towards us, their gaits indicating exhaustion and a lack of sleep. Some head towards the river, whilst the rest retire directly to the Lodge. After they enter, others exit from the structure and disappear into the woods, taking their place. The silence continues undisturbed, as if they were never there.

"We work in shifts," Aiesha finally says. "The more experienced Elementals patrol the forest throughout the night, whilst the rest take watch during the day. Unlike the

Apex, we work alone to ensure that we cover maximum ground. We are the only Marks who get to venture off as far as we wish, as long as we stay in our allocated territories. The Apex, however, are bound to defend the areas just outside of camp. Simply put: they hunt for food, we hunt for new drops."

"New drops?"

"Kids."

She turns to me, but I fail to respond. "I spoke with Skylor and she agreed that I could take you with me if I worked the day shift."

This snaps me back to life. "You want me to go back into the forest?" I ask warily, seeing that I almost got eaten the last time.

"I'll guide you," she reassures me. "Besides, you serve no use to us sitting at camp all day. Until we figure out what your mark means, this will have to do."

My phone is still pressed against my leg, unscathed and out of view. Rusty was furious when I refused to hand it over. So far, I have only witnessed stressed reactions when any sort of device was in question. Technology is clearly a very rare resource on this planet.

"That first boy, did he break someone's watch?"

"No," she answers.

"Then why were you so angry?"

"I wasn't angry," she stands up. "We don't have the luxury of getting angry at our own kind. Only disappointed."

Our kind. I take note of these words.

She gathers her composure as quickly as she lost it. "I never cared about the watch. I care about the person it was attached to." She sighs. "He failed to save a drop, so he retrieved the watch instead."

I look down at my feet and see the remains of the watch glower and melt into the ashes. We finish our meals in silence, then set off into the unforgiving grasp of the forest.

CHAPTER 14

The trees loom over us like bending skyscrapers, casting monstrous shadows. Massive roots lift patches of ground, creating treacherous bulges around every corner. As we venture deeper into the heart of the wild, the world seems to come alive around us. Buzzing, chirping and something I can only describe as a *click-clack* sound emanates from the branches above. Down below, minute creatures scuttle away as we approach, whilst some pay no regard to our presence at all and continue to casually wander about.

Astounding colours illuminate the plants of the lower plains that are concealed from the suns' rays. Aiesha explained that poisonous liquid courses through most of them, causing the surrounding shadows to radiate with an entire spectrum of glowing pigments. In this mystical paradise filled with forbidden fruit, we are able to experience nature like never before.

Talking doesn't seem to be an Elemental's strongpoint; at least not when it comes to Aiesha. The lonely days spent out here in the unknown must have an effect on her. Unless she's always been this quiet. Perhaps this is one of the very reasons she was chosen as a Green.

Every few minutes, Aiesha stops and bends down to inspect the uneven terrain. Then she pushes three fingers into the ground, scoops up some mud or sand, and smears it across her face. I obediently follow her example, still not understanding why. Surely the first handful of sooty charcoal was enough camouflage to last an entire day. The Elementals don't seem particularly keen to wash it off, either. Most I encountered inside the Lodge were covered in it. If the main goal of having dirt on your face is to blend in with the surroundings, then why keep it on at camp? If anything, the camouflage draws more attention to the Greens when among the rest of the Marks.

After about an hour has passed, when the second sun announces its arrival with a threatening glower, I decide to get some questions off my chest.

"If your job is to catch drops, why don't you just wait for them at the Clearing? You won't need to chase them if they don't run away in the first place."

"It's not that simple," she replies flatly.

"Is it because of those creatures?" I ask, remembering the monstrous lizard that chased after me in the forest. My knee is still healing where the acidic saliva splashed it.

"The Reptants? They're hardly a problem." She jumps over a giant tree root and lands on her feet with a dull thump. "It's the drops that cause the real trouble."

"What do you mean they aren't a problem? One almost killed me." I try to hop over the same root Aiesha cleared so easily but fail miserably.

Her green eyes watch me from the other side with a hint of amusement. "They only register movement," she explains, before lending me a hand. "If you simply remained still, it would have gone away eventually."

I think back to the encounter and recall the creature acting strangely after I fell off the cliff. The Reptant could easily have killed me when I lay defenceless on the ground, yet it didn't. The creature simply walked off.

"Reptants surround the Clearing at all times," she continues to explain as we walk down the pathway of gnarled trees. "At first we tried to signal directions to the drops from the nearby bushes, but they would run towards us instead, giving away our positions and endangering everyone's lives."

We cut through dense undergrowth and turn a corner. Hidden by the canopies, a small stretch of open land appears, discreetly concealed from the outside world. Aiesha progresses onward and finally comes to a stop next to a small waterhole. The inky water swallows most of the light that touches its surface. In return, it produces a dark shimmer. Purple flowers and saplings bloom lavishly, surrounding the pond in circular spirals.

"I discovered this waterhole a while ago," she says. "The others use the stream back at camp to wash themselves, but I prefer this one. It's more secluded." She inspects my dirty clothes with a suspicious stare. "And you look as if you haven't bathed in days."

I survey the breach in the ground, hardly even two metres wide. "It's not very big," I suggest unsurely.

"It's big enough," she replies and gives a wink before turning around to undress. I feel my face redden and quickly look away. Following her lead, I fumble with my laces until they are untied, and pull off my shoes along with begrimed socks. I tug my shirt over my head and add everything to a bundle before piling it on top of her clothes under a large tree. I decide to keep my pants on.

When I turn back, Aiesha is already sitting at the edge of the hole, readying herself to climb in. Wearing nothing but a tightly wrapped piece of cloth around her upper torso and lower half, deep-ridden scars stretch across her entire body. Three parallel lines, beginning at her stomach, protrude from beneath the cloth and stretch around her back, morphing into a single red line ending right beneath her neck.

She steadily lowers herself into the water until it is up to her shoulders. With a swift movement of her wrist, she beckons me to follow, before disappearing underneath the surface. I walk closer, expecting her to resurface, but she doesn't. There is no sign of her.

At first, I think she's teasing me by staying under the water so long—but after a minute, I begin to worry. Something is wrong.

Alarmed, I dive into the hole. What if she swam too deep and got caught in some tree roots, or can't find her way back because of the dark? I expect my hands to touch the bottom within seconds, but instead I continue to sink down. As I go deeper, the water turns colder and the tunnel darkens. I begin to fear that I might not make it out in time. Even if I do find her, my oxygen is running out.

The hole narrows, and the walls begin to graze my arms. I'm about to turn back when faint, shattered rays of light become visible from below. The bottom appears so I stretch out my arms, blindly feeling around for Aiesha's body between the soil and loose debris. She isn't there. Instead, more light floods into the pit from a tunnel stretching sideways. Without hesitation, I kick away and swim through the murky water leading to the horizontal passage.

A gleaming trail brings me to an open body of water. I follow the source of illumination and excel upwards as fast as my tiring limbs allow. I finally resurface and greedily inhale the damp air like an infant who just exited the womb. A voice echoes through the cave.

"It took you long enough."

Regaining my breath, I glance around the curved stone walls surrounding us. Light filters through multiple cracks in the rock ceiling and illuminates the cave floor where Aiesha is sitting. I paddle to the edge and hoist myself up next to her.

"Welcome to my private quarters," her eyes twinkle with mystery. "This is where I keep my secret stash."

Next to her lie various items. Everything from nuts, berries and fruit to weapons and tools forged from animal skin and bones.

"I thought most plants here are poisonous?"

"Yes. Those that grow in the wild tend to be inedible." She picks up a prickly purple plum-like fruit and hands it to me. "Although rare, an Elemental will occasionally find a new strain of fruit that contain little to no toxins. We then go about collecting the seed groups and replanting them at camp. It makes harvesting easier."

"Does it work?"

She shrugs. "Nobody has died yet."

Aiesha chooses another piece of fruit and plucks the hairs from it before biting into its soft skin. She allows the pungent juices to flow down her chin and drop onto the already wet cave floor. "Have one. I bet you'll like it."

Not needing much convincing, I pluck the hairs until the plum-looking fruit is bare and bite down. The initial taste is sweet, but it leaves a sour aftertaste. I work my way down to the centre and take hold of the pit in the curve of my palm.

Aiesha looks pleased. She removes the pit from my grasp and pushes it underneath the cloth around her chest. "We can replant the seed later."

My gaze falls upon the green symbol on her arm. Luminous emerald vines tightly wrap around each other, twisting and morphing into several branches that stretch out towards the edges of the mark. Then again, they could also represent the roots of a tree, reaching to an unknown source within.

At the far end of the cave, I spot a piece of paper resting on a raised rock. This intrigues me, so I stand up and walk over to it. Aiesha quickly jumps in front of me, blocking my way. "Don't touch it. Your hands are still wet."

"What is it?" I ask.

She hesitantly turns around and looks into the distance. I wasn't supposed to notice it. I don't know why Aiesha brought me down here, but it might be her way of trying to build my trust. Keeping secrets this early on in our relationship will render this whole exercise pointless, and she knows it.

Aiesha walks to the large rock and reluctantly picks up the paper. "It's a photo of my family."

Having touched the water once, the thin layer of ink on the photo has faded into a greyish brown. Two smiling parents stand in the background. Before them, seated on plastic chairs, are four boys and a girl.

"Back in India, I used to work in the fields for extended periods of time before I was allowed to return to my village. I always carried this with me, to remind myself why I needed to work while my friends had the luxury of attending school. Luckily, I still had it on me when I was taken." She carefully places the photo back on the rock.

"Luckily," I say, but the words escape my mouth as being more sarcastic than genuine.

She looks at me for a second, then takes my arm and pulls me towards the water. "I want to show you something."

She dives in, and once again, I follow.

In contrast to the tunnel, the cave water is clear and iridescent. We swim down, where crystals of various colours cover the rocky bottom. Scattered beams of light leak into the cave, piercing the water's surface and filtering through the currents. Time stands still as we drift around, free and without care.

I resurface before Aiesha does. When she pops up, the surrounding water turns a muddy brown and the remainder of her camouflage runs down her face in dark streams. She wipes it off and for the first time, I can clearly see her face.

Aiesha's skin flows like that of melted amber, highlighting the sharp features that emphasise her emerald-like eyes, still analysing me. Always analysing.

"Are you ready to go back?" she asks.

"I guess so."

"Good. The trip back up is more difficult. Take a deep breath and stay close." She disappears in the water. I fill my lungs with as much air as they can hold, then begin my descent into the tunnel. After every turn, I make sure that Aiesha is still in my sight. She propels herself through the water with the grace of a sea nymph. This isn't her first time feeling her way along the tunnel.

My eyes are still bleary and adjusting to the brightness as I lie gasping and spread out on the welcoming bank of the waterhole. For once, I appreciate the hot air. Within a few minutes, I am completely dry. I walk over to Aiesha, who is waiting underneath the tree, staring at the empty spot where our clothes had been.

"I suspected it," she mutters to herself.

"Suspected what?"

"We've been followed."

CHAPTER 15

"We have to go back to camp." She makes no attempt to hide the urgency in her voice.

"Naked?" I ask.

"That's hardly a problem," she responds, irritated. "My weapon is missing."

She scans our surroundings for branches and subsidiary tools, quickly concludes that none will suffice, then rushes off into the forest like a cat spotting its prey. I dash after her and attempt to keep up but swinging branches and vines tear into my skin like whips, making this task almost impossible.

"You're an Elemental!" I shout in fear of getting left behind. "Can't we just lay low?"

Before completely disappearing out of sight, she stops. I catch up with her and gather my breath.

Aiesha stares me down, furiously gesturing at the scars lacing her body. "Do you think laying low worked when I got these?" She begins to walk on but then stops again. "Having a green mark doesn't make me invincible out here. It just means that I know when we're in trouble."

"Are we?" I ask.

"Without a weapon, we are screwed," she states.

A large snap erupts a few metres away, sending an icy chill down my neck. The peril of our situation becomes evident when I see the expression on Aiesha's face. Until now, I didn't know she had the capacity to experience fear. Helplessness. Aiesha lowers her hand, signalling that I should remain where I am. With swift, distinctive movements, she disappears into the dark forest.

I stand there alone, my only company consisting of two stubby creatures chasing each other up and down a tree trunk. They stop playing at the sound of movement in the nearby shrubbery, and their bushy tails quickly vanish into the thick canopy.

The atmosphere becomes overwhelmingly fraught with the prospect of danger. I feel like I'm being watched. Then again, I *always* feel like I'm being watched. I want to run away like I did when I found myself in the middle of the Clearing, but leaving Aiesha behind wouldn't sit quite right with me; even though she is more than capable of looking after herself and is probably much better off without me slowing her down.

She emerges from the undergrowth and hushes me closer, leading me to a small gap in the bushes where a gigantic footprint left a metre-wide indent in the ground. What bothers me most isn't the size, but rather the lengthy claw marks. Four determined strokes part the soil like lines of waves in a stormy sea. They point towards the haze of down-hill shadows, leading farther into the depths of the jungle.

Aiesha is uneasy. In her hunched position, the dark scars across her torso are more noticeable than ever. "There's only one creature big enough to make those tracks," she says nervously. "But it doesn't make any sense."

"Why?" I ask, hesitant.

She looks up at me with a stark crease between her brows. "Shriekers are supposed to be nocturnal."

As soon as her words escape into the air, a thundering howl rips through the bushes. Both Aiesha and I jump into defensive positions. The wail is immediately followed by stomping, growing closer like a rampaging herd of cattle. I push my back against Aiesha's and survey the opposite side, not sure about the direction of attack. I notice movement behind a tree and prepare to act swiftly.

The tension is cut short when several Red Marks reveal themselves. Aiesha swings around and doesn't even attempt to cover herself.

"Kyle!" she confronts him with rage. "What is wrong with you? Even for an Apex, stealing my spear is just beyond stupid. If something decided to attack us, we would have been left defenceless."

Kyle strolls closer, whistling a triumphant tune. His gaze lingers over her exposed body. "If you were attacked, then you wouldn't have been a worthy Elemental, would you?" he says with a smug expression.

She grabs her spear from his grasp. "Now give our clothes back," she snarls.

"I don't know, I think I prefer you without them," he says with a smarmy grin.

"Just give them back," I demand, impatient.

"It speaks!" he shouts, loud enough for every creature in a square kilometre to hear. Kyle laughs hysterically and turns around to the other two Apex for approval. They both snigger. He turns back to face me. "What's the matter, don't you want everyone to see how special you are?" He points to my mark, now clearly visible without a shirt to cover it.

This time it's my turn to confront him. "What is your problem with me?" I demand.

"He's jealous, John," Aiesha laughs, taunting him. She knows exactly which buttons to push to elicit an anger-fuelled response.

Kyle takes serious offence at this. He looks at her with hatred. "You're just a filthy, feral Green," he snaps. "You'll say anything to get your way, even if it means treating us like the animals you stalk all day." He moves closer, leaving an uncomfortably small space between the two of them. "But that's all you Elementals are good for, isn't it? Playing with people."

He takes another step closer, but she retaliates by pushing him away. She could easily have used her spear, but she chose not to. He takes advantage of this, grabbing one of her wrists and pulling her closer. I immediately leap forward to intervene, but before I can touch Kyle, he whistles to the other Apex, who force me into a tight chokehold. Kyle now grasps both of Aiesha's arms and thrusts her to the ground.

"Let go of her!" I scream as loud as I can, with the hope that someone on a different patrol might hear me. Aiesha can only look on helplessly as Kyle pins her down and the other two tighten their holds around my neck.

The trees swirl and morph into abstract shapes as my blood flow is cut off, and Aiesha's face soon fades away. When I fall onto my side, the ground beneath me begins to tremble. The two pairs of legs alongside me dash away, fleeing into the forest. Aiesha pulls me up and tugs me along in the direction of camp. It's only after regaining my senses that I hear the noise escalating behind us.

Something *did* hear my shouts.

CHAPTER 16

We run the rest of the way, even though the noise stopped shortly after it had begun. When we finally reach the camp, Aiesha pulls me back into the shadows.

"They dropped this after fleeing," she says in a hushed voice, handing over my clothes. "We should dress first, or people might get ideas."

I nod and start to tug on my shoes. If I weren't still in shock from the recent attack, I might have had a grin on my face right now. The thought of us exiting the forest naked is quite something. I can just imagine the stares I would have received back at school; but then again, I don't really know how these kids would react. I don't know anything about them.

A warm breeze winds around the tree trunk that conceals us from the camp's line of view. It gently pulls at Aiesha's dark locks, waving them in my direction. Her hair hasn't completely dried yet, and the curls give off a pleasant, sweet smell. I noticed it on our first encounter with the landmine but thought it was just the surrounding forest air.

"Are you wearing some kind of perfume?" I ask, curious.

"It's a mixture of herbs," she explains. "I need them to mask my scent from predators."

I hold back a chuckle. I think she just wants to smell nice but won't admit it. It's working, after all.

"Be cautious of Kyle," she whispers behind me. "He's trying to assert his dominance and will challenge you again."

I fasten the last button on my shirt then look back in her direction, but she's already gone. I leave the shade of the forest and walk out into the open, then spot Aiesha heading to the Lodge. It seems she's trying to hide the fact that we arrived together, but I can't place why. Surely, she isn't embarrassed to be seen with me? She might still be shaken from the incident with Kyle. Unless the Apex often attack unsuspecting Elementals, I'm probably to blame for what happened. If nobody knows what my mark means, then it's very likely that the Apex were following me, and not Aiesha. They were trying to test my strengths before I could discover them myself. Before I could use my skills against them.

Tired and weary, I walk across the verdant field. I decide to avoid the Lodge and go straight towards the campfire. At first, I hesitate when I spot a Red Mark sitting there. I couldn't get a clear view of the other two faces who accompanied Kyle in the forest. I just know that they were Apex. I reach the fire and greet him. He doesn't respond, so I ignore him and pick a log that faces the other way.

The camp is surprisingly quiet during the middle of the day. The Elementals are either in the forest or sleeping in the Lodge, the Neuros rarely leave the Cave, and the Apex aren't back at camp until they've gathered enough food for the day. The boy sitting beside me seems to have killed a dog-sized rodent and is now consuming his share of its flesh. Aiesha said that the Reds hunt together in pairs, yet this one appears to be alone.

I ask his permission to take a small portion for myself. When he remains silent, I lean forward and tear off a cooked piece of meat. Germ told me that the food at the fire is anyone's to take. I sniff the strange animal and concentrate on chewing around the smaller pieces of broken bone until a voice interrupts me.

"It won't work, you know."

I look up at the boy. "Did you say something?"

He continues to stare down at his meal, but then I clearly see his mouth move. "You think I'm gullible, but you can't fool me."

I hesitate. "I'm not sure what you're talking about."

He throws the remainder of his food into the dirt and yells at the top of his lungs, causing me to almost jolt off the log I'm sitting on. "I know what you are!"

"Whoa buddy," Germ steps out from behind me. "He comes in peace."

The Red Mark glares accusingly at Germ, then turns around and stalks off into the woods.

Germ shakes his head with a sigh. "That boy is going to wind up a Feral one of these days."

"Are all Apex just pricks?" I ask him.

"This one isn't really part of the pack. I actually like him quite a bit. He reminds me of myself in a way."

"How's that?" I wonder since nothing about Germ's physical appearance suggests even the most remote similarity with an Apex.

"Isn't it obvious? He's a man of conspiracies. Someone who seeks a truth that is not consistent with the perceivable reality," Germ says with an air of pride. "That's why he was acting so weird. He believes that every single person on this planet is actually part of a far more intelligent community, merely playing along to deceive him. He thinks we're all just aliens in disguise."

"What if he's right?" I play along.

Germ pauses for a second, then smiles keenly. "And *that* is why I hang out with you, Johnny." He plops down beside me. "Speaking of hanging out, where did you run off to this morning? I was afraid that you might have gone Feral on me."

"What on earth's a Feral?" I finally burst out.

"You're not yet ready for that conversation," Germ laughs. "So, stop avoiding the question. Where were you?"

"Aiesha showed me around the forest," I tell him.

Germ does a double-take. "Wait. Aiesha took you into the forest with her?"

"Yeah," I shrug. "Skylor said she could."

"How peculiar," he muses. Something about this clearly bothers him. "Well, at least you were in good hands. She is the top-ranking Elemental, after all."

This information grabs my attention. "How can you tell?"

"Quite easily, actually. You've most likely noticed by now that each time the Greens reach a new terrain, they cover their faces with the surrounding elements for camouflage. Therefore, the most experienced Elementals will travel the farthest and have the most dirt on their face to show for it."

Germ is getting worked up again, like he tends to do when he's talking about a subject that he knows a lot about. I'm quickly beginning to realise that this is, in fact, every subject.

"Greens are able to tell where other Greens have been just by looking at their faces," he continues. "As the gossip around camp goes, you've already encountered a landmine on your first day and lived to tell the tale." He pauses just long enough to create the necessary amount of suspense, but short enough so I do not have to ask. "Apparently, black soil can only be found next to landmines, as its void of any minerals. Aiesha knew perfectly well what she was doing when she rubbed it onto your face. She knew the other Elementals would show you some respect when you arrived."

I remain silent. If this is true, then I owe Aiesha a great deal of gratitude. Not only for saving me but ensuring that my transition at camp went a bit smoother than my initial encounter in the Adjustment Shack. Most kids I met were already wary of my black mark. If I want to fit in here, I'm going to need all the help I can get.

"Anyway, the Neuros are working on some cool stuff. I thought you might want to see."

I nod, and we set off towards the Cave, though I doubt that Rusty will welcome me with open arms.

Upon entering the Cave, I begin to pick up on details that went unnoticed on my first visit. For instance, the workstations are all situated near the entrance in one big mass. A familiar article dangles from the Cave opening, giving the cold working environment an almost comical office atmosphere. I stare long enough to catch it in motion.

The analogue wristwatch is pinned to the wall, held there by some kind of plant substance that acts as an adhesive. The accumulated layer of dust on its surface indicates a significant passing of time, so to speak. Yet, the black dials tick on. 11:35—definitely nowhere near the correct hour of the day.

I scan through the hunched figures. "Where is Skylor?" I ask Germ.

"She doesn't work in the Cave."

"I thought all Neuros worked here?"

"Not Sky. She's stationed at the Adjustment Shack so she can monitor new drops and injuries. She will check up on them, though."

I give this some thought. "Is she the only Neuro with medical knowledge?"

"No," he responds. "In fact, the Elementals are much better with medicinal herbs. If Sky runs short on medicines, they'll scavenge for it."

I decide to push the matter further. "So why is Skylor the leader? Why not Aiesha or Kyle?"

Germ laughs. "I knew this question was coming." He takes a seat on one of the benches and turns to face me. "Sky was one of the first. So was Aiesha."

"What does that mean?"

"It means they arrived here first, dummy. There was a day before this camp existed, and drops were left to wander the planet alone. One day, three Marks ran into each other. A Blue, a Green, and a Red: the First."

"Skylor, Aiesha, and Kyle?" I guess.

"Almost, but not quite. Kyle hasn't been here that long. Adam was the first Red. He wasn't like Kyle at all. He was brave and righteous. From there on out, the First stuck together. With their abilities combined, they somehow managed to overcome the impossible. They survived. As the weeks progressed, they began to come across other kids. When there were ten of them, they settled down and built this place."

"And Adam?" I ask. "What happened to him?"

And then he tells me. "The First insured that this camp became a safe haven for Marks of all kinds. Unfortunately, it also became a target for predators. One day, the growing noise of children attracted a group of Reptants, killing almost half of them. They would have slaughtered the entire camp if it weren't for Adam. He fended them off, before dying from his own injuries."

I think of Kyle, who wouldn't even help open a walnut if you asked him to.

"After Adam's death, Skylor established a strict system to prevent something like that from ever happening again. She appointed herself as the camp's official medical worker and ordered the Apex to build the Adjustment Shack. Aiesha assumed charge of the Elementals and assigned them to explore the wild and gather as much research about the wildlife as they possibly could. By then, the Apex already did most of the hunting, but now they were ordered to do so only around the camp border. Guarding the territory became a priority, to prevent another incident from ever occurring. As the Marks carried out their orders, Skylor began to receive casualties on a regular basis. One day, a delirious new drop was brought to her Shack; one that would change Skylor forever. It was the first White. The little boy awakened at camp and became hysterical. Before anyone could figure out what to do, the young boy ran back into the forest. Skylor panicked and made the mistake of chasing after him. Searching for the boy was no mistake, but not alerting an Elemental first was deadly. When she eventually tracked him down, she couldn't find her way back. Aiesha took control of the camp and sent the Elementals into the forest in shifts. Instead of searching for resources, Aiesha instructed them to begin their search for humans. They didn't find Skylor, but Aiesha's endeavours were not fruitless. New drops appeared in droves with the Elementals' strategic help. Three months later the camp was flourishing, and a new norm was quickly established.

That is until Skylor returned looking better than ever. The Neuro somehow managed to survive in the wild all on her own. We didn't even have to vote. The decision was unanimous to make Skylor our leader."

"How long ago did this happen?" I ask.

"It's been a while," Germ adds unsurely. "About two years back."

As we make our way deeper into the Cave, I trail my fingers along the curved walls. The rough texture scrapes into my skin, leaving a black residue on my hands. The beams of sunlight that do make it into the Cave reflect against the walls, causing a sort of luminous glow. We reach the farthest corner and stop in front of a large object displayed on a table. Squinting, I struggle to see in the low light. I suddenly recognise the oddly shaped metal structure.

"How did this get here?" I gawk at Germ.

"The Elementals were over at the Ashfalt when they stumbled upon it," Rusty emerges beside me. "It was just sitting there, as if it had dropped from the sky."

A gramophone. I play with the thought. *An old-fashioned record player on the middle of another planet in who knows what galaxy.* I share Rusty's bafflement.

"Whoever left this here purposely didn't want us to get our hands on advanced technology," says Rusty. "A gramophone hardly has any components of value to us. This one is entirely mechanical. No electromagnetic aspects at all."

I look around the Cave and at the different projects being worked on. Almost all of the Blues are fidgeting and tampering with watches or phone components that arrived with the other Marks.

"What is the point of leaving it here for us to find, if there is no record to play?" I ask.

"They like to mock us," Germ says with distaste. "Stay here long enough and you'll see."

Rusty flashes a condescending glare. "If he lives that long."

CHAPTER 17

When the second sun goes down, the level of light becomes insufficient for work. We leave the Cave along with the Neuros and go to the campfire. There, we are met with a variety of sliced meats on the flat rocks surrounding the fire. This is the first instance I've actually made it in time for dinner. The feast of pure flesh is astonishing to say the least. The Apex are already helping themselves. I guess it makes sense that they get the first pick.

The Neuros carefully inspect the texture and colour of the meat slices, making sure that everything is edible and thoroughly cooked. Once satisfied with a pick, they'll carefully lift up the stone and carry it to a seat, using the rock as a plate.

I can't help but cringe inwardly. Why didn't anybody tell me I was eating incorrectly? Pretending that I knew all along, I inspect the meat for a few seconds, then choose the first plate that looks like it contains Rodback.

I spot Germ and walk over to him. He didn't take a stone like the others. I sigh. No wonder I got the wrong impression. I join him on the log and place the stone on my lap. The moment I bite into the crunchy flesh, I know it isn't Rodback. "Nice piece of Ptera you got there," Germ chuckles. "You should have taken a wing. At least it would have some bite to it."

I look at the flattened piece of meat then back at Germ. "You call those birds 'Pteras'?"

He shrugs. "They look like Pterodactyls, so we call them Pterodactyls."

As the final sun creeps towards the horizon, a few of the Elementals exit the Lodge and join us around the fire. Aiesha is among them but doesn't look my way. We sit in silence, appeasing our ravaging hunger. With everyone gathered at the same location, I notice the absence of the White boy and his sister. When I ask Germ about them, he just says, "They don't eat with us."

When the horizon glows with an orange array of scattered lights, the day-shift Greens begin to exit the forest. One of the older Elementals puts his stone on the ground then stands up to peer at them. His initial size shocks me, making me glance twice at his mark, wondering why it's not red. His nose is much darker than the rest of his face, having been exposed to its fair share of sun. Hazel eyes reflect an almost palpable weariness. Unfortunately, his captivating gaze is not enough to distract me from the patches of melted skin on his face. Looking at his horribly deformed features, like that of a burn victim, I can't help but lose my appetite.

"That's Skeith," Germ whispers to me. "The African shaman I told you about."

Skeith stares into the distance until the final few Elementals exit the forest. For several more moments he stands in silence. Then he announces loudly, "Two of mine have not returned."

I immediately recognise his voice from the night before. The Green Mark on the boulder. He looks over to Aiesha.

"All of the night shift Elementals checked in with me," she tells him. "These went missing during the day."

I gather that she and the burned boy are responsible for different shifts. He lingers a bit longer in hope of their return, then orders a younger Elemental to call Sky. The Green Mark scatters off to the Adjustment Shack and quickly returns with Skylor on his heels.

She arrives at the campfire, visibly shaken. "What is it, Skeith?"

"Two Elementals have not returned," he repeats.

She immediately counts the faces around the fire, then starts to yell out orders like a drill sergeant.

"Germ, fetch the Whites and keep them in the Adjustment Shack until I return." He nods submissively and rushes off towards the river.

"For the rest of you, it's the usual protocol. Neuros, go into the Cave, secure your work at the back, and defend it with your lives. Elementals, search the forest in groups of two, don't leave your partner alone for a second. Apex, guard the Cave and the Adjustment Shack. Supply the rest of the Marks with weapons."

With urgency and a collective fear, the group begins to move. Before anyone can leave, Skeith shouts at them to stop. Skylor turns to him impatiently. He raises his arm and points to the edge of the forest. The missing Elementals have returned. They are carrying something—it's hampering their movements as they struggle forth. I can now see why. There's a third person.

"It's a new drop!" Sky exclaims excitedly. She rushes forward, and the rest follow.

A feeling of dread overcomes me as the two Elementals carefully lay the girl down on the grass. Sky inspects the pale, young drop, who is covered with bruises and abrasions. Her blue mark seems fainter than Skylor's and all of the other Neuros who kneel beside her with medical supplies at hand. The girl's light hair falls on the ground in soft curls. A faint touch of mascara clings to her eyelashes, and her lips are painted a glossy pink. Elegant long legs stretch out before her, partially covered by a short summer dress. I can't help but notice the finer intricacies of the girl's attire. Her wedge sandals, although dirty and torn from running, would have complemented her sundress perfectly. It must have been a beautiful day outside when she was abducted.

"She's dead," Skylor states flatly.

We stare at the girl for a long time. She would have been the third female Neuro at our camp.

Sky looks at her for a few more moments, then turns her furious gaze to the two Elementals. "What happened?" she demands, a threatening undertone in her voice.

The bigger of the two steps forward. "I was next to the Ashfalt when I saw her being dropped in the Clearing, but she ran away before I could catch up with her. The last time we tracked her trail, she was heading her way." They turn to Aiesha now.

Skylor looks at her and repeats the question impatiently. "What happened, Aiesha?"

Aiesha responds quickly. "The girl never crossed my path. I would have seen her."

Laughter erupts behind me. Kyle shoves his way into the middle of the group. "You couldn't have seen much, since you and John vanished into that waterhole."

Aiesha flinches as his words take effect. There are a few sniggers from the group. I feel my cheeks burn.

"We were just washing," she insists.

"For an hour?" he asks sarcastically, causing more Marks to mumble under their breaths. Skylor doesn't appreciate the disorder in her meeting. She looks at Aiesha, her eyes blazing.

"John came with you?"

A mere glance at Skylor's expression makes it clear that she was unaware of our trip. The look on her face snuffs out the laughter in the back of the group.

"I thought Skylor gave you permission to take me?" I ask Aiesha, who is now inspecting the Blue girl's scratched knees, avoiding eye contact.

She lied to me. That's why she was acting so strange when we returned to camp. I was never supposed to go back into the cold claws of the forest. I almost died because of Aiesha's little outing.

She ignores both our questions and explains, "The new drop couldn't have entered my territory. Kyle was following us and would have seen her running past." She sounds more like she is trying to convince herself than the rest of us.

Skylor now turns to Kyle. "You left the camp perimeter?"

Kyle seems surprised that the blame has suddenly shifted to him. "Yes, but—"

"Do you think this is a game, Kyle? That you can just frolic about wherever you like, leaving us open to attack?"

"We just wanted to keep an eye on them," he scrambles for an excuse. "The Apex have a duty to protect others."

"You don't have the jurisdiction!" she screams.

Kyle is visibly taken aback by her outburst. For a swift moment, I can even make out a hint of fear in his eyes. He starts to talk back, but then decides against it and doesn't say anything.

Skylor turns to me, her face red with anger. "You had no place being in the forest, John."

I look over at Aiesha for support, but she is still avoiding my gaze.

Sky bends down and kneels next to the girl. She lightly caresses her sides, then pulls off a wristwatch and hands it over to the other Neuros. She stands up and straightens herself, calming again.

"Alright everyone, return to your prescribed duties." As the group departs, she turns to us again. "As for you, Kyle, you are demoted from your privileges and are to remain within the camp's boundaries until further notice."

"Are you kidding me?" Kyle exclaims. "What about her?"

"Aiesha is our most valuable Elemental," Sky states in a matter-of-fact manner. "I cannot dispense of her over a mere altercation. She is to continue with her shifts for the good of the camp."

Skylor turns to me. "However, her actions will not go unpunished, John. You will accompany Aiesha to the Clearing to attend to the lifting ritual. Is that clear?"

I nod, even though I don't know what I'm agreeing to. "I'd like to speak to Aiesha in private now," Sky says, dismissing me and Kyle.

I gratefully oblige and create some much-needed distance between myself and the others. Kyle quietly follows me, strolling along the edge of the forest. When he's certain that we're out of hearing range, he says to me in a hushed tone: "I thought it fitting to let you know that we *did* see the Blue girl run past. If you were actually doing your job instead of snogging with some filthy Elemental, you would have been able to save her."

I stop in my tracks and turn to him, astonished. "You *let* her run past?"

"Well," he replies in a cocky manner. "Like Skylor said, it wasn't our job to catch her, it was Aiesha's. If it wasn't for you," he pushes his finger into my chest, "she wouldn't have died." He walks off, leaving me alone to process the severity of his statement.

Skylor walks away too, returning to the Shack. I march to Aiesha, who is still standing next to the girl's body.

"What is a lifting ritual?" I ask angrily, not hiding the feeling of betrayal in my voice.

She doesn't respond with words but wipes away a stray tear rolling down her cheek. "Can you carry her?" she finally asks softly. I look at her tormented expression and then at the pale girl who appears to be sleeping.

My questions can wait.

Pushing both of my arms underneath the girl's back, I roll the limp weight onto its side and clasp the body in a firm grip before lifting it up. Without saying a word, Aiesha walks into the forest.

Carrying the cold corpse, I follow her into the darkness.

CHAPTER 18

We reach the Clearing and stop in the middle of the circle where we all began this futile struggle for survival. I'm more at ease this time around, knowing that the Reptants only respond to movement. I still try to tread lightly, but the dead weight in my arms makes it difficult.

"Here," Aiesha whispers, indicating to the sandy patch in front of us.

I kneel, and carefully lay the girl down on the rough surface. The stray lights in the sky illuminate the Clearing, so the sand around her gleams red. Aiesha slowly leaves the circle and I hesitantly follow. She comes to a halt just beyond the first bushes and sits between two groups of shrubs, concealing herself almost entirely.

"Aren't we supposed to perform some ritual?" I ask, unsure.

She doesn't respond, instead pointing to another grubby bush a few feet away. Too tired to protest, I part its leaves and sit underneath. From this position, I'm able to see the entire Clearing.

Loathsome bugs bite at my exposed skin, causing itchy bumps to sprout across my arms and the nape of my neck. For two hours I alternate between swatting and scratching myself, struggling to keep my eyes open.

My mind is all over the place, making it difficult to focus on one thought at a time. They alternate between the girl lying in the Clearing, and the one who is hiding in the bushes. I want to know why Aiesha would go through the trouble of saving me from a landmine yet go on to betray me and place my life in danger the very next day. I can't shrug off the feeling that she was testing me. Like she wanted to find the meaning of my mark. How can I possibly trust someone who is willing to risk my life in the forest for some sick experiment? Kyle said it himself. Elementals will say anything to get their way, even if it means treating others like the animals they stalk all day. Whatever her reason was, I hope she got her answer. I hope it was worth the death of another.

I need to be more careful from now on. Not just in the forest, but also around the other Marks. Kyle was just as eager to get me alone in the forest, though it could have been Aiesha he was after. He spoke so viciously of the Elemental that I can't help but wonder what he would have done to her if I weren't there—if the noise in the forest hadn't scared the Apex away.

Like a merry-go-round, I'm thinking of Aiesha again. This time I'm wondering if she's okay. I should be furious, but my contempt for Kyle somehow diminishes what I feel towards her. She didn't intend for this accident to happen, but Kyle did. In a way, she is also a victim of today's events.

I'm on the brink of leaving my hiding spot to check up on Aiesha when a familiar droning sound stops me. Every fibre in my being wants to get up and run to safety, but the insidious noise anchors my limbs in place. Like an underwater torpedo propelling towards its target, it rapidly grows louder until directly above us. The ground beneath me begins to vibrate while the layer of sand covering the Clearing shakes incessantly.

The sky lights up with static electricity, and sporadic white beams shoot down on the Clearing like lightning bolts. Stray flares bounce off the treetops, splitting the night sky into millions of broken fragments. The sand floor rises into the air and hovers in place like a cloud of red mist.

At first, the sparks of searching blue light play around the girl's chest in undulating currents, causing her to twitch uncontrollably. Then slowly, her limp body lifts into the air as it's moved by some invisible force. She rises into the sky until she passes the tips of the highest treetops. A cloud of mist swallows her and the droning simply stops. In an instant, the sand drops to the ground in a wave of dust. The girl is gone.

I rise and step out of the bushes. Aiesha is already standing behind me when I turn to her.

"I'm sorry," she says, her voice barely audible. Without an explanation, she proceeds to walk off into the wrong side of the forest, leaving me behind. I take a final look at the empty Clearing that now looks strikingly similar to my mother's painting. A sanctified grave, preserved for those who have not yet fully lived.

For a brief moment, I consider throwing myself into the Clearing. I feel an overwhelming urge to go home—and this might be the only way. I want to see Mom and Carter again, but my stomach sinks as I realise the truth. I'm only leaving this planet if it's as a limp corpse.

With a load far heavier than the body I carried, I trudge back to camp alone. I head directly to the fire and scan the faces around it until I spot the person I'm looking for. Despite her cold stance, Rusty's eyes appear unusually warm and longing tonight. I clutch the cold satellite phone in my front pocket and toss it into her lap. I won't be needing it anymore.

As I walk to the Lodge, I become aware of a salty taste in my mouth. My face is soaked in tears.

CHAPTER 19

*Seattle, 34th Avenue West: Five
months before abduction*

"*I'm telling you man, another kid disappeared this week and
the government ain't doing jack squat about it.*"

"*Jeremy, don't you think you're taking things out of propor-
tion again? I mean, not to twist your handles or anything, but
you weren't exactly right about Area 51. Or the crop circles. Or
the pyramids.*"

"*Ryan, I get it.*"

"*Or aliens building Stonehenge.*"

"*Alright Ryan—*"

"*Or that Atlantis is hidden in the Bermuda Triangle.*"

"*That's* enough, *Ryan! And I wasn't wrong, I just haven't
acquired the necessary proof yet.*"

"*I am not going on one of your rampages again, Jeremy. We
nearly got arrested the last time. Don't you remember? Or did
the 'aliens' probe your brain when I wasn't looking?*"

"*Okay, I don't blame you. It's just…. It just feels like something big is going down right beneath our noses. Bigger than all
of us. And nobody even seems to notice.*"

"*Nobody cares.*"

"Yeah, but I do, Ryan. People are ignorant of the truth, until it sneaks up on them one day and bites them in the face. Then, nobody believes them either. Ironic, isn't it?"

"Yeah dude, bittersweet."

"I'm serious. I'm going to find out what has happened to these kids, even if it gets me killed this time."

"I'll delete your browser history when you're dead."

CHAPTER 20

Life around here has become dull and pointless. I haven't seen Aiesha since the lifting ritual. She switched back to night shifts and sleeps during the day. I suspect that she's avoiding me. I've run out of things to do within the first two days of my arrival and now spend my time wandering aimlessly around camp. Kyle has remained completely out of sight for the majority of his suspension. Until now.

I sit back, leaning against a tree near the edge of camp. It stands on a slight slope, allowing me to look out over everyone, and envy the children who are hard at work. I'm annoyed with them for having a purpose. Frustrated at the lack of mine.

In the distance, I spot a person leaving the Cave and slowly making his way in my general direction. Just by looking at the bent figure's odd gait, I can recognise Germ from a mile away. He finally reaches me, slightly out of breath from the brisk walk.

"Hey Black Jack, I've spent the entire morning helping the Neuros with some tech research, and if I told you I was starving it would be one hell of an understatement. Let's go grab something to eat."

"I'm not hungry," I mutter without looking up, and continue to draw flesh-eating worms in the moist ground with my stick.

"What do you mean you aren't hungry? You're still sitting in the same spot I saw you in five hours ago. And I know it's been five hours, because Rusty's watch never skips a beat. You must be starving."

He's right, and this annoys me even more. I've been to the campfire several times today, but Kyle has been squatting there since the break of dawn and hasn't moved once.

Germ looks over to the fire and then back at me, as if reading my thoughts. "Do you want to get some water instead?"

I nod, deciding that anything is better than an empty stomach. He yanks me up by my forearm and leads me down the scenic route towards the river in order to avoid Kyle. We navigate our way across the arch that spans the Cave exterior. On our left lies the desert and the various juvenile sprouts of green saplings that decorate the otherwise lifeless terrain. On the shaded side of the mountain are the Adjustment Shack and the lulling river. The angle of the rocky hill keeps the camp out of the suns' rays for most of the day, protecting us from the worst of the heat.

Germ pretends not to hear my stomach crying for nourishment, but alters our path towards the campfire nevertheless. I decide not to argue with his scheme to get me fed and keep my thoughts on our surroundings instead.

"You can't avoid him forever, you know," Germ says. "Sooner or later, you will have to face Kyle." He chuckles to himself and adds, "I'll protect you," as he walks away to get some food.

For some reason, the idea of a pale, thin kid like Germ having to protect me, makes the corners of my mouth stretch into a grin. I pull myself out of my funk and follow him to the fire. If Kyle wants to confront me, then let him.

When we arrive, there is no food in sight. Germ suggests that we wait for the next batch of meat to arrive and takes a seat. I cautiously join him, even though I spot the charred chunks of uneaten flesh sticking out from beneath the ashes. Someone purposely spoiled our food.

What follows is an extremely uncomfortable silence. When a Neuro or Elemental comes to check up on the food, they turn to each of us suspiciously before going back to their work empty-handed. When everyone is out of sight and the suns hover above us in full blaze, Kyle breaks his five-day streak of quietude.

"So, what exactly do you do around here?" he inquires, looking at me with disdain. "You don't hunt, you know nothing about technology, you clearly can't catch drops," he flashes a smirk, "and you don't even water the bloody plants!"

I don't give him an answer. Not because I'm ignoring him, but because I don't have one.

"So basically, you can't do anything," he concludes. "Okay, we've figured it out, guys!" He stands up with his hands cupped around his mouth, as if proudly announcing it to the entire camp. "A black mark means worthless!" He sits down with a grimace. Looking me flat in the eyes, he triumphantly adds, "A jack of all trades and a master of none."

Before I can decide between passiveness and retaliation, Germ chimes in. "Is often times better than a master of one."

Both of us turn to him.

"What the hell are you talking about, Germ?" Kyle spits out the words. The way he said 'Germ' made it sound filthy, as if the name itself is an insult to his character.

"Well," Germ continues, obviously not sensing the threatening undertone in Kyle's question. "That was only half of the saying. The full phrase goes: *A jack of all trades but a master of none, is often times better than a master of one.*" He straightens his glasses with his index finger and adds, "If you are going to use poetic literature to mock someone, at least do it right."

Kyle sits frozen in place, eyes locked on Germ. His face reddens as his jaw clenches shut and his back tenses up. Without so much as a verbal warning, he jumps to his feet and tackles Germ, smashing him face-first into the ground. There's a *snap* as Germ tries to roll out underneath Kyle, his broken glasses slipping off in the process. Just as well, because in the same held up breath, Kyle swings at him and lands a punch directly in Germ's face, sending blood shooting out of his nose.

I quickly find myself on top of Kyle, trying to pull him off with every ounce off my strength. Germ isn't even attempting to fight back, yet Kyle shows no sign of stopping. I somehow manage to wrestle him off Germ and hurl him to the side.

If Kyle was angry before, he's furious now. I position myself between him and Germ just before he throws another fist through the air. I barely dodge it, stepping to the right and swinging my left elbow in his direction, catching him straight on the edge of his jaw. Disorientated, he staggers backwards and holds his chin. Kyle looks at me in disbelief. He spits a mouthful of blood-laced saliva at my feet, then reaches for his back pocket.

I stand alert, watching for Kyle's next move while Germ moans in pain behind me. My stance quickly changes when I realise what he's reaching for. Kyle pulls out a knife and flicks it open with his thumb, revealing a curved blade. Rays of light emphasise its sharpness, bouncing off the steel and giving it a shimmering glance. He had to be carrying it on him when he got abducted.

I can sense the growing unrest in the air around me. Even the forest is louder than usual as the animals titter and howl in anticipation. When I lock eyes with Kyle, the last shred of hope drains from my body. His stare is like that of a sociopath—not just filled with his usual contempt for me, but yearning bloodlust, as if I'm just another prey in the forest. An obstacle separating him from his next meal. A grim glower forms on his face as he lunges forward.

Through the noise, none of us noticed the commotion escalating within the depths of the forest. Trees snap like twigs under the brute force that tears through them, growing closer until it reaches a deafening climax. A creature, bigger than any living land animal I have ever known to exist, leaps out from the forest and lands between us. My heart drops when I hear the scream of this beast from Hell.

It's a Shrieker.

CHAPTER 21

It releases a fierce growl, then turns to Kyle and bites into his shoulder, tearing off a chunk of flesh. Kyle lets out a wail and immediately drops to the ground, clasping his wounded arm. The beast bends over and turns around to face me. My eyes dart around for a weapon. I spot Kyle's knife, but it's too far away. Even if I could reach it, it would be as useful as jabbing a bear with a stick.

I slowly tread backwards, but the beast follows, steadily approaching me. Its face, now an arm's length away from mine, engulfs me in its massive shadow. The smell of rotting flesh assaults my nostrils as waves of putrid breath blow in my direction.

By now, an anxious weapon-bearing crowd of Apex and Elementals has formed at the campfire. None are willing to intervene, as they will face certain death. Meanwhile, I'm like a deer caught in the headlights, unsure if I should stand my ground and stare the beast down or avoid eye contact altogether. With limited options, I make my decision.

I gaze into its eyes and am mesmerised by the rapid contracting and expanding vertical slits of black pupils. It stares back at me, but I quickly realise that it's not my eyes the beast is looking at. It's staring at my mark.

The Shrieker pushes its snout into my heaving chest, almost causing me to lose my balance. It quickly inhales my scent. Seemingly satisfied, it bows its head, revealing a swarthy crown. I'm dumbfounded.

Does it want me to touch its head?

With measured movements, I raise my arm as slowly as I possibly can, preparing for the possibility of losing it. Carefully placing my hand on top of the creature, I allow my fingers to caress the black patch of fur. To my amazement, the creature pushes its head forward in appreciation.

As the crowd around us grows, the Shrieker becomes uneasy—its movements more abrupt. It shifts its attention to the others, turning its back on me and releasing a deep, threatening growl. Leaning forward on his two front legs, its ears prick up and its tail stiffens. Having seen more than one dog do this back home, I quickly recognise the creature's alarming body language. It's preparing to pounce. Some of the Elementals have noticed it too and are urgently trying to urge the group to move back.

I have to do something. I step forward and push my hand against the Shrieker's coat, this time letting it sink down all the way to its tough skin. My unauthorised movement startles the Shrieker and sends it spinning back to me—teeth bared and nostrils flaring. For a creature large enough to massacre us all, it seems uneasy and confused. Instead of retracting my hand, I slowly begin to stroke its exposed stomach. The Shrieker seems torn between what to do. Even if I'm just able to distract it long enough for the others to get away, I'll have succeeded. Before it gets a chance to turn back to them, I decide to risk petting it with my other arm too. I gradually bring my hand up to its face but stop when it bares its teeth again. Peering over its broad shoulders, I see a few of the Apex have already managed to carry Kyle away to the Adjustment Shack. Germ, however, has refused to leave and is now sitting in a puddle of his own blood, gaping at the events unravelling before him. I commit the mistake of making eye contact with him.

When Germ sees me looking at him, he shouts as loud as he possibly can, "Run, John!"

The beast jolts away in response to the noise. Bright colours ripple across its body, morphing into different formations like that of a chameleon. Before I can react, it pushes its snout between my legs and jerks its shoulders upwards with an overpowering force, sending me spiralling into the sky. Helpless, my body flails through the air, unable to grab onto anything. When my momentum changes and the ground gets closer, I brace myself for a very painful impact.

Before I hit the hard surface, a blur of black fur enters my vision and moves underneath me, breaking my fall. The Shrieker doesn't slow down, and careens into the looming wilderness with me on its back.

CHAPTER 22

Every time I try to jump off, the beast gives a loud grunt and keeps me from doing so. As we pass different scenery, the Shrieker's colours change sporadically. It moves at an overwhelming pace, zipping past the Clearing and then the hidden waterhole. Within ten minutes we have already covered a greater distance than Aiesha and I managed to travel within hours. Even if I remember how to get back to camp, at this rate it will take me days to return on foot.

A few Reptants pick up on our trail, but the Shrieker easily outruns them, altering its course to find higher ground. I spot a cliff in the distance up ahead, but the Shrieker shows no sign of slowing down. This is a problem. A disastrous one. If we cross that ledge and I manage to escape somewhere down the road, I won't be able to get back at all.

I pull on the beast's hair and kick at its sides, but this makes it run even faster.

"Stop!" I yell, as if it's able to understand me. Ignoring my pleas, it runs up to the cliff and leaps off the edge.

The impact of the landing knocks me off its back and onto the black soil, which sticks to my clothes when I roll over. Ignoring the pain, I jump to my feet and put as much distance as I can between the creature and me. The Shrieker doesn't seem bothered by the elements—or me for that matter—and strides a few feet before finding a satisfactory spot in which to sit and rest. I suspect that it's taunting me, since there's nowhere for me to hide and no probability of outrunning it. Doesn't it know that it's considered bad manners to play with your food?

I peer up at the ridge that we dropped down from, and feel all hope drain from my being. There is no conceivable way I'll be able to make it back up again. The angle is far too steep and climbing it would be impossible.

I turn back around to face the stark scenery before me—or rather the lack of it. Kilometres of black land stretch out as far as the eye can see, with not so much as a single tree in sight. Sore and tired, I kick a heap of dirt, revealing a lighter layer of soil underneath. Contrary to what I thought, the soil itself isn't black. It's covered with a thick layer of ash. It's as if the whole area burned down. I shift my attention back to the Shrieker, who seems to have lost interest in me.

"Are you going to kill me or what?" I ask the beast impatiently.

It ignores me. Every time the Shrieker's eyes blink, it's almost indistinguishable from its surroundings. Its black pelt blends into the sooty ground like a woven furry carpet. When it breathes, the terrain practically appears to be moving. The Shrieker rolls over and closes its eyes, completely disappearing from view. Frustrated, and left with no other choice but to wait for its next move, I sit on the ground and lean back on my arms, staring into the sky.

One strange thing on this planet which I still haven't gotten used to is how almost everything has multiple shadows. At least, out here in the open. In the forest, some trees can have up to three shadows in the same vicinity, each dark shade stretching in a different direction. Each of the three suns has its own orbit, so there is only a small fraction of the day when all of them are clearly visible at the same time. The Marks call this the time of the Trinity, and it only lasts a few minutes shy of an hour.

At some point, I must have dozed off, because when I open my eyes again the Shrieker is gone. I pat the ground where it lay, in case it's just blending in with the environment again. When I stand up, I'm startled to see human footprints all around me, embedded in the ash. Some are clear and others blurred, all leading to an object a few feet away. I walk over to the item and lift it up to my face. It's a black disk the length of a ruler, with circular rims and ridges that twist into a continuous spiral.

Out of the corner of my eye, the Shrieker comes into view. I begin to step backwards, clasping the heavy item to my chest in an attempt to shield myself from any potential blows. Ignoring my frantic display of self-preservation, the beast continues to trudge in my direction, its tail hanging low and its head wearily swaying from side to side. Before the tip of its wet snout is able to stain the disk I'm holding, it takes in a long whiff of my scent.

With an uncoordinated movement, I leap away and accidentally bump my elbow into its jaw, leaving a long streak of saliva on my right forearm. Expecting it to retaliate, I

159

drop the disk and sink to my knees, clasping both arms onto my head and neck in a protective brace.

Feeling more vulnerable than ever before, I remain in a foetal position as the Shrieker hovers over me. Its loud breaths escape in quick, rapid bursts. I flinch as the creature's drool drops on my forehead. The sticky liquid seeps into my hair and over my sealed eyes. When it begins to force its way towards my mouth, I roll away and bury my head in the crook of my arm, rubbing it from my face.

I slowly straighten and get back on my feet, facing the Shrieker from a few metres away. The beast remains seated, patiently waiting for me to regain my composure. A coat of sand covers its snout. Looking closer, I notice the sliced skin underneath its eye socket. That wasn't there before. Something attacked the creature while I was asleep. The fur around the injured area is stained with a steady stream of blood, still running down its chin. I suddenly feel sorry for it. Is it even possible to develop Stockholm syndrome when your captor is a Shrieker?

I take off my shirt and bundle it up, before approaching the wounded creature. It remains surprisingly calm and allows me to push the fabric against its warm skin. After my shirt has soaked up most of the blood, the Shrieker pulls away and starts to dig in the ground. It continues to do this until a small patch of green appears. It bites onto it and swiftly pulls it out with a ripping sound. My mouth drops open. It's a beetroot. As the creature chews the plant, red fluid drips down his chin. It continues to do this until a bunch of half-eaten beetroots are scattered across the ground. Growing increasingly hungry myself, I begin to consider a strategy. The cliff still looms over us, a formidable barrier. I don't wish to remain on the wrong side of it. I realise that I'll only be able to go back the same way I came here in the first place: on the Shrieker's back.

"Hey," I try to get its attention without getting too close. "We need to go back."

It ignores my request and continues to inspect the ground like a sniffer dog.

I drop to my knees and begin to search for beetroots alongside him. Tugging fiercely at the purple plants, I soon have a small pile of my own. Envious of my growing pile, the Shrieker nudges its head underneath my arm. I quickly use my bundled shirt to cover the beets, wrapping them inside. Testing the Shrieker's reaction, I pull a single beetroot from my bundle and throw it towards the cliff. Like a ravenous dog with a bone, it bolts to where it landed and gobbles it up. Tying the bundle around my waist, I approach the awaiting Shrieker with a grin.

I reckon that I made it this far, so what do I have to lose?

An arm, the voice in my head answers.

I tuck the black disk into my pants and retrieve another beetroot from my bundle. Before the beast is able to bite it, I jump onto its back and hurl the beet as far as I can into the direction of the camp. Unconcerned with the weight on its back, the Shrieker bolts forward and begins to scale the fatal ridge.

CHAPTER 23

"You're back!" Skylor throws her arms around me, but then quickly retracts them. "We sent two Elementals looking for you, but your trail vanished into thin air."

I take this a bit personally. "Only two?"

She hesitates. "In my defence, they were looking for a body."

"That probably makes sense."

She takes a few steps back and looks at my shirt, now stained dark with blood. "Do you need medical attention?" she asks, her eyes widening.

"No," I reassure her. "The Shrieker was wounded, so I used my shirt to stop the bleeding."

By her perplexed expression, she isn't sure what to make of this. Her gaze darts around, as if she expects the beast to jump out at any moment.

"Don't worry," I laugh. "He isn't here."

My plan worked perfectly until we reached the Clearing and I ran out of beetroots. The Shrieker got impatient when I stopped feeding him and refused to move another inch. I climbed off and showed him my empty hands, to which he responded with a loud huff, turned around and walked away.

"Are you sure?" she asks.

"I'm sure."

Skylor sighs. "No wonder we thought Shriekers only came out at night. They're practically invisible." She looks frustrated as she contemplates the idea. "It's not even supposed to be possible, you know. The Elementals told me that mammals don't change colours like that. Even less so when it comes to their hair." She thinks about it some more, but then returns to her usual collected demeanour. "I'd wash that shirt if I were you. Don't want the scent to attract any other uninvited guests." She turns around and begins to walk away, but I stop her.

"Skylor?"

"Yes?"

"I was meaning to ask you about earlier, when Aiesha and I went into the forest. Why were you so upset that I went along? We don't know what my mark means, so I should test all the possibilities to find out, right?"

Sky appears visibly uncomfortable with my question.

"Is it because I'm inexperienced? I can assure you, Aiesha kept me safe. If it wasn't for her—"

"I can't talk about this right now," she interrupts me. "I need to check up on Kyle. He's hurt very badly."

Before I can push further, she elaborates on her list of tasks.

"And after that, they need my guidance at the Cave. The Neuros are on the verge of making a breakthrough."

This gives me a sudden burst of hope. "A breakthrough on what?"

Skylor starts to walk towards the Adjustment Shack, forcefully cutting off the conversation. "You wouldn't understand, John. You're not a Neuro!" she shouts from far away.

I want to stop her again and show her the disk, but then decide against it, tucking it deeper underneath my blood-stained clothes.

The river isn't very far away from the Adjustment Shack. Apparently, this water source is the main reason the First chose to settle here. The water drains out of the mountain and disappears a few kilometres ahead into the underground storage basins. I was hoping to be alone at the river, but farther upstream the two White children are washing rocks. I peer at the objects in their hands. The flat rocks look like the ones we eat from. A giant heap of them lies next to the river where the two children are hunched over, scrubbing away.

With the disk hidden beneath my shirt, I can't really afford to wash the blood out of my clothes. The risk of someone spotting it is far too big. I peer over at the children, uncertain as to what I should do next. The alluring water gently flows between the rocks and pebbles, the white grains of sand polished smooth by the timeless force of the current. Giving in to the temptation, I take off my shoes and tread into the stream until the bristling water reaches my knees, and I walk over to them.

The boy is hardly able to hide his excitement when he sees me. "Hi John!" Matthew greets me.

Talaya avoids eye contact and continues to scrape the old food off the wet stones.

"Why do you have to wash everyone's plates?" I ask.

"It's okay," the boy assures me. "We like washing them."

I study them closely. Their clothes are dripping wet and stick tightly to their bodies. The girl's hair, which she uses to hide behind, is tangled with knots. The Whites are choosing their words carefully. They're scared.

"You can be honest," I try to reassure them. "It doesn't look very fun."

The boy looks at the girl, then at me. He smiles. "It's not. But sometimes, when nobody is here, we play in the river."

I laugh. "I won't tell anyone." I look down at my shirt, wondering if I should take the risk.

"Did the monster hurt you?" Matthew asks, concerned.

"Can you keep a secret?" I whisper, enticing them to lean closer. I glance from side to side, making a show of it.

Matthew nods his head aggressively then looks at Talaya, who also nods eagerly. I look around, as if to make sure that no one is listening. Then I carefully retrieve the disk from its concealment, giving it to Matthew to hold.

While they stare at it in wonderment, I pull off my shirt and begin to wash it in the flowing stream. The blood slowly dissolves into the surrounding water, but some of it refuses to leave the fabric. I use two of the flat rocks to loosen the fibres by rubbing them against each other with the shirt in between. Once I'm satisfied that the stain has at least faded, I rinse off the shirt and pull it back on again. I return to the Whites, only to see them holding a completely different object. A gleaming golden disk.

"What did you do?" I ask amazed.

"We washed it," Matthew says excitedly. "It was all dirty, so you couldn't see the words."

I take the disk back from him and inspect it closely. Engraved across the surface, the words *SOUNDS OF EARTH* are visible. It's very clear now why this thing weighed so much. It's plated with solid gold. With a new-found appreciation of the item in my outstretched palms, I shove it back into my trousers and securely tug the bottom of my wet shirt into the waistband.

I spend the rest of the evening helping the Whites carry the rocks to the fireplace. After making a few trips to the river and back, my arms begin to cramp up underneath the weight of the stones. I'm able to transport four at a time, which is a lot more compared to the two of them, who can only manage one in each hand. Without my help, this menial task would have taken at least twice as long.

When the final stones are washed and placed next to the fire, the two children sit down to catch their breaths.

"Are you hungry?" I ask them. Talaya nods, but Matthew doesn't answer. His attention is focused on the group of older boys heading out of the Lodge.

"We can't eat now," he says. "We still have to water the plants."

"Are you sure?" I ask.

"Yes," he takes Talaya's hand and pulls her in the direction of the river. "We'll get in trouble if we don't."

I stare after them, suddenly very concerned for their wellbeing. These children are far too young to look after themselves, much less to labour away all day whilst suffering from malnutrition. I make the decision to help them whenever I can from now on. At least it will keep me busy until I'm assigned a real job to do.

I inspect the stones and choose the biggest two I can find, before making my way to the fireplace. Hunching between the smouldering coals, I carefully pick the softest scraps of meat and pile them on top of each other until the plates can carry no more. Then I amble back to the river where the Whites are still sitting, their feet in the water. To their surprise, I place the stones between them, the tender meals large enough to satisfy the hunger of a full-grown Apex.

They finish all of it.

CHAPTER 24

The Lodge is practically empty except for the night Elementals, who are all still asleep. I recognise Aiesha among them, her body turned away from the door. I wish I could wake her and tell her about the Shrieker or show her the disk. She's been avoiding me since the incident with the new drop. I don't know whether it's because of guilt or the fact that Skylor told her to stay away from me. Either way, I wish she wouldn't.

I scan the room before taking out the disk and sliding it beneath the cushioning of my bed. It should be safe here. Just as I get ready to leave, a large group of boys enter the Lodge with Germ leading the group. His face is mildly swollen and the skin around his nose is discoloured from the fight with Kyle.

"Hey, it's the Shrieker whisperer," he says, flopping down on the foot of my bed. The others eagerly gather around.

"Jeremy says you tamed a Shrieker," Conner says sceptically.

"He did!" Germ insists.

"While *he* kept Kyle away from you," Connor adds.

I look at Germ, who gives a shy chuckle in return. The rest of the Neuros quickly fill up the space between my bed and the next, trapping me inside the narrow cubicle. I sit down and uncomfortably shift my legs into a position that will best hide the protruding edge of the hidden disk. The Blue Marks mumble in unison, their shoulders rubbing against each other as they try to lean closer.

This is the first time I've seen the majority of them together in broad daylight. The Neuros do not often leave the protective enclosure of the Cave. Come to think of it, most Marks tend to avoid those who aren't their own kind. It might be a territorial thing, or just a general fear of the unknown. If this planet has taught us anything, it's to fear everything.

"I saw what happened," announces a booming voice at the back.

A tall, dark Elemental steps forward with his arms crossed. A cynical expression comprises the lower half of Skeith's face, but that might just be a permanent feature that goes with his malformation. It looks as if someone poured boiling water down his head, leaving every inch of his face scoured, except for his eyes and mouth. Skeith pushes the Neuros out of his way and stops at the side of my bed.

"The Shrieker submitted to you. The animals on Damnatus don't behave like that. Every single creature is dangerous, territorial, and most importantly, wired to kill us."

Aiesha silently joins the back of the group along with the others, wiping the sleep from her eyes. She shows no intention of intervening.

"So, tell me why the apex predator of this abominable ecosystem would risk its life to save you?" Skeith presses. "What makes your life more valuable than the countless Elementals who have been slaughtered by that *thing* in the forest?"

The clear disdain in his voice takes me by surprise. Some of the Elementals at the far edge of the Lodge have been woken by the ruckus, and now stand next to us. All of them stare at me with contempt. I suddenly feel very vulnerable. No one is willing to help or defend me, because I'm not like any of them. I don't have a group of my own and am therefore alone. I lift myself up from the bed and take a step closer so I can look Skeith in the eyes.

"I never said I was worth saving."

He continues to stare whilst analysing my movements, then he lowers his guard and turns to the others, raising his voice. "Now, will you all shut up? Not all of us get a free pass when a Shrieker shows up. We need our sleep." He shoots me a last glare before striding away. The Elementals return to their sleeping quarters and a few of the Neuros exit the Lodge. But Germ continues where he left off as if nothing happened.

"He's just mad because a landmine got him in the face," Germ shrugs. "Anyway, while you were away, we came up with some names for your Shrieker."

I wonder how Germ could be so oblivious about the situation. One of the Elementals' leaders just conveyed his distrust and even disapproval of my interaction with the Shrieker, while the other leader did nothing to stop him. Does Skeith not know that the alternative outcome would have meant my death? Does he care?

"Isn't 'Shrieker' good enough?" I groan.

"No. That's like calling your dog, Dog." He rolls his eyes. "We all like Kyle-Eater, but Red-Eater will do just as well—a bit more arbitrary."

"Or we can call him Russell," one of the younger Blues pipes up. "My dog's name was Russell."

"No," another chimes in. "Claws sounds better."

"How about Fluffy?" Conner suggests.

Germ takes offence to this. "Fluffy sounds like a glass of dirt."

"His name is Beetroot!" I exclaim.

Everyone stops talking.

Germ's face sinks. "You can't be serious, John."

"I am serious."

There's a general mutter of disapproval from the crowd. Good.

"But why?" Germ prods.

"He likes them."

"There aren't any beetroots on this planet."

"Well, *Beetroot*," I purposely emphasise the name and watch Germ's face crinkle up. "He found some underground."

With that said, the excitement dies down and the remaining boys start to disperse. Alone again, I ponder this daunting situation I'm in. I might constantly be surrounded by people in camp, but at the end of the day, I have nobody.

I spot a pink mark on the edge of my peripheral vision and realise that someone else is in a similar position. Maybe that puts us in a group—the outsiders. I quickly stop Germ before he reaches the door. "Hey, Germ?"

He turns around, visibly upset.

"When he ate the beetroots, red juice flowed out of his mouth."

"And?" he asks, irritated.

"It kind of looked like blood."

Germ's face lightens up. "I knew you'd give him a cool name." He hesitates, but then lifts up one of his hands and points to his bruised nose. "Thanks, by the way. For stopping him."

I shrug. "It's nothing, I helped just like anybody else would have."

Germ slowly shakes his head. "No John, nobody else would have."

CHAPTER 25

People treat me differently after the Shrieker incident. There's a certain look in their eyes; one that wasn't there before the attack. Fear. I keep having the same nightmare where I wake up to find my bed surrounded by children. I know it's a dream, because they don't have marks and their bodies are painted black. Usually, they just stare down at me like inanimate entities. I've learnt to ignore them by now, brushing them away as figments of my imagination. The dreams wouldn't bother me at all, if it weren't for the beds around mine slowly emptying.

Matthew and Talaya still remain, however. I recently discovered why they always end up in the same bed. Whenever I find myself between recurring dreams, a familiar child's voice pulls me back awake. Talaya gets nightmares too and will crawl in with Matthew when she gets scared. The boy will then try to console her, softly singing the same song over and over again.

"Don't be scared,
They're in your head.
Away they creep,
So go to sleep."

Kyle is still in the Adjustment Shack, fighting an infection. Skylor says it shouldn't be fatal, but I don't know what to make of this. I wouldn't say I feel satisfied, but I don't feel remorseful either.

There's been a noticeable drop in the food supply since Kyle's absence. The Apex are struggling without him, and often return with nothing but injuries of their own. They insist that Kyle's presence makes no difference and blame something else entirely. Apparently, a much larger animal is chasing the prey away and feeding on our grounds. I have a sneaking suspicion of what it is, and I'm almost certain that I will face repercussions if I don't intervene soon.

"This chocolate mousse tastes extraordinary," Germ groans, relishing the brown paste on the tip of his tongue. I follow his lead and clutch my food between my fingers. A loud crackling noise escapes my mouth as I bite into it. "Well, my black pizza is seasoned just right."

"I've heard of that," he says after slurping down another mouthful of gunk. "Some restaurants add a bit of vegetable charcoal into the dough, then call it gourmet and double the price."

"You sound like the type of person who would have hated red velvet," I laugh between crunching bites that leave my teeth feeling brittle.

"I detested it," he agrees unenthusiastically. "Oh look, this cupcake is red! Now buy it, you sheep."

"But Germ," I say mischievously. "There's a red velvet cupcake sitting right there in front of you?"

"Oh yes, I see. How delightful." He sighs and grabs the red chunk of unknown origin. I watch as he pinches his nose shut and closes his eyes, swallowing it down whole.

174

A few weeks ago, Germ and I invented a game for the days when the suns were at their hottest and the food was scarce. Without much to choose from around the campfire, we were each only allowed to eat what the other told us to and could not refuse a suggestion. Naturally, we chose only the most grotesque offerings.

I peer down at my crusted Ptera wing and inspect its surface. "They even added banana as a topping, just how I like it."

Germ gags. "John, that's disgusting. I'm trying to eat here." He bites into a particularly repulsive mud beetle. "Oh no," he moans as the watery liquid squirts out of the insect and oozes onto his clothes. "I spilled some sauce."

After we've consumed as much food as our stomachs can bear to keep down, we wash up at the river and find a tree to rest under. I lean back against the calloused bark of the tree while Germ lies on his back, wedged between the overgrown roots. He rolls over to me and inspects my mark.

"Those look like obelisks," he says, adjusting his glasses and peering over the crooked frames, bent out of shape during his scuffle with Kyle. "They seem to be guarding an entrance of some kind."

"What are obelisks?" I crane my neck to get a better view of my own mark.

"Depends on who you ask. Obelisks were normally used in pairs in front of temples and tombs. The Egyptians raised them in honour of a great king's accomplishments, but also used them to praise the solar gods. The pointed tops reflected the sunrays, and the first and last light of day would always touch their peaks."

"Why are there two of them?" I ask.

"In keeping with the Egyptian values of balance and harmony, of course. It was believed that the two obelisks on earth were matched by two in the heavens."

I frown at him. "Why would Egyptian symbolism be used on my mark?

"It isn't. You're implying that aliens have attempted to recreate Egyptian culture. If anything, the Egyptians were imitating them."

I peer over at the pale arm that's propped underneath his head. The pink mark has no patterns and is almost as blank as the white marks that could just as well have been cut from crumpled pieces of paper. Unlike theirs, Germ has a single circle in the middle of his mark, almost as big as a marble, coloured an even darker shade of pink.

"What do you think yours means?"

"There's not really much to it, is there?" He presses his finger into the centre of his mark, where the single bold point resides. "Looks like the Japanese flag. A very simplistic approach if you ask me." Pinching his skin together, he plays with the outer edges of his mark. "Then again, it might be a sort of binary code. The dot could represent a one, and the outlining of the symbol a zero."

I twist my head at an uncomfortable angle and strain my eyes to try and see what he is referring to. "What does the code mean?"

"Utter gibberish. You'd need a lot more ones and zeros to formulate anything of real value."

I take a few steps back and kneel next to him on the ground. Covering one of my eyes with the palm of my hand, I try to view the pink mark from a different perspective. "From afar it looks like an eye." I lift my hand like it's a camera lens, and pretend I'm look through it. "The middle looks like a pupil." I pause for a moment. "Isn't an eye the symbol of the Illuminati?"

Germ bursts out laughing. "That's not a can of worms you should be opening right now. We'll be sitting here all day, talking about the significance of eyes." He hesitates for a moment and scratches his forehead. "The connection with the Illuminati is plausible though, I'll give you that." He considers this theory for a few moments, then he turns to me and asks the question that is on everyone's minds. "So, what are you planning to do about Beetroot?"

"I'm not sure."

The question isn't whether I should intervene with nature and attempt to reason with a Shrieker. It's whether I can. Whatever prompted Beetroot to spare my life might not be present anymore.

What if he turns on me?

"What does the camp expect me to do?"

"Well, you have two options. Either train him or get rid of him. Not that the second option is possible, so that really leaves you with only one option."

"Nobody has even seen Beetroot this week. What if I can't find him?"

"Don't you get it? He protected you. And I think it has something to do with *that*." He points to my arm.

"How can you be so certain? You weren't attacked either. Maybe the pink mark means Shrieker whisperer."

Germ lets out a deranged laugh that rises in volume with each passing second. "Only one way to find out!" he screams before pushing me to the ground. Mimicking the cry of a Shrieker, Germ screeches at the top of his lungs and climbs on top of me. Still laughing hysterically, he shouts, "I'm going to kill you!"

Immediately, a booming uproar escapes the nearby shrubbery. I knock Germ off with a rapid thrust of my hips and jump to my feet. Beetroot is bolting towards us, his ears perked and his eyes wide. His mane changes rapidly from one dark colour to the next. I stand before Germ and raise my arms as far they can stretch.

"No!" I yell at the animal.

Beetroot comes to a halt in front of me and attempts to claw into Germ's exposed legs.

"Stop it!"

Beetroot seems troubled. He pushes his snout into my shirt, still stained. He recognises the scent of his own blood and takes a step back, letting out a wail. A few Elementals bolt out of the Lodge but hover when they see the Shrieker. Having studied most creatures in the area, they're still not used to seeing Shriekers, who have remained invisible until recently. It's an obvious threat.

I attempt to silence Beetroot by carefully caressing the fur around his wet snout. He leans into my hand and lets out a built-up breath of damp air. I do the same, slowly letting my guard down. As I pull my hand away, a string of drool peels off my fingers. I signal the Greens to go back into the Lodge, but they do so reluctantly and at a slow pace. Aiesha stays behind, ignoring my gestures. Standing a safe distance away from us, she looks on suspiciously.

Germ stands up and wipes the soil from his clothes. "I told you so," he boasts.

"Why would you do that?" I growl at him, more annoyed than impressed.

"It worked, didn't it? Beetroot only protects you."

I drop down on my knees and stare up at the towering beast. We're the same, in a way. Alone and misunderstood. Breathing in his musky odour, I close my eyes and am transported back into the forest where the cliff sloped down and met an ash-laden desert. If the Shrieker wanted to kill me, he could simply have left me there to rot. Instead, the large beast allowed me onto his back, carrying me back into walking distance from the camp. The Shrieker is drawn to me in a way that I cannot put into words. I feel it too.

"Do you really think this is what my mark means?" I ask Germ.

"It appears so. You should train him."

And so we do.

* * *

Every day when the suns are at their warmest and the Trinity begins its cycle, Germ feigns an attack and I play

179

along. Without missing a beat, Beetroot storms out of the forest, rushing to my aid. Aiesha does the same, running out of the Lodge to watch our interactions. I know what she's doing, because it's the very nature of an Elemental. Aiesha is observing and learning.

It's become obvious that Beetroot is lurking near the camp border, always watching me. It's quite possible that he's been following me before the incident, only making his presence known when Kyle attacked me.

Kyle. The name sends off danger bells for a variety of reasons. This isn't the first time the Apex leader has laid his hands on one of my friends. He isn't confident that he can beat me in a fight, so he targets my companions instead. First it was Aiesha, now Germ. If it wasn't for that deafening shriek in the forest causing the Reds to flee, Kyle might have seriously hurt Aiesha. Something scared him off before he could.

My eyes widen as I notice a pattern that's too significant to ignore. *Was Beetroot protecting me back then already?*

As time passes, I stop roleplaying a fight with Germ and simply begin to scream very loudly. To our relief, it has the exact same effect, alerting Beetroot of potential danger. After every encounter, I reduce the intensity of my voice. I repeat this process until I'm no longer required to scream and a mere shout is sufficient to get the Shrieker's attention. Just like calling a dog.

The rest of the camp has grown used to the exercise by now, barely looking twice when the elephant-sized beast comes storming onto the campgrounds. With time, his presence shifts from a threatening intrusion to a welcome source of security. A calm atmosphere has once again settled over the camp.

That is until Germ decides we need a control group. He heard the phrase 'control group' from one of the Neuros and is now adamant about using it. "Help!" he screams, falling to the ground. "I'm dying!"

"It's not going to work," I shake my head disapprovingly.

Germ writhes on the ground, clutching at his chest. "Our experiment needs me as scientific control. How else will we know if Beetroot isn't just responding to any person who is in danger?" He rolls onto his stomach and pushes himself onto all fours. Crawling forward, he proceeds to make gurgling noises like a choking cat. I can't help but laugh.

"Oh, the pain!" he howls.

"What's wrong?" Rusty exits the Cave and runs toward us. "Do you need help? Should I call Sky?"

"Not necessary, Elizabeth. We have everything under control!" Germ shouts.

She looks over at us, dubious.

I decide to put an end to the show and call Beetroot with a quick and simple, "Here boy!"

The Shrieker trots out from behind the bushes and takes a seat next to Germ, who has given up on his experiment.

The Neuro's curious nature soon gets the best of her, and by the end of the hour she's lying between us, playing with Beetroot's retractable claws. Rusty discovers a neat trick by stroking Beetroot's stomach. Like an imbedded reflex, the animal's fur pigment warps into the colour of the luminous green terrain it is occupying.

We discuss various reasons for this and decide on a favourite—which just happens to be my idea. Seeing that Beetroot is an omnivore, we're assuming that he needs to stalk his prey when he hunts. Generally, lions and tigers stoop to the ground, crawling until ready to pounce. Perhaps Shriekers do this as well; the only difference being that when their stomachs rub against a surface, it triggers a cloaking mechanism that allows the creature to change colours and blend in with the environment.

"Good boy!" Germ brushes Beetroot's tail after he turns a bright green.

Aiesha passes us on her way to the fire. It's almost time for her shift to begin.

"It's a girl, you know," she mentions apprehensively, not stopping to explain why.

"What! Are you serious?" Germ whines.

Rusty bursts out laughing. "Why, does that bother you? Can't you handle the fact that a girl could shred you to pieces?"

Germ gags. "No, even you could probably do that if you wanted to."

I look at Beetroot and caress her fur. "It changes nothing."

"I still don't believe that she found beetroots. You just wanted to mess with me," Germ insists.

"She really did," I assure him. "She took me to a giant black, burned down field and dug some up beneath the ashes."

Germ's eyes widen. "You went to the Ashfalt?"

I shrug. "I don't know."

"Not even the Elementals are allowed to go there," he says. "Why?"

"Because of the Feral," Germ whispers, his eyes lighting up like he's telling a ghost story. "Legend says that there were other Marks who came, even before the First. They were living in the Ashfalt, but back then it wasn't called that. It was filled with plants and animals, just like our camp."

I find it very hard to believe that any sort of life once existed on that barren stretch of land. It's about as unlikely that aliens once wandered the plains of Mars. Germ scratches Beetroot behind her ear and tries his best to recall the gritty details.

"They weren't like us, though. It was different back then. Everyone spoke different languages, so they weren't able to communicate properly. After a while, the Marks stopped speaking altogether. They went crazy struggling to cope with it all and started behaving like animals. Feral. One day, they simply had enough and set the entire forest alight. Everything burned down to the ground or died in the process." A giant grin stretches across his face. "They say that all the drops who don't find their way to camp, or are simply too freaked out to fit in, eventually wind up Feral."

"That's just a story, Jeremy," Rusty says.

He frowns at her. "It doesn't matter. They would have starved by now anyway."

Rusty winks at him. "Who knows? Maybe they eat beetroots all day." She playfully punches him in the arm and they both burst out laughing.

"There were beetroots!" I insist.

"Prove it," Germ says.

A sudden idea enters my mind. "I will."

I stand up and bolt towards the Lodge. When I reach my bed, I carefully slip my hands in between the twine. The cold metal rim touches the edge of my fingers. Relieved, I pull it out and run back to Rusty and Germ. Their expressions change drastically when I show it to them.

"Where did you get this?" Rusty demands.

"At the Ashfalt. I told you, I was there."

"Is that what I think it is?" Germ's face grows pale.

Rusty doesn't answer him. Instead, she grabs the disk from my hands and runs off with it firmly clasped against her chest. We follow her into the Cave and join her at the back.

"It can't be a coincidence that the Elementals found a gramophone at the same location," she mumbles to herself. Using the handle, she winds up the spring-driven motor and fits the small needle into the groove of the record. Sitting in the corner of the Cave, the gramophone whirs to life.

Beethoven's Fifth Symphony works its way up the diaphragm and bursts out of the metal horn. The familiar, yet foreign music trails out of the Cave, captivating all who can hear. Within seconds the stone enclosure is crowded with Marks, their faces filled with expressions of euphoria and simultaneous disbelief. Without turning it off, Rusty picks up the gramophone and carries it past the mesmerised children, who follow her outside.

As we walk, Marks push and shove to get closer to the sounds that escape the contraption. Germ stays behind, longingly staring after them.

"What's wrong?" I ask, intrigued by his sudden perturbed demeanour.

"It's just too much of a coincidence," he mumbles, still deep in thought.

"What do you mean?"

"It was gold, John," he says with a hint of fear in his voice. "Have you ever heard of the Voyager Golden Record?"

"No, but it rings a bell."

He rambles on. "It's a record NASA shot into space mid-1970s, hoping that it would reach intelligent life. They made it out of gold-plated copper and recorded different languages and songs onto it, in case anybody ever found it."

"Well, something did," I realise aloud.

We look at each other, sharing a brief moment of mutual understanding.

When the third sun vanishes from the sky, the entire camp surrounds the fire, listening in rapt silence. Even the night Elementals were reluctant to depart for their shifts, claiming that they didn't want to miss any hidden messages. This was of course just an excuse to hear it again, as we'd listened to the entire album two times already.

When the needle reaches the end of its course, Rusty fiddles with the pointed piece of metal until the mesmerising sounds again flow from the twisted horn speaker.

Greetings in sixty different Earth languages echo into the air, followed by various snippets of classical music and aquatic animal noises. These sounds bring about a profound longing for a life I once knew. Perhaps I didn't cherish it enough. I focused too much on the things I couldn't change, like the absence of my father, and not enough on the things I could, such as my relationships with the people around me. Could that be the reason why I was ripped away from everyone I loved and cared for?

"Why are we here?" I blurt out. The moment the words escape my mouth, I regret it. I expect the group to ridicule me, but no one so much as flashes a grin.

"Do you want to discuss theories?" Connor asks, his tone serious.

"I'd like that," I answer.

"Alright, you first," he refers to me, as the others look on expectantly.

"Okay..." I hesitate. "We've been abducted."

"No shit, Sherlock." He seems rather disappointed in my answer. The Neuro was expecting more from me.

I concentrate a bit harder before making a second attempt, taking my time. I remember watching a certain movie with my dad when I was a child. Trying not to sound too cliché, I hazard a second theory based on its content. "What if," I start, "we never actually left the Earth."

"Go on," Conner sounds intrigued.

"We only think we did, because we travelled back in time. That's why the atmosphere is so different and why the animals resemble dinosaurs."

Connor smiles, pleased. I clearly said what he wanted to hear. Everyone turns to him, waiting for a response.

"Solid theory, John. Unfortunately, it's false." He takes a deep breath. "We are definitely on a different planet. Besides the fact that we're surrounded by entirely different constellations, your theory falls flat in the face of gravity. The planet's size and mass determine the gravitational pull you experience—or your weight, if you will. You might remember feeling abnormally exhausted the first couple of weeks after your arrival. That's because you weigh significantly more on Damnatus than you did back on Earth. This planet is much larger, disproving your theory."

Undoubtedly in his element, Germ tries to contribute as well. "What if we're dreaming?" he asks eagerly.

"Pinch yourself then," Connor shoots him down.

We wait a few more moments until a familiar voice from the back speaks. "We've all died and gone to Hell." Kyle sounds tired and sore, but he seems utterly serious.

Instead of dismissing his theory off the bat like the rest of ours, Connor chooses his words more carefully with the Apex. "Just one little problem with that. I don't really remember dying." He looks over to the opposite side of the fire. "Do you?"

Kyle doesn't answer him.

"So, what's your theory then?" I ask Connor.

He takes a moment to structure his idea. "I think we're being tested. To see which type of Mark survives."

"Shouldn't we just kill each other then?" Skylor suggests as she approaches the group.

"Obviously not." This time it is Connor's turn to defend his theory, but Sky doesn't show any intention of holding back her critique.

"Why not? If we're being tested to see who lives, why not just go to war and get it over with?"

"It's not that simple!" Connor is getting frustrated. "There are many questions we could ask. Why do we have marks? Why are only children abducted? Take the Clearing, for example. It's as if the Reptants are purposely placed there to kill new drops, yet they only sense movement, assuring that no person who is still unconscious will be devoured." He looks to Sky, who doesn't seem to share his enthusiasm. "We are thrown into a world where literally everything— even the plants—are out to kill us, yet we are still ensured a fighting chance. Why?"

"You tell me." Sky seems offended for some reason, as if she's taking this debate more personally than she should. "You're the one who seems to have all of the answers."

Connor is about to give up but decides to offer his last bit of input. "There is definitely something more to this. None of you can deny it." He stands up, making his point as clear as possible. "There's a very specific reason we were brought here, and I don't think you'll like it one bit."

For a moment the campfire is silent. A strange feeling overcomes me as Connor's harsh words set in. I think we all feel it.

"Unless you're a restless sleeper," Germ attempts to break the awkward silence. "Then the Reptants will eat you before you even wake up."

A few chuckles resonate around the group. Even Kyle comments, "Lucky bastard."

Although the mood has lightened, a heavy feeling sticks with me. I can't quite shrug it off. There was something very real to what Connor said—an uncomfortable truth that none of us want to face.

Avoiding the light at all costs, a stealthy figure creeps up on me from behind. When I turn around, I catch a glimpse of the silhouette disappearing into the shadows of the forest where the fire's fiery arms can't reach. No one else noticed, but I clearly heard the whisper.

"Go to the Clearing at dawn. Alone."

The voice vanished as quickly as it came, leaving only the sounds of animals and other distant messages from a seemingly unfamiliar planet.

CHAPTER 26

India, Maharashtra: One hour before abduction

Magic seeds. She pierces the barren soil with her hoe and wipes the sweat from her brow. If she had the good fortune of attending school, she would be able to tell her parents that these were GM seeds. Promised to be entirely immune to disease and free of pests, the Western travellers made promises too good to ignore. If only she could explain to her starving parents that even genetically modified seeds were not entirely free from fault.

To the contrary, the air now smells of pesticide, used to rid the fields of new and even worse pests. Unfortunately, this is not the only reason homes are filled with its stench, for in these dark times many farmers see it as an answer to troubles much greater than an unsuccessful harvest. One use for pesticides proves a lot more morbid. It's no wonder that children are being orphaned throughout the village.

At the first sign of a discoloured stalk, Aiesha had secretly snuck away in the dead of night. Knowing better and aware of her parents' ignorance, she bought normal cotton seeds and began to plant them sparsely, yet thoroughly. Not enough to raise suspicions, but an adequate portion to ensure a successful harvest when it would be needed most.

It had been twelve hours since they left home to work the fields. The polluted, overcast sky blocks the Sun's diminishing light and the children decide to call it a day.

"You should go," Aiesha tells her younger brothers. "I'm not done with my plot."

"Are you sure?" the youngest of the four asks. "I can help?"

"No, Khalif." She pushes him into the direction of the others. "Mother will worry."

He seems reluctant to leave her, but hurries onwards to catch up with his siblings. Once they are out of sight, Aiesha retrieves the pouch hidden around her waist and begins to plant the cotton seeds. She struggles in the dimming light and uses her hands to scratch around in the loosened soil.

Soon, steps become audible from the direction of the village. She sighs. The little one always comes back when he falls behind with the others. The plants before her shake.

"Khalif?" she calls out into the darkness.

Nobody answers, but there's another rustle, and the stems sway forward.

The girl slowly lowers herself to the ground until her chest grazes the soil. She abandons the bag of wheat and reaches for the sharpened metal tool instead.

The movements have stopped now. She knows she's being watched. The only question troubling her is by what. Fight or flight? She must choose quickly, for the only thing worse than picking the wrong option is executing neither of them.

Her sympathetic nervous system causes her heart to race, readying her for action. She listens to the noises of the night but doesn't hear anything. She draws a fast conclusion and her eyes dilate. If she isn't able to detect the entity with any of her trained senses, then it can only mean one thing. It's not human.

Like a trigger being pulled, she shoots off into the fields and away from the village. If she can't outrun it, at least she'll be able to lure it away from her people. With the insidious silence of an underwater torpedo, it trails after her with a propelling speed. She follows a random course, winding around plants with rapid, twisting movements. Reaching the outskirts of the open unsown field, she skids to a halt. Turning around, she clenches the tool between her hands and raises it before her.

As silent as a serpent in the grass, the Bengal tiger crawls closer, salivating in anticipation. It seems to be fighting itself, as if struggling to win back control over its own body. The animal's expanded pupils roll back into its head until both sockets are entirely black, like the dark side of the moon. It jerks its head backward, resisting the temptations of an unknown force. Like a possessed puppet controlled by invisible strings, the animal twitches, and lurches forward.

CHAPTER 27

When I awake, the sky is still dark and filled with stars. Since I cannot rely on an alarm or ask anyone to wake me later, I grab my shoes and quietly head into the forest. After about an hour of walking, I come across the trademarked bones. As the corpses increase, I know I'm heading in the right direction.

The trees begin to give way, and before long the insidious ring of sand appears. In fear of attracting Reptants, I avoid the Clearing's centre and slowly tread around it instead. The first shimmer of orange shines through the treetops, casting shadows on the flaxen plain that resemble the arms of a ticking clock.

"Were you followed?" a voice asks.

"No," I respond, but a rustle in the nearby shrubs proves otherwise. I spin around and peer into the darkness, only to find mirages of overlapping shadows and a distorted patch of bushes that stands out from the rest. When I call out to it, the object changes into a familiar shape, slowly morphing into pure blackness. It's Beetroot.

"She won't bite," I lie.

"Good, I need to show you something." Aiesha jumps out of the nearby tree and lands beside me.

"What is it?" I ask, glad to see her again.

"You'll see."

For the first few minutes we walk in silence, carefully moving like silhouettes between the trees. To avoid the other Elementals, Aiesha purposely heads off into her own territory, starting on the same route we took last time. When we reach the waterhole, she changes direction, leading me through kilometres of dense foliage. The first sun rises and its throbbing heat nags at my exposed neck. Once we have travelled far enough into the unknown, Aiesha begins to speak.

"The moment I saw Beetroot, I knew something wasn't right. Only ectotherms are able to change their skin tone like that. Not mammals. At first, I thought it was due to some kind of sporadic mutation, but then she protected you like a wolf does for its pack." Aiesha looks around nervously, surveying the area for other Marks. "It's just too much of a coincidence. It's as if she was genetically modified."

We approach a stretch of land where the line of trees ends abruptly. In the skies, Pteras soar freely, their wings spread out like overhead planes. Aiesha stops beneath a protective shield of branches and drops to her knees.

"This stretch of terrain is called the Dengar. It's the farthest point any Elemental is allowed to go." She takes a handful of sand and rubs it onto her cheeks. Her expression grows more serious. "I need you to be quiet from here on out."

I agree and smear some sand on my face.

Aiesha reaches underneath her blouse and plays with the tightly wrapped strapping until she retrieves a small pouch, held between her fingers. Constructed out of animal skin, the leather bag is tainted copper and stained slightly brown around the crumpled edges. It releases a sharp scent when she pulls the cord from the hem. She instructs me to hold out my hand, in which she empties half of the saturated contents.

"Do you like coffee?" she asks.

"I drink it every now and then," I answer, unsure. "Caffeine makes me jittery."

She tries her best to grin, but the tension in her jaw only allows her lips a pursed twitch. "Well, prepare for a caffeine overdose," she says while spilling what's left of the mixture into her outstretched palm. "I whipped it up this morning."

I lean closer and inhale a better whiff of the soggy, black substance. Without having to raise the question on my mind, Aiesha puts my fears to rest.

"I gathered what I needed from the plantation and brewed it in some river water over the campfire. It's entirely safe for consumption." She looks at me with a trace of challenge in her eyes.

"Cheers," she finally says and lifts the substance to her craving lips. Knowing better by now than to question an Elemental's methods, I mimic her movements and choke down the pungent mixture of ground beans. Once the bitter extract grazes my taste buds, it sends a wave of nausea up my throat, forcing me to hold back a gag. Aiesha shows no discomfort in the slightest and licks the leftover residue from her fingers.

Bitter bile slides down my throat, leaving a strange herbal aftertaste on my tongue. My stomach burns in response, causing my neck to break out in hives and my eyes to tear up. My heart beats faster and louder within my chest, and air escapes my lungs in quick, compact bursts.

"Your breathing has hastened," Aiesha observes. "Good."

Suddenly feeling the urge to stand up, I rise to my feet and jog on the spot. The amount of adrenaline that's flooding through me needs to be controlled or released. Beetroot notices the change in my behaviour and becomes agitated, trotting around me in circles.

Aiesha gestures to the open field in front of us. "There's only one way to go about this, and that's to run as fast as you possibly can. The field ends where those bushes begin. It's a thirty-second sprint, twenty-five if you're fast. The Pteras can't get you once you're between the trees—they're too big." Aiesha turns her back to me and looks up at the sky. "Don't stop. Don't think. Just run."

She bolts onto the field. I dash after her. Beetroot is on my heels but easily surpasses me. The soles of our feet crunch into the sand and send clumps of soil flicking up from underneath our heels. I ignore my own breathing and concentrate on Aiesha, who grunts every time she forces the air out of her throat.

With alarmed outbursts of screeching, the Pteras in the sky shift their focus on the intruders beneath. In a gust of wind, they descend toward us. I urge myself to ignore them and keep running as fast as my legs will allow me. Halfway across, I make the error of looking up.

About a dozen Pteras swarm above us, their talons exposed and beaks pointing downwards.

I'm not going to make it.

Aiesha has a good few feet on me and is closing the distance to the bushes much quicker than I am. The Pteras must have realised this as well because they're all bearing down on me instead.

I glance over my shoulder. Maybe if I run back to the shelter, it might confuse the birds and throw their trajectories off track. Even if I don't reach the trees in time, it will give Aiesha enough time to get across. I slow down and swing around, looking to the sky as I do so. The Pteras clumsily flutter into each other, then shoot upwards, readying for another attempt to dive down.

I manage to progress a full twenty metres before a hard blow knocks the wind from my chest. The creature grabs onto my clothing and swings me upwards, carrying me into the opposite direction. Within seconds, Beetroot is at my side, snapping at the air. Startled by the Shrieker's attack, the bird releases its hold on me. Beetroot circles around and stops me from running any farther. Knowing the drill by now, I climb onto her back and cling to her fur as she runs towards Aiesha, who is already under the tree.

The Pteras claw at the Shrieker's back, which changes from one bright colour to the next. I try to protect her lower body by kicking at the birds with full force. Except for a few lucky blows, my resistance has little effect. If anything, this only irritates the birds. One of the Pteras avoids most of my attacks, and glides next to us. I kick him in the beak, but he retaliates by sinking his claws into my chest and ripping me from Beetroot's back. Blood seeps out of my wounds as the bird carries me into the sky. I inhale a deep breath, but refuse to let it out, as it will most likely be too painful to take another.

The other Pteras claw at my body like a piece of meat, excitingly screeching in celebration of a successful hunt. Their victory is cut short when my attacker releases me. I fall through the air and land on the ground, the Ptera dropping dead beside me. A rigid spear sticks out of its greasy chest. Aiesha runs past me and pulls the spear from the bird's torso, then helps me to my feet, supporting my weight on her shoulder and acting as a crutch for the rest of the way.

Beetroot makes it to the shelter before us; her wounds minimal. The rest of the Pteras flock down to the ground, eagerly tearing into the flesh of their fallen companion. When Aiesha and I have breached the first border of bushes, she rests me against a tree and inspects my body closely.

"Let me see," she instructs, her tone concerned.

I pull up what is left of my torn shirt and look down at the growing traces of blood. Aiesha wipes it away with a shaky hand. Her fingers carefully trace the abrasions along my heaving chest. The Ptera's claws left three deep gushes across the front of my body. In my back, I can feel a fourth gash where it grabbed onto me.

"You're lucky. It's just a flesh wound," Aiesha sighs with relief. She uses the tip of her weapon to tear off a part of the cloth that was wrapped around her body. With a copious amount of pressure, she holds it against my wounds in an attempt to stop the bleeding. Leaning over me with her arms outstretched, I notice that the scars across Aiesha's body look strikingly similar to the wounds that now mark mine.

"We'll have to disinfect the lesions back at camp, but it will have to wait." She releases her grip on my chest and helps me off the ground. "This is far more important." Again, she reminds me to stay quiet as we set off into the woods.

The farther we travel, the more agitated Aiesha becomes. Our pace has been altered significantly to avoid making any noise as we step over loose rocks and crunchy leaves. At the moment we barely move at a regular walking speed. Within an hour we come across a river but stop when something moves down its lower banks. The figure hunches over and scoops up water with his hands.

I point to the boy. "A new drop."

"It's not a new drop," she informs me.

I don't understand what she means. I've never seen him before at camp, and besides, nobody is allowed to travel this far. We follow the boy for a while, steadily keeping a safe distance between us. It's clear that Aiesha doesn't want us to be seen.

Finally, the boy disappears behind a large, wooden structure. A towering two-storey shelter that makes the Lodge look like a rundown shack in comparison. Once a formidable work of craftsmanship, all that remains now is an infested assembly of dead wood. Strains of blue mould run down the tilted walls and meet the ground, where swarms of insects have gathered to nest. Not unlike the Lodge, this building lacks a roof as well. It must have fallen off long ago, as it now lies on the ground, slowly rotting away.

We skirt around the building, choosing a route that leads to higher ground. Once we have scaled the hill and are narrowly able to see the structure peeking out from underneath the treetops, we get down on all fours. As we peer off the edge, my eyes widen in disbelief.

The hollowed-out hill is filled with Marks. Dozens of children walk around the area, each bearing a symbol on his or her arm. I don't recognise any of them.

"Who are they?" I ask.

"It's another camp," Aiesha whispers.

I count the number of figures that I can spot below. There are fewer people in this group—hardly even thirty.

"I've been spying on them for months now," she says. "Skylor instructed me to do so in secret. I report back to her on a weekly basis."

"Why?"

"She only told me that it's for the good of the camp, and that it's better if they don't know of us and we don't know of them."

"Why would she say that?" I ask, my trust for Skylor gradually deteriorating. How could it possibly be a bad thing if we knew of each other's existence? If anything, we should work together and form a bigger, better camp.

"That's why I brought you here," she continues. "Something doesn't feel right about all of this, and an Elemental's instincts aren't usually far off."

I look around the camp, paying more attention to the finer details. They only have Red, Blue and Green Marks. Nobody seems to be talking either, and a gloomy atmosphere hovers over the camp; the kind one would find at a cemetery or abandoned amusement park. The children look mournful and stricken with famine. This place gives off a dark feeling that I can't quite shake. Something is clearly not right.

"We should head back to camp before they notice we're missing," I suggest to Aiesha, looking for an excuse to leave the area.

"No, wait John. There is something else I want you to see."

Before I can prod again, a low resonating growl emerges behind us. Beetroot snarls, this time more threatening and imminent. I swing around and survey the threat but find myself frozen and unable to react. Aiesha is better prepared, pushing me onto Beetroot's back and jumping up in front. She begins to rally us back to camp, but someone grabs me from behind and pulls me to the ground. I watch as Aiesha disappears around the corner, before I'm gagged and blindfolded.

The Black Mark didn't say anything. He only smiled.

CHAPTER 28

I finally open my eyes, but my hands are still bound. The blindfold is removed from my head and my mouth is free to move again. The building's upper-level floor is hidden beneath a thick layer of animal fur. The shaggy black carpet clings to my legs and softly cushions my back. In the corner of the room, dozens of similar black pelts are piled on top of each other to form a large, comfortable bed.

A wooden chest stands at its side, carved with extravagant patterns. In the centre, the frivolous designs are replaced with cave-like paintings of wolves, feasting on the bones of fallen gazelle. A closet leans against the opposite wall with its doors wide open, displaying a wardrobe of well-maintained shirts, pants, jackets and male underwear. Its doors are also decorated with dark sketches of wolves, most of which are growling and baring their teeth.

A row of well-maintained shoes are stacked at the foot of the bed. Boots, sneakers, sandals and even a shiny pair of loafers lie next to each other, all about the same size. I look at the possessions in awe. How does one accumulate so many riches on a planet like Damnatus?

After I was pushed to the ground and blindfolded, more Marks approached me and tied my hands together with some rope. I couldn't see who was talking, but I distinctly remember a very aggressive voice shouting demands, ordering the others to take me away to his chambers. I was led down the hill and into the wooden building where I was pushed up two flights of stairs and into a room.

Although I was subsequently tied to a wooden post, great care was taken to make sure that I was comfortable. One of the Marks even went as far as placing a pillow beneath my head before leaving. Left alone for an hour, someone eventually came back to untie me.

I look to the far corner of the room and spot the Pink Mark.

"Germ?" I ask hesitantly.

The figure jumps up and strides towards me. Dressed ridiculously, he's flaunting nothing but bare skin laced in pink. Pink sandals smack the floor as he walks towards me, while tight pink leggings stretch up to his hips, which is also covered in a pink skirt. Apparently, pink shirts were out of stock because he has chosen to go shirtless and wear a pink scarf instead.

"Who is this Germ you speak of?" he asks in a high-pitched voice that bubbles over with cheerfulness. "There are no germs here, none at all! You could even lick the ground if you wished!" he sings merrily. "Royalty should never lick the ground though, oh no," he corrects himself and gracefully leaps around the room before returning with a dish in his hands. "Here, a meal instead, fit for a king!"

He humbly bends over and hands me a tray that is covered with food, most of which I have never seen before. Luscious fruit hangs over the edges, still attached to their long, twirling vines. A variety of meats and sauces rest in the centre, topped with a sprinkle of potent smelling spices.

Where did they find all of these delicacies? And why is there so much of it? When Aiesha and I observed the camp, half of the Marks were just days away from starving. The boy before me looks no different.

"Who are you?" I ask.

He does a little twirl. "My name is Jester, for that is what I am."

"You're a jester?" I ask suspiciously. What does that even mean?

"Well, of course I am! My purpose is to provide entertainment and entertain you I shall!"

He proceeds to drop down on all fours, using his pink scarf as a make-shift trunk. "Can you guess what I am?" he trumpets. "I'll give you a clue. I am the largest land mammal on a little planet called Earth. You might have heard of it!"

I feel uncomfortable. This teenager is putting on a show for me; the type you might find at a young child's birthday party. His behaviour is wildly inappropriate for his age.

"Are you an elephant?" I humour him.

"Yes! That is exactly what I am, well done!" He trumpets again and waves his scarf around in the air. "Now, although I'm the only mammal that can't jump, I can do other nifty tricks, like use my trunk as a snorkel when I swim!"

He flops to his stomach and starts to mimic swimming movements. "I also need to consume about a hundred and fifty kilograms of food every day and can spend up to three-quarters of my day eating. Do you want to know the worst part?"

"What's the worst part?" I have to stop myself from rolling my eyes.

"Up to half of my meals often leave my body undigested. What a waste!" He stands up and brushes off his clothes. "Speaking of waste, you haven't touched your food." Jester leans closer, inspecting the buffet. "Is it not to your liking?" he asks nervously.

It certainly is. It took an exceptional amount of self-control not to indulge in the extravagant display before me. On this single tray, there is more food than there was available for our entire camp yesterday. My mouth is watering, yet I cannot help but feel that something is very off about all of this. Jester is nothing but skin and bones. His ribcage stands out like an eye sore, and his knees are all knobbly. The Pink Mark's sunken eyes watch me with great interest.

"Eat with me," I finally suggest.

His expression changes drastically. For a moment, Jester drops the act and his face is struck with fear. His gaze quickly bounces to the door, as if expecting someone to enter the room. He looks back at me, and for a fleeting second, considers my invitation. Then he pulls himself away from the dish and switches back into character.

"Oh, no, no," he laughs heartily with his hands on his hips. "This is a test! Oh yes, a test. And I almost fell for it. They should call you the jester!"

"I'm not going to eat until you have some first," I state outright.

"You're getting angry," he notices nervously. "Please don't get angry, I will do anything you want. Absolutely anything."

I pick out a thick, glazed piece of meat. The biggest serving I've seen in weeks. I slowly stand up from the floor, kicking the rope to my side. Eye-level, I hand the Pink Mark the heavy meal. "I want to you to eat until you can't fit another bite."

He nods then lifts the food to his mouth with shaky hands, his eyes still betraying a sense of distrust. "I really shouldn't," he whispers, but bites into the tender meat anyway. A long sigh escapes his lips, one of pleasure and delight. I place my hands on his shoulders, pulling him down to the ground with me. He gives in and takes a seat next to me on the soft, embracing carpet.

Satisfied with his compliance, I help myself to the second biggest serving—a buttery meat patty, rich in flavour and seasoned to perfection. The taste is foreign, yet welcome. It's not a Rodback, Leaper or Ptera, but an entirely different species that our Apex have not spotted before. Or never managed to kill.

I quickly swallow it and move on to a purple fruit that looks like a slice of watermelon. Eagerly slurping down the syrupy juices, a quarter of it leaks down my chin and stains my shirt. I hand Jester some fruit as well, which he takes without protesting. We continue to eat in silence, momentarily taking breaks to let out wind. When we're both too stuffed to eat any more, we lean back against the wall and groan. More than half of the food still remains on the tray. It's enough to feed several people.

"You're like a shrimp, whose heart sits in his head," Jester says. "Yes, a shrimp you are."

I turn my head to the side and glare at him. "Are you being forced to talk like this and play the fool?" I ask him, to which a trace of panic makes its way to his face again.

For a long time, he doesn't say anything. He just stares at the heavy tray of food, contemplating many things. Then, he finally turns to me and executes a very slight nod. I knew it.

"Is he bothering you?" a loud voice booms from the doorway. Jester jumps away from the food like a startled cat. The large Apex approaches him and pushes him into a corner. As he inspects the traces of sauce in the corners of Jester's mouth, his face turns red with fury. "Did you eat the food?" he asks Jester, grabbing him by the neck and shoving him against the wall.

"He thought you were trying to poison him," Jester gasps for air. "A smart man he is! He requested that I be his royal food taster, less he ended up dead like the Roman Emperor, Claudius!"

The Red turns to me, unwilling to release Jester from his tight hold. "Is this true?" he asks me. I find it strange that he trusts the word of a stranger more than one of his own.

"Yes," I declare. "He's telling the truth."

"Lucky you," the Apex spits at Jester. "Now get him ready, the tournament is about to begin." He marches out of the room and down the stairs.

Jester takes a deep breath, regaining his composure. "Thank you," he says. With a spring in his step, he walks over to the closet and presents the rack of clothing with jazz hands. "Time to get dressed."

"Are you talking to me?" I ask. Surely, he's the one who needs to revaluate his wardrobe choices.

"Of course, I am! You can't meet the king looking like that."

"I'll stick to this outfit," I brush him off.

"Oh, but you must! The king is putting on a great show in your honour!"

"Why?" I frown. "What makes me so special?"

"Well, your mark of course! For yours is the same as his!"

That explains it. The fancy food, clothes and impeccable service. They've made the conclusion that I'm some kind of royalty, merely because my mark is the same colour as their so-called king's. Surely, it's just a convenient incident that a Black Mark has managed to rise to power here. I'm just a Shrieker whisperer who strolls around camp all day, wishing I had some greater purpose. All of this must be a big coincidence.

But what if it isn't?

I examine my shirt, which is torn and stained. It hasn't bothered me until now. My running shoes are still holding out, even across the most hazardous terrains. My pants, on the other hand, have shrunk quite a bit over the last few weeks and feel tight around my waist. I suppose it won't hurt to replace some of my clothes.

Jester sifts through the rack of clothing, picking out the items that he likes best. He holds up a navy polo shirt with a proud glint in his eyes.

"This one was mine," he exclaims. "I wore it to school on most days. It's the perfect blend between casual and formal." He hands it to me, almost reluctantly. "It allowed me to fit in with the kids during school hours and hop straight into the public library when the final bell rang." He sighs. "Oh, how I miss the library. I have an eidetic memory, you know. After reading every book in the building, I quickly ran out of things to do. The librarian offered to hire me as an assistant, and I'd already memorised everything there was to read—so I thought why not?"

He finds a pair of skinny jeans along with some khaki shorts. Jester seems to consider the fashionable choice for a second, but then comes to his senses and tosses me the khaki shorts instead.

"Do you want to know how I got abducted? It's quite silly actually. I was on my way home from the library when I spotted a strange-looking book lying on a park bench. It was already dark outside, but the book sort of glowed under the starlight. I thought someone threw it away. I couldn't believe my luck."

He pulls opens a small drawer attached to the closet. The contents inside rattle as he scours through them, but he eventually retrieves a pair of sunglasses and an inhaler. I shake my head, refusing both. As an accessory the glasses are simply overkill, but the inhaler bothers me for a different reason. It likely belongs to someone who really needs it. Or at least it used to.

Jester takes a puff from the inhaler and puts on the tinted glasses, now looking even more ridiculous than before. "I remember thinking to myself, this is how you're going to get kidnapped, Roderick. Forget strangers in a van with a bowl of candy. That's not going to cut it. A big new book on the other hand—that will most definitely do."

"So, what happened?"

"I barely touched the book before I blacked out. When I woke up in the circle, I was quite upset that the book had vanished. They could at least have brought it along, you know?"

I chuckle at the Pink Mark. He reminds me a lot of Germ. I think they'd get along very well. He takes off the sunglasses and looks at me for a second. Jester might be prone to talk a lot when he's nervous, but it's the small, hesitant pauses that give him away. He's still afraid of me, but wary to show it.

"Here, I want you to have it," he gives me the shirt.

"But it's yours?" I protest.

"The king confiscated it soon after I arrived. I'd rather see you wear it than have it shoved away in a closet, unappreciated."

"Alright," I agree. "I'll take your shirt and the khaki shorts, but I'm not changing my shoes. They haven't failed me thus far."

He nods approvingly. "I'll leave you to dress then."

Jester takes a last, longing gaze at the leftover food. He ties the scarf around his forehead, so the two ends hang to the sides like an old-fashioned jester's hat minus the bells. "Oh, before I forget," he reaches deep into the closet and tosses me a pair of underpants.

210

"Did you know that King Tutankhamen was buried with 145 pairs of underpants?"

"No, I didn't."

"You're welcome." He executes a graceful bow and shuffles down the stairs.

I pull off my clothes and exchange them for the new, cleaner outdoor wear. The fallen roof of the two-storey building has been replaced with large green leaves that block out most of the suns' heat. I consider escaping through them but fear the drop might be too steep. Even if I manage to get away from the camp undetected, what would I do then?

I can't cross the Dengar on my own. It's far too dangerous without Aiesha's help, and I don't know where she is. I wonder if she'll distance herself from me again, fearing that Skylor might find out about our journey. A part of me hopes that she's still hiding in the bushes, keeping an eye on the situation. If things get rough, she could always send for reinforcements.

The chest against the wall vibrates, startling me. I can see the carved wolves from here, snarling at me. Another quiver shoots through the chest, I didn't imagine it. I walk over to the doorway and glance down the stairs. Jester is out of view, and so are the others. Their faint voices trail into the building from far away. I turn around and hurry back into the room. When I reach the large, wooden chest, I yank it open and peek inside.

I gasp. It's filled to the brim with confiscated electronics. The device that's responsible for causing the vibrations is a silver flip phone. An alarm accidentally triggered it to go off. I quickly dismiss the notification and bury my hand between the other mobile devices. Most of them are dead and drained of battery, but I manage to find two that turn on when I play with their buttons.

Not wasting any time, I take off my shoes and loosen the laces. With a growing urgency, I place a phone in the forepart of each, then manoeuvre my toes beneath the metal slabs and tie the laces into sturdy double knots. I test my weight on both heels, making sure that the phones are pushed firmly in place. I can't afford one to slip beneath my foot as I'm running away from this place.

Gently closing the chest, I make my way down the stairs.

CHAPTER 29

When I reach the lower level of the building, a pungent smell overwhelms me. To my left is a doorway that leads to the outside. To my right, a large hall stretches into complete darkness. The offensive odour is coming from inside. It should repel me, but I find myself drawn to it instead. Wanting to investigate further, I avoid making noise and sneak deeper into the hall.

As my eyes slowly adjust to the lack of light, my stomach turns to stone. Countless Marks are strewn across the floor like discarded ragdolls. Some are curled up in cold corners while others bundle together. Unlike the room above, there is no carpet to provide any sort of comfort down here. The ground beneath my feet is moist with body fluids and adds to the sour dampness that's trapped inside.

I try to count the bodies as they pass, but struggle to see the children that are tucked away in the farthest regions. Those who sit in groups are quietly murmuring to each other, but many have chosen to keep to themselves. One such person is slanted against the middle of a grey wall, exercising a watchful gaze over the others. Many lie around her, writhing in pain and discomfort. She makes turns to console each of them but remains vigilant as I approach.

"What's going on here?" I whisper to her.

"Are you new?" she winces at me.

"I just arrived here."

She eyes me up and down, then pats the ground next to her. I sit down and lean towards the jaded girl. "What's wrong with them?"

She wets her hands in a bowl of water and softly pats the boy lying next to her on the neck. He moans again, but the water appears to help. "This one has heatstroke," she rubs his back. "The other two are suffering from exhaustion."

"What happened?" I ask.

"The king sent them into the forest. He told them not to come back unless they found something worthwhile."

"What did he mean by that?" I frown.

Skylor would never give our Elementals such a vague demand. Neither would Aiesha. Telling them to search for food or new drops is a reasonable request. It's one that has a clear purpose—unlike sending them off on a goose chase to discover something *worthwhile*. This king is either a mad hatter, or he knows something that I don't.

"Nobody knows," she pushes her face into her palms. "I haven't seen Gabriel in two weeks. He used to help me with the injured, but his missions take forever these days. Some of the Greens are so scared of returning empty-handed, they don't come back at all."

She lifts the bowl of water to the Elemental's mouth and urges him to take a sip. "I envy them. If I could survive out there, I'd leave this place for good."

"Why don't you?" I ask her. "Gabriel could keep you safe."

"We're not allowed to leave…" her voice trails off.

I don't like the sound of that. This hall is starting to look more like a prison than a camp's sleeping quarters. That explains the lack of beds and windows. She lifts her head and notices my concerned expression.

"What am I doing?" she groans. "You've barely settled in and I'm already terrifying you."

"It's okay."

"No, it's not. There are enough things to be afraid of here, and I'm not one of them."

I smile at her, even though she can't see it in the dark. She speaks like a Neuro and communicates in a very matter-of-fact way. This quality might be off-putting for some, but I find it endearing. Time is the most valuable resource we have on this planet, and Neuros know not to waste it.

"My name is Henrietta," she says. "Most of us in here have blue marks, meaning we're pretty smart. Personally, I got to skip a few grades in high school. I was already doing a university calculus course when I was taken away."

"I hated maths," I chuckle.

"Then you're certainly not a Blue," she giggles. "There aren't too many Greens in here. Like I said, they're always being sent away. Those who return are in a dire state."

She moves the empty bowl away from the Green whose eyes are fluttering shut. Henrietta shakes her head with grief. "Once he is able to stand on his own two feet, the king will order him back into the woods."

"Can't you stand up to him?" I suggest, refusing to use the word *king*. "There are so many of you in here."

"There are even more of them," the words leave her mouth in a hiss. She points her finger to a solitary figure propped up against the wall. He isn't interacting with any of the other Marks and appears injured. "The Reds are the king's personal bodyguards and make up more than half of the camp. Those that end up inside with us are few and far between. This one is as good as dead."

"Why is that?" I play dumb.

"They're like wild animals, constantly fighting each other to prove themselves worthy. When the Reds are not mishandling us, they're killing each other. This one lost a fight."

I try to imagine Kyle in a camp where there's no one to stop him from doing as he pleases. He could fulfil his wildest desires, while committing the most heinous of acts. The idea gives me goosebumps and isn't one I'd like to dwell on. I've seen what he is capable of doing, even when others are nearby.

"Don't sympathise with the guy," Henrietta warns. "If given the chance, he'd be the first to bash you silly."

She takes a gander at the two Elementals who haven't woken since I arrived. Both toss around restlessly, unable to escape their dreams. It must be difficult to switch off your defences if sleeping in the forest has become the norm. Out there, one must be able to reach wakefulness at the drop of a hat.

Henrietta shifts onto her knees with great difficulty. "Help me up, will you?"

"Are you injured?" I ask, concerned for her well-being.

"No, just starving."

I take hold of her hand, pulling her up from the ground with remarkable ease. The Neuro wasn't exaggerating at all. She weighs less than Carter, though her height surpasses mine. The girl is nothing more than skin and bones. Although we're standing inches away from one another, she leans closer to get a better look at my mark through the gloomy atmosphere.

Hesitant at first, she takes a step back and laughs. "It's so dark in here, for a second I thought you had a black mark."

"I do," I tell her.

"Don't make jokes like that," she responds, her voice sounding less relaxed than it did a moment ago.

"I'm not joking," I insist, lifting up my arm so she can see it more clearly. Henrietta doesn't respond immediately. She leans closer again and squints her eyes. Then, she begins to scream. "Get away from me!"

I lunge away and almost trip over a Mark. The others grow quiet and turn to us. "What's wrong, Henni?" Someone shouts from across the hall.

"He's a Black Mark!" she cries, desperately trying to get away from me.

Like a herd of frightened sheep, the others do the same, all of them attempting to distance themselves from the wolf wearing the darkness as sheep's clothing. The Neuro loses her footing and falls to the ground.

"Leave her alone!" one of the others shouts.

"I didn't do anything," Henrietta sobs.

I back away from the girl as my heart pumps wildly in my chest. A small square of light shines from the doorway at the end of the room. I race towards it like a moth to a flame. Just a moment ago this girl was eager to confide in me. Somehow, my mark changed all of that.

We might have been friends, in an alternate reality. If only she'd turned right instead of left at the Clearing. She would eventually have reached our camp instead of this one. I can't guarantee her safety, but at least I can offer some food and a bed to sleep in. Skylor could even put her skills to use in the Cave. Perhaps I can still make that happen.

A wave of fresh air greets me at the door as I step outside. Looking back one last time, I'm met with fear and animosity. The Marks are all bundled together in the farthest corner, watching me with terrified gazes. The Red hasn't moved from his position and remains seated against the closest wall. He stares at me with curiosity, a faint glimmer of amusement in his eyes.

CHAPTER 30

I back away from the building with a new goal in mind: to liberate these Marks from their so-called king. I scan the peripherals of the strange camp. Now is the perfect opportunity to make a dash for it, but Aiesha is nowhere to be seen. Without her guidance and Beetroot's speed, I'll just be caught again. It's not even worth the risk.

An oversized Apex appears next to me, making me jump. "The king requests your presence," he announces.

That hardly sounds like a request. I play along and follow him across the campgrounds. In the centre of the camp lies a large field where most of the grass has died and turned yellow. It reminds me of the broken spirits of those Marks inside the hall. The terrain has been stepped on millions of times, until finally every strand turned crisp and withered away.

We walk past other residents, all of them bearing red marks. In turn, each of them meets my gaze and executes a slight nod. Some go even further and acknowledge my presence with a graceful bow. They exhibit a characteristic that the Apex at our camp lack; one that still continues to ignite a lot of unaddressed conflict. Obedience.

These Reds are properly controlled and militarised. They march around the camp with expressionless faces, eyeing the building's entrance and camp borders like trained hawks. They're better fed than the Marks inside, as well as properly dressed. The Apex are well aware of this too, and strut around with a spring in their step. Unlike Jester, they got to keep the clothes they arrived in. At least I'm assuming it's theirs. It's quite possible that the king rewards them with the belongings of lesser Marks.

We reach a shade-bearing tent made entirely out of branches and leaves. A total of ten Apex stand guard at the entrance of the structure, all of them stationed in a straight line. The two in the centre appear to be the highest-ranking Reds, and tower over the others. Both carry a spear more than two metres in length, holding it erect at their sides and pinned to the ground. Acting more as a deterrent than anything else, the spears seem longer than they are practical. The rest of the squadron are equipped with wooden shields and batons. When I stop before them, all but the two in the middle take a knee and place their weapons on the ground before them as a sign of respect. Those still standing execute a coordinated salute. They lift their spears and march to opposite ends of the line, clearing the way to the entrance.

I hesitantly step inside, unsure what to expect after that bizarre performance.

Jester gallops forward and grabs me by the arm. "Please, do come in your majesty! The suns aren't nearly as generous as our king!"

He leads me to a table and two chairs. A boy already occupies one of them, watching me with great interest. I scan the rest of the tent in search of the king. When I turn to Jester with a questioning glance, the boy in the chair stands up and strolls towards me. Unlike the Marks outside, his clothes are exceptionally well-kept. A dark school blazer sits in sharp contrast to his mismatched cargo pants and hunting boots. A golden glow surrounds him as rays of light trickle through the leaves and splash onto lavish curls of blonde hair.

The Black Mark smiles at me like he did in the forest. It didn't put me at ease then, and it doesn't now. His demeanour is relaxed, and not at all threatening. This throws me off.

Jester pretends to blow into an invisible horn, then shouts, "I now introduce the king!"

"Please, call me Azon." He extends a warm, open hand and says, "It's so heartening to finally meet you."

I meet his gesture accordingly, not yet ready to burn a bridge that I might need to cross later. Once our palms meet, he surprises me by lifting his free hand and enclosing mine with both of his. For a moment, my dominant hand is subdued, leaving me vulnerable for an attack. Azon squeezes tightly, then let's go. A firm, yet friendly handshake.

"What is your name, weary traveller?"

I consider giving a false name, but what would be the point of that. "My name is John."

His eyes light up. "It's an honour to meet you, John."

Jester prances around us, also in high spirits. "John, John, the Englishman!"

"I'm not British," I tell Jester.

"Oh no, but King John was! You're alike, you see?"

He runs in circles while doing elaborate jumps and spins. Azon doesn't seem to mind. In fact, he appears to be enjoying the show. "The youngest of four, they thought him a bore! Never meant to inherit the land, they cruelly dubbed him John Lackland!"

"Does this story have a happy ending?" Azon asks sceptically.

"Of course, sire! All your stories deserve happy endings!"

Azon nods and waves his hand, hurrying Jester along.

"John never gave up and worked on his goals, but his brothers revolted and fell like stubborn poles." Jester grabs onto his chest as he falls to the ground, gasping for air. He pretends to die of a heart attack, but his performance isn't very convincing. Dead people don't blink their eyes like that. He keeps peeking at Azon, who seems to be getting impatient. Jester jumps up and wraps up the story. "In the end, he became Henry's favourite son and the eventual King of England!" He takes an over-exaggerated bow and slips out of the spotlight, into the corner of the airy tent.

"That's quite the destiny you have there, John." Azon ambles back towards his chair and taps the back of the other one with his knuckle. "Please, take a seat."

I join him behind the round, wooden table. There's a distinct difference between this camp and the one back home. For one, they have actual furniture. I haven't seen something as simple as a chair since I got abducted. At our camp, we make do with logs and boulders. Given the circumstances, I'd like to think that practicality takes preference over aesthetics. The table's flat, polished surface is engraved with the same ferocious wolves that decorate his chambers. They prowl over the tabletop, searching for vulnerable prey. The boy sitting across from me resembles the art, in an uncanny way. His golden mane sprouts in thick strands, covering his head in smooth waves. Beaming green eyes watch my every move, probing for more information. His luring smile displays two rows of white teeth. I can't tell whether he's planning to charm his way onto the cover of Damnatus Weekly or feed on some unsuspecting gazelle.

"I trust you've been fed?" Azon enquires.

"I have, thank you."

"And was it to your liking?"

"It was overwhelming, to be honest. I haven't eaten properly in days."

"You'll get used to it," he winks. "It's the least I can do to reward your successful journey. With all those flesh-eating beasts crawling around, it's truly a miracle that you managed to get here all on your own."

I flinch, unintentionally breaking eye contact. That's not what happened. Aiesha and Beetroot were next to me when I was snatched, and the Black Mark was there when it all transpired. He's testing me.

"I received help," I tell him. "There was a Green girl who led me to safety."

He nods, satisfied with my answer. "Now that you mention it, I do recall a green blur moving away from the area. I thought I might have imagined it, because the girl was riding on top of a large beast. What a magnificent creature!"

He leans closer and purrs, "Tell me John, how did she tame it?"

"I—don't know," I stumble over my words. "She didn't really speak."

Azon sits back in his chair, disappointed. "The Greens like to hold on to their secrets."

He inspects his trimmed fingernails, deep in thought. "I'd give anything to subdue such a mighty beast. Think about it John, we'd be unstoppable!"

An Elemental enters the tent with a tray of fruit. Exhausted, he trudges towards the king and falls to his knees, presenting his findings before him. Azon leans closer and critically judges the large portion.

"Another successful gathering!" he finally exclaims. "You've really been stepping up to the plate these last few weeks, Gabriel."

Jester inspects the fruit and pushes his face comically close to the tray. "What beautiful colours!" he marvels aloud. "A glorious find. Truly terrific!"

"Indeed," Azon smiles. He commands the Elemental to stand up. "Go to my chambers and find yourself some new pants to wear. You've earned it."

The Elemental's weary eyes widen. "Thank you, sire." He bows low.

Jester helps him up and escorts him out of the tent. "There's a pair of shorts that will compliment your figure very nicely! Just stay away from the skinny jeans. They tend to make one's thighs look fat."

Azon sniffs the tray and bites into one of the purple fruits. "Please John, help yourself."

"Thank you, but I'm stuffed," I insist.

The abundance of fruit seems extreme, similar to the tray I was presented with in his chambers. These large meals are reckless, considering that half of the Marks are starving,

"Shouldn't we share this batch with the people in the hall? They seem very malnourished."

My suggestion catches him off guard. "You went into the hall?" he asks.

"I was a bit lost."

Azon shakes his head with remorse. "It's sad, truly. There are too many people in this camp, John." He lifts up another piece of fruit and stares at it while deep in thought. "This might be a hard pill to swallow, but there isn't enough food to feed everyone here. This places me in a very difficult position." Unhurried, he extracts the black pits from his meal and flings them to the ground. One by one, they leave his hand and disappear between the tall grass.

"Have you ever heard of the trolley problem, John?"

"Not really," I frown.

"Let me explain it to you," he suggests. "Imagine that you find yourself next to a railway. Up ahead, there are five people tied to the tracks and unable to move to safety. Next to them lies another set of tracks, with only one person tied to it. All of the sudden, a massive runaway trolley comes into view. If it continues on its current path, it will kill five people."

Azon looks at me intently. "Now, here's where you come in. There is a big lever to your side. If you pull it, the trolley will switch to the other set of tracks, killing only one person instead of five. Will you pull the lever, John?"

"Do I know who the people are?" I ask.

"You do not. They are too far away, and your time is running out."

I hesitate. "I pull the lever, changing the direction of the trolley."

A sinister grin creeps across Azon's face. "Congratulations, you just killed one person."

"But I saved five. Wouldn't you do the same?" I ask the question.

"Believe it or not, most people wouldn't," Azon responds, not answering my question. "The trolley dilemma places you in the position of a mere bystander. A witness, if you will. It's not your fault if the trolley kills five people. If you intervene, however, the death of one will be on your hands. The average person would rather walk away guilt-free than intervene."

I'm not like most people, then.

"Interesting," is all I say.

"Interesting, but problematic," he adds. "You see John, this ethical dilemma relieves a person of all responsibility because he's merely a bystander to the event. So, I went ahead and changed it a little bit." Azon picks out another purple fruit. He seems to like that one in particular. "Imagine that you find yourself in a similar situation, except this time you actually own the trolley company. It's your job to make sure that everything runs smoothly. Now your predicament has changed entirely. Even though you didn't tie the people up or place them on those tracks, you are responsible for what happens whether you decide to act or not. No matter what you choose, the public will blame you for the resulting deaths. In this scenario, the answer is quite obvious. Most people will pull the lever. Do you see the difference, John?"

"I do."

He stands up and tightens the watch around his wrist. The formal accessory fits him so well that I might have believed it was his if not for the circumstances. Like a businessman trying to sell his idea to a conference room filled with investors, Azon paces behind me with heavy steps.

"So, answer me this. What if you're the leader of a large camp filled with starving children? Again, you have two options. One, you can simply choose to sit back and do nothing, allowing the entire camp to starve. Or two, you can send the Greens out into the forest every single day. You'll order them to bring back as much food as they can manage, even when it means pushing them far past the point of exhaustion."

He sighs and takes his seat again. "No matter what you choose, you will be blamed for the deaths of many. You are responsible for what happens, no matter if you caused it or not. Most people will forever remain the innocent bystander, because they don't have the guts to step up to the plate. The people in this camp are perfectly content with others dying, as long as they don't have to carry the blame. Does that not make them worse in a sense?" Azon takes a last bite out of the swollen fruit and then puts the remainder back on the plate. "Are you sure you don't want anything?"

"I'm sure."

He calls Jester back into the tent.

"How can I be of assistance, your majesty?"

"We're done here," he points to the tray of fruit. "Take this to the hall."

"Oh splendid! What a generous serving." He prances out of the tent, balancing the tray on his head for show. If the serving was meant for one person, it could well have been called generous. In reality, the contaminated tray of fruit is supposed to feed an entire hall of people. By the time it reaches Henrietta in the back, not so much as a seed will be left.

The two spear-carrying Reds enter the tent and kneel before Azon. "The tournament is about to commence, your majesty," one announces.

"That's great news!" Azon rises from his chair. "Escort us to the pit."

The Apex salute before standing erect and marching out of the tent. We follow them in an orderly fashion, while the other eight Reds fall to our sides and cover the rear. Most of the Apex who were patrolling the campgrounds have now flocked to the hall entrance, where the other Marks swarm out in dozens.

Every person who can walk or limp is heading into the same direction. At the base of the hill that borders a small portion of the camp, there is a noticeable indent in the ground. Almost as large as the Clearing, the circular dent serves as an arena of sorts. Azon and I are shown to the edge of the pit, where two chairs beneath shadow-bearing trees await us. The rest of the Marks file into a line and situate themselves on the hill in rows, each one higher than the next, like a colosseum. With a clear view of the pit, they wait in silence.

"What exactly is the tournament?" I ask Azon, who is barely able to suppress his excitement.

"We play all sorts of games in the tournament!" he replies.

"What kinds of games?"

"Today we'll be playing the circle game."

Jester makes his way to the edge of the pit, then hops in. "Good evening, ladies and gentlemen! Our generous king has invited you here today to celebrate the safe arrival of your new prince, John!"

My heart stops beating. *Did I hear that correctly?*

"Surprise," Azon grins.

The crowd gives a polite round of applause, but their faces reveal no joy. The Apex lingering among them intimidate the Marks into submission.

Jester continues with his speech while circling the ditch. "When our king created the pit, he only had greatness in mind. He knew something to be true—something that most of us chose to deny. If we are given the freedom to do as we please, man is wolf to man."

"Homo homini lupus!" Jester screams.

"*Homo homini lupus!*" The crowd echoes back.

"We will now commence the circle game!"

The Marks cheer enthusiastically, their expressions slowly changing.

"All of us have played this game before, when we woke up in the circle. Today, one of you will play the game a second time."

A frightful growl emanates from the top of the hill. Grey scales emerge from the trees as three Elementals coax an agitated Reptant towards the pit. Taking turns to lead, they jump in front of the creature, acting as bait. Each time the Reptant's tail gets into striking distance, the Green in front freezes up like a statue until one of the others takes his place. Only able to sense movement, the creature is quickly distracted by the faster target and dashes around the immobile Mark. Aside from the bloody lacerations stretching down their naked legs, this strategy seems to be working so far.

The tight leash around the Reptant's neck does not appear to serve much purpose. Just like the Reds' spears and Jester's theatrics, it is merely for show. If the creature chose to spin around at any point, the Green girl holding on to it would go flying through the air. They're trying to convince the crowd that they have control over the situation.

Azon steals the audience's attention away from the impending wreck. He leaves my side and addresses them with a booming voice that demands to be heard. "It has come to my attention that someone has been stealing from the royal food tray!"

The people turn their gazes away from the Reptant. It takes a few seconds before the weight of his words sets in. The already restless Marks are hardly able to contain their outrage, and exchange foul words among each other. Azon doesn't stop after his first remark. Instead, he chooses to fuel their anger.

"I do everything in my power to feed you, but it is never enough! Our numbers keep growing and so does the demand for food. One of the Reds has been caught stealing from the people's portions! This behaviour is unacceptable, don't you think?"

The crowd calls back in an overwhelming *"Yes!"*

"You will continue to starve and suffer, unless we eliminate the weakest links!"

"Yes!" they shout back at him.

"The parasites need to go!"

"Yes!" they scream.

"Homo homini lupus!" he bellows to the crowd.

"Homo homini lupus!" they chant back.

Azon looks back at me for a brief moment, then signals something to the spear-wielding Apex. They salute him and march to the end of the line that consists of Azon's personal guards. Suddenly, they grab onto an unsuspecting boy and start to pull him towards the pit. Shocked, the young Red attempts to flee, but instantly gets knocked to the ground.

"I didn't do it!" he gasps.

They pick him up by the arms and drag him farther down the hill. He fights back, all the while protesting his innocence. "I've been framed, I swear it!"

Azon continues to address the crowd, riling them up even further.

When the Apex reach Azon, they release the boy, who drops to his knees. "Please your majesty, you must believe me!" he begs.

The Black Mark looks down at the boy with disgust. Using the Red as a stage prop, he continues to play to the gallery. With his chances of freedom slipping away, the boy does something unprecedented. He disregards Azon and turns to me instead. "Prince John, don't let them hurt me!" he cries.

Something in me breaks when I hear those words. I stand up from my chair and run towards the edge of the pit. With dozens of Red eyes on us, it would be impossible to stop Azon with brute force. Unfamiliar with the rules of the camp, I'll have to take a chance instead. Using my new title and the authority that goes along with it, I begin to reason with him.

"We should reconsider this," I tell him firmly. "There are other ways we can punish the boy."

Azon finds my behaviour amusing. "What do you propose, John?"

"We'll send him into the forest," I suggest. "He will accompany and protect the Greens as they search for food. The punishment should fit the crime, don't you think?"

The Apex boy nods furiously, showing a clear preference for my suggestion.

Azon appears to consider it for a second. At least, he pretends to. He places his arm around my shoulder and explains why that won't be allowed. "Remember the trolley problem, John? I am prepared to do what most people wouldn't." He lets go of me and plants himself before the boy, eyeing him with contempt. Like a member of a firing squad about to execute a prisoner of war, he shouts, "I'm pulling the lever!" He kicks the boy in the stomach, launching him backwards into the pit.

The crowd cheers while Jester prances around in the circle. "The Red has been caught red-handed!" he cackles aloud, ridiculing the winded boy.

The Red gasps as he tries to find his footing. The other Apex leave their stations and begin to take their places around the pit. When all of them border the arena, it creates a perfect replica of the Clearing—almost mockingly so. One of them reaches down and helps Jester out of the hole.

"What is your weapon of choice?" the Apex asks the boy.

The terrified Red yells back for a spear.

"You heard it here folks, the traitor wants a long, pointy stick!"

Laughter bursts from the crowd. One of the Apex reluctantly throws his oversized spear into the pit. The boy fetches the weapon and jogs to the middle of the arena. He practices his swings in the air, spinning around with each thrust.

"The rules of the circle game are simple!" Jester shouts to the Marks who are now standing to catch a better glimpse of the fight. "Only one may leave the pit alive!"

One of the Elementals reaches the edge of the arena, and the provoked Reptant quickly follows. With nowhere left to run, the Green girl feigns a hard left, then jumps to her right instead. The creature doesn't react fast enough and clumsily stumbles onward. With a calculated blow, the two

Elementals in the rear shove the beast forward with all their might. A surprised hiss reaches my ears as it falls into the pit, landing with a loud thud.

A cloud of dust shoots into the air, momentarily obstructing my view. When it settles, I see the Reptant scrambling to its feet. It lays its reptilian eyes on the only target in sight and prepares to take its frustration out on it. The boy freezes on the spot, resting the spear on his shoulder. He slowly shrinks into a ball and stays in that position.

"Let the games commence!" Jester announces.

The beast sniffs the air, disorientated by the noise of a screaming crowd. He stares in the direction of the boy but doesn't see him anymore. The Reptant's weakness appears to be well known, even at this camp. Not detecting any movement, the creature looks around aimlessly. A wave of relief rushes over me. The boy can use this knowledge to his advantage. The situation looks promising until the Apex behind the boy begin to beat the side of the pit with their clubs. The beast's eyes widen and the flaps hanging around its neck shoot open like that of a Cobra snake. It rushes at the boy—but its sight remains on that of the Apex leaning over the edge.

With no choice but to dodge the attack, the boy leaps away, betraying his position. This was clearly the intention of the other Reds, who have stopped moving again. The boy sprints around the pit and tries the freezing tactic a second time, but the Apex behind him bat away at his head, luring the beast closer again. This appears to be the goal of the circle game.

At various points, the boy lifts his spear in preparation for a strike—but he never gets a clear shot. The shaft is too long to be used as a melee weapon and will snap in close combat. He only has one chance at throwing it, but he struggles to put sufficient distance between himself and the predator. The pit isn't as big as the Clearing and manoeuvring away from the Reptant's spiked tail is a lot more difficult.

The young boy begins to tire, his legs dragging beneath him. He props himself up against the wall and reaches for the ledge. The Apex hit his hands bloody, forcing him to let go. He jogs to the opposite side of the arena and reaches for the ledge again. At first it seems his escape attempts are in vain—but then the boy does something that makes me suppress an excited laugh. He grabs onto a Red's baton and pulls down as hard as he can. The girl tumbles into the pit, her arms flailing.

She doesn't stir after hitting the ground. Not because she's injured, but because it's her only chance of surviving. Before the Reptant can reach her, the Apex on the other side of the pit furiously start shouting, doing everything in their power to get its attention. The sudden change of mood is unsettling. Just a moment ago they were attempting to murder one of their own. Something has triggered an invisible switch.

The Apex run around the pit and bundle together on the same side of the arena, managing to lure the Reptant towards them. Some even throw their batons at it, but none jump in to help her out of the pit. The girl peeks through her fingers but refuses to rise.

While all of this is transpiring, the boy slowly lurks behind the beast, his spear raised and ready. When his shadow touches the tail of the unsuspecting Reptant, he takes the shot. The spear shoots across the pit, stopping where it sinks into the back of the beast's head. The Reptant collapses to the ground, dead on the spot.

Well done, I think.

The crowd disagrees. They voice their disapproval by booing like a bunch of undisciplined children. Do they really believe that this boy stole food from them? Is that why the Apex are treating him differently than the girl? Azon doesn't take kindly to their reaction. He struts up to the edge of the pit and addresses his subjects with a fierce tone.

"The rules were very clear! Only one may leave the pit alive!"

The girl's face twists in horror as she realises the implication of this rule. Still lying in the depths of the pit, she turns to the boy with hatred in her eyes. He knew this would happen if he forcefully involved her in the circle game, yet the desperate boy did it anyway.

He doesn't show any remorse. Instead, the boy pulls his spear from the Reptant's skull and shifts his focus to the bruised girl. He never intended to overpower the Reptant. He merely had to pick an opponent that he could. The fall disoriented her more than anything, but she grabs her baton with a fierce determination and pushes herself off the ground.

"Homo homini lupus!" Jester waves his scarf like a flag in the wind.

"Homo homini lupus!" The children repeat, their lust for blood growing by the second.

The girl grips the wooden baton in both hands, swinging it from side to side like a baseball bat. Her weapon is much sturdier than the spear, but places second in length. With the advantage of range on his side, the boy takes aim at the girl. I instantly regret standing up for him. These children have descended into savagery, their minds polluted by the Black Mark's tyranny.

Azon referred to the boy as the weakest link. A parasite. If an Apex can be called a burden, then what chance do the others stand? Roderick is dressed up in pink and forced to play the fool. The Blues are locked away in the hall where the sight of them can't scare off new arrivals, and the Greens are sent into the forest to slave away in search of delicacies. And the Whites—

Come to think of it, I haven't seen a single one. What did Azon do to them? If the Whites were as young as Matthew and Talaya, they wouldn't have stood a chance. Azon has no use for small, defenceless children. I wonder how he disposed of them without raising suspicions.

Perhaps he sent them wandering into the forest to look for food. Knowing Azon, he could easily persuade the people that White Marks were meant to be gatherers. *Small hands can reach into small holes*, he'd say. But that would be too easy. It doesn't involve a show with a crowd of bloodthirsty onlookers. He likely accused them of stealing as well. It would have prompted another tournament, and some ridiculous game.

I picture Talaya and Matthew in the pit, desperately trying to outrun a Reptant. I close my eyes, but the image doesn't fade. They'd try to stay together but eventually fail. Matthew would lead the creature away from Talaya, but the Apex would bash their sticks against the walls, making this task impossible. Matthew would be the first to perish, and a crying Talaya follows—all while the crowd cheers ecstatically. The idea makes me sick to my core.

The Red boy takes a step forward, then launches his spear across the arena. It misses the girl's neck by mere inches, leaving him without a weapon. She lunges forward, taking advantage of his blunder. Slightly taller than her opponent, she lifts her baton into the air, bringing it down on his head with a sickening force. An ear-splitting crack echoes through the pit as the boy's knees give in beneath him.

The girl discards the broken weapon and picks up another. She strikes his head a second time. The boy starts to convulse, his body jerking uncontrollably. She hits him again and again, all while the crowd cheers ecstatically. The applause grows louder with each swing, while his movements slowly lessen. As the final bit of life seeps out of his head and reddens the floor of the pit, the Marks on the hill jump up and down in a frenzy. They scream until their voices hoarsen and the Apex force them back into the hall.

"Homo homini lupus!"

CHAPTER 31

I haven't uttered a word since we left the pit. My mind has fled from this world and wandered back home. Mom is cooking beef stew and telling me about her day. She wants to paint a family portrait but can't find the right shade of blue for my eyes. She says the colours she mixed together were either too dark to capture my determined energy, or too light to portray the depth of my character. She's worried that the picture won't be done in time. I'll be leaving soon.

Carter sits next to me while listening to her story. He looks healthy and optimistic, untroubled by real-world events. I take comfort in knowing that he is safe. Dad enters the room and takes off his jacket as if he's merely been out hiking all this time. He kisses Mom on the cheek and pats my brother on his shoulder. I feel left out, knowing that I won't be able to feel his touch. This is just an illusion after all.

Mom tells everyone to sit down for the painting. She wants to get a good look at us before I leave. Dad walks past me and takes the seat on the opposite end of the table. He glances over at me and suggests that we take a photo instead. It will last a lot longer than a memory. Mom likes the idea so much that she leaves the room in search of a camera.

I gaze after her as she disappears into the dark hallway. I've missed her so much. The simplicity of our little home brings me immense comfort. I wish I could stay here forever. I turn around in my chair and survey the area. The kitchen window has been bolted shut from the inside. I should be proud of Mom's efforts to secure the house, though I can't help but wonder how I'll get back in if I ever return.

Dad tells me to stop moving. I need to sit still for the photo or else they'll forget what I look like.

"That won't happen," I say.

"Of course, it will," he laughs. "You barely remember my face."

I frown at the man before me. I can smell his sharp cologne, and his laughter is almost palpable, yet I'm struggling to see him clearly. Dad's finer features have not materialized fully. The more I concentrate on his face, the less real it becomes. I feel a pang of anxiety when it becomes clear that he's right. I can't remember what my own father's face looks like.

The food on the stove starts to burn, but nobody gets up to stir the pot. Mom emerges with the camera and prepares to take a photo. She politely asks me to stop crying, because she can't see my eyes. She doesn't want to forget the colour of my eyes.

* * *

"You remind me of my former queen," Azon laughs.

We're back in the tent made of leaves and branches. Nine Apex now guard the entrance, the tenth one still lying in the pit. I threw up on my way back, while the Reds only stopped to look and snigger. I can only imagine how pale my face must be. Azon continues to eat his fruit, not at all perturbed by the events that took place earlier. His appetite is unquenchable.

"The games weren't to her taste, either. She remained in my chambers while they took place."

"Is she dead?" I blurt out.

"Far worse! She went mad and ran off into the woods."

So, it's not impossible to escape this wretched place. I finally manage to look him in the eyes. I've been avoiding his gaze since the tournament concluded. A thirsty wolf stares back at me, his fangs no longer concealed.

"Oh, but what a beauty Claudia was! A bit too outspoken for my taste, but pretty, nevertheless. Her hair was long and brown, and I've always fancied brunettes. I had her all to myself most of the time, until she started sneaking off to make small talk with the people in the hall. Half of them left with her that day." Azon scoffs. "What a waste of potential."

I growl at him. "Can't you just pick another queen?"

He snarls back at me. "I didn't *pick* her. She was gifted to me."

Jester shuffles around the table, quickly trying to break the tension. "A rare gift indeed! It's not every day a Black Mark falls out of the sky."

I pause. "She had a black mark?"

"Of course," Azon snaps. "Who else would be worthy of such a title?"

Another Black Mark. What was she like? Or what was she good at? He mentioned that she didn't approve of the games. She didn't approve of him either, because she ran away. That has to mean something. Perhaps a black mark doesn't mean I'm a terrible person. Its meaning might still be entirely unknown to me.

I have to suppress my emotions. It won't be easy, but I need more information out of him.

"It doesn't make sense," I say.

"What doesn't make sense?" Azon's voice is still on edge.

"I mean, you treated me so well when I arrived here. Jester helped me into some new clothes and made sure I was adequately fed." I try my best to sound sincere and feign innocence. "Why would anyone want to run away from that?"

Azon relaxes a bit. He's still a bit tense after my remarks, but that won't deter him from accepting a compliment.

"She befriended those dirt people," he states.

"Dirt people?"

"Yes," he elaborates. "Those savages who kept sneaking into our camp at night. Always covered in dirt."

I hesitate. The description matches the dreams I've been having these last few weeks. Of the shadow children without marks. Come to think of it, I wouldn't be able to see the marks if they were covered in dirt.

"We caught one a few months ago," he smirks. "Claudia was conspiring with the filthy muck behind the hall. They were scared real good when my Reds caught them. I demanded to know where the grimy kid's camp was situated, and why his friends kept coming back here. He refused to talk, so we made a nice example out of him. My queen received a lighter punishment, of course." He boasts about this as if his mercy was admirable. "We were never bothered by them again."

"Is that before or after half of your camp ran away?" I sneer.

Azon sits back in his chair, folding his hands together.

I didn't do enough to hide the sarcasm in my voice.

The wolf bares his teeth again, hiding his true feelings behind a smile. "You're acting strange, John."

Jester paces faster around the tent. He senses the growing tension and is thinking of a way to diffuse it. I don't know what happened in the past to cause him such anxiety, but it couldn't have been good. I'm still numb after watching a boy get murdered. Seeing another terrified kid having a panic attack only angers me.

"Who wants to hear the story of Claudia Octavia, the neglected Roman Empress?" Jester announces nervously. "The resemblance is quite uncanny."

"Shut it, Jester," Azon states slowly.

"Of course, of course!" Jester chatters away. "I only jest!"

I'm sick of Azon pretending to be something he's not. Our collective circumstances on this planet are tragic enough as it is. If you find yourself on an alien planet and decide to seize the opportunity as an evil monarch, then at least be upfront about it. I want to see who is hiding behind the mask. I'll tear it off myself, if I have to.

"I don't like the way you're running this camp," I state outright.

Jester almost faints.

Azon doesn't flinch. "I'm always open for constructive criticism."

I take a deep breath and stretch my legs, just in case I need to make a run for it. "For starters, there are a bunch of starving Blues locked away in your disintegrating hall. It looks like a concentration camp."

"We already discussed this," Azon responds. "I can only feed so many."

"That doesn't explain why they're not allowed to leave," I quickly retaliate.

"I am responsible for keeping them safe, and it's easier to do that when they're in the building. Those with blue marks are defenceless out in the wild."

His point is a valid one. Skylor keeps our Neuros cooped up in the Cave all day, because it's the strongest structure in our entire camp. The only difference is that our Blues are allowed to wander around camp as they please. Azon seems to read my thoughts.

"They're allowed to leave," he insists. "They always have been."

That's not true, I think to myself.

"The Reds," I state.

"They're a difficult bunch," he admits. "It took me a long time to figure them out. They respect power, so I took it away from them and convinced them that they never had any to begin with. It's the only way to keep them under control. By rewarding them with bits of the power they always held."

"The Apex slaughtered one of their own," I blurt out. "Is that the sort of power you're referring to? Killing children in cold blood and getting away with it?"

"The Apex?" he raises an eyebrow questioningly.

I instantly regret losing my temper. "The Reds. My tongue slipped."

He cackles aloud. "What a funny joke! Are you taking notes, Jester?"

"Yes sire!" Jester laughs.

"I'm the alpha," Azon states with no uncertainty in his voice. "There are no 'apex' here. Just a ruler and his subjects."

I shift uncomfortably.

"Apex," he muses. "You said it with such conviction as if it were their real name."

He analyses me from a different angle, tilting his head as if to get a better view. "Black Marks act differently than the rest of the pack, this is true. Yet, I found it strange how unfazed you seemed on your first day here. It's almost as if you were already used to it all. Like you've been living somewhere else before."

His eyes grow wide as the realisation finally sets in. "Somewhere where they call the Reds, Apex."

Jester's eyes grow wide with horror.

"How could I have been so blind? Here I am calling you a prince, when you are already a king! That Green girl was your servant, and so was the beast!"

He jumps up with excitement. "You found my camp and decided to test my alliance first. A very wise move indeed. We'll be unstoppable when we combine our forces."

I shake my head, but it has little effect. Azon is convinced.

"So, John, where is this camp of yours?"

Jester steps closer but remains behind Azon. He shakes his head profusely and waves his arms to signal that I should keep quiet.

"I don't have a camp," I say softly.

"Oh, come on. Surely, I passed your test?" His tone becomes a bit more aggressive. "Is your camp bigger than mine? Do you think I will steal it from you?"

"You've got it all wrong. I'm not a king. Or even a prince. I'm just a normal guy."

He grabs me firmly by the shoulders. "You're wrong, John. Nothing about you is normal. Don't you feel it in you? The way people listen when you talk. How the weak rely on your very actions to survive? We're meant to rule, John. The marks merely label those who are beneath us."

I stand up from my chair, now eyeing the opening of the tent. Jester is telling me to go.

"Don't you see?" Azon grins. "You've been here just a day, and already my jester is trying to protect you."

Jester's face turns pinker than the scarf around his neck.

"He thinks you're different than me, but he doesn't see what I see. People like to think that they're innocent, when they're really just harmless. Is a wolf cub more innocent than a fully grown male, merely because its claws have not yet come in? It won't hurt you yet, but only because it can't. Just wait until it is fully grown and tastes power for the first time. It will feast on the blood of those who have no claws, and they will fear his wickedness." He looks down at his own hands, inspecting his nails. "And now I have to punish my jester," Azon states.

"Don't," I warn.

"It's the law of nature, John. Power corrupts all who wield it."

"That's not true," I speak out. "Power doesn't corrupt. The corrupt seek power."

Azon's face transforms as he snarls with rage. He grabs Jester's scarf and pulls it tightly around his neck. The Pink Mark begins to choke and gasp for air. I leap forward and use all of my weight to shove Azon onto the ground. He knocks his head against the table, cracking the wooden surface. I pull the scarf away from Jester and rip the fabric to pieces.

"I don't trust you, Azon," I growl. "I don't like the way you treat people."

He remains on the ground, looking at me with contempt. "You are free to go now."

"I may leave?"

"You always could," he lies.

CHAPTER 32

I run away from the camp as fast as my legs can carry me, hoping that Azon won't change his mind. A wave of relief hits me when Aiesha becomes visible near the Dengar terrain. I knew in my gut that she wouldn't leave me behind. I don't know what Aiesha sees in me, but she clearly values my life more than she does Skylor's rules.

"Did you see the tournament?" I pant.

"I saw everything," Aiesha responds, still clutching onto her spear.

We arrive at camp on Beetroot's back. Not much has changed since we left, and a strange, comforting sensation overcomes me when the camp perimeters finally close in around us. I'll never take it for granted again.

I burst into the Adjustment Shack with a score to settle. Aiesha is right on my heels but shows no intention of stopping me.

"Why didn't you tell us there is another camp?" I demand. "You knew there was another Black Mark and didn't tell me."

Skylor's face grows pale in an instant. She ushers the two sickly Marks out of the Shack and closes the door behind her. The Neuro turns to Aiesha, her eyes wide and filled with fear. "What did you do?" she says slowly.

"It was John's right to know," Aiesha defends herself. "In fact, it was both of their rights to know of each other, and now they do."

Skylor's mouth drops open. *"He saw you?"*

I become aware of genuine fear in Sky's voice. "They know we're here now. We aren't safe." Without an explanation, she opens the door just a crack, cautiously peeking outside.

"We didn't tell them where the camp was," I bark.

"They would have followed you," she says quietly, afraid that someone else might be listening. "I was just trying to protect us from them." Skylor looks like she's about to burst into tears.

"Protect us? We could have helped them!" I exclaim. "What makes those children so different from us? It's not their fault for winding up at the wrong camp."

She looks to the ground and then at my new shirt and pants, her mind clearly racing. She closes the door behind her. "I can explain everything," she says. Trying to buy herself some time, she walks to one of the cupboards and extracts a cloth and bowl of liquid. When she joins us at the table, she points to my shirt. "Your wounds will get infected if I don't clean them."

My lesions have not yet closed after the Ptera attack, and the blood has already stained Jester's polo shirt. I allow the assistance and pull off what is left of my clothes. She soaks up the potent liquid with the grey rag and rubs it against my chest. The antiseptic stings, and I clench my teeth to endure it. Skylor uses my discomfort to her advantage and begins to tell her story.

"By now the rumours must have reached you? How I survived in the forest on my own."

"Yes," I clench my jaw.

"They're not entirely true," she releases an anxious sigh. "I wasn't alone."

"I knew it!" Aiesha yells with outrage. "That's the only reason you are the leader of this camp! You gained everyone's respect with that outrageous story of yours, including mine. Wait till the others hear of this," she threatens.

"No!" Skylor sounds desperate. "You don't understand. The rest is all true."

"Stop talking rubbish, you're just scared because you're caught." Aiesha reaches for her spear. "A Neuro could never have survived in the forest as long as you did."

"Let her speak," I urge Aiesha, who throws me a furious look in return.

"Thanks John," Skylor says. "As I was saying, the first part is true. I was lost for several days, and the experience was truly terrifying. It felt like I was walking in constant circles, and the White boy wouldn't stop crying and making noise."

She gazes deeply into my eyes, hoping to find a morsel of empathy. After all, I've been there, too. I've experienced the same hunger and thirst that could drive a person mad with desperation. I've heard the ominous cries from creatures and children alike, though I could never tell the difference. I've also seen the monstrosities with my own eyes. Creatures that have no right to exist among defenceless children.

Skylor manages to break past my wall of reluctance and continues when she finds the bit of sympathy she's been searching for. "You can just imagine my relief when we stumbled upon another camp. They thought us both to be new drops, so they took us in."

"That still doesn't explain why you lied," Aiesha interrupts.

"Listen," Skylor insists. "They had different ways of doing things back there. Everybody lived in constant fear of their leader, Azon."

She fetches a clean cloth from the cupboard and tightly wraps it around my skin. Slowly recalling the events, she shudders.

"He forced the Elementals to explore deadly lands, each time pushing them to go farther than the last. Nobody could object, because the Apex punished anyone who disobeyed his orders. On many occasions, the Elementals would take weeks to return from their journeys, some never returning at all. One day, Azon's relentless pursuits paid off. A Green Mark came back, claiming that he found something big in the desert. A massive structure, clearly created by intelligent beings. From afar, it looked like a silver dome."

Sky picks a black t-shirt and hands it to me. I pull it over my head and cover the unsightly bandages. Aiesha frowns, distrusting Skylor's attempt to win me over.

"What was it?" I ask, feeling a spark of hope.

"Exactly what Azon was searching for." She announces it softly, still suspicious of who might be overhearing our conversation. "A way off this planet."

A surge of heat rushes to my face. It sounds too good to be true. The idea of home has long ago faded away in exchange for a more realistic outcome. This camp is the closest thing we have to a home, and that's exactly what we settled for. I feel ashamed for growing so accustomed to this godless place. It's not a home. That's just the lie we've been telling ourselves to get through the long, tiring days. It's nothing more than a temporary shelter.

Skylor shakes her head, her shoulders drooping with the weight of grief. She continues with her tale. "A week later, Azon disappeared and took all of the Apex and Elementals with him. He left the rest of us behind to fend for ourselves."

"He didn't take you with him?"

I shouldn't be so surprised. Azon made it very clear that he valued power above all else. What's the point of taking the others along if they'd only be a burden? *Getting them home to their families.* The answer seems obvious enough.

"Azon said we were too weak to make the journey," Skylor sighs. "Perhaps he was right. Within a week, all of the Whites had starved to death, along with most of the Neuros."

My face flushes red with anger. "What about the White boy who accompanied you?"

She slowly nods her head, answering my question. Looking away with guilt, Skylor seems to be holding herself accountable for his death. "When Azon finally returned, there were only five people with him. A part of me wanted to believe that he succeeded, that he came back for the rest of us. Only, it couldn't be further from the truth. Everyone else had died."

"Was the dome real?" I ask.

"It is real. All of them confirmed its existence. They couldn't enter it though. Apparently, each group of Marks only gets one chance to escape this planet, but they blew it somehow."

"Blew it?" The way Skylor said it makes it sound like they failed some sort of test. Or maybe they were never supposed to find the dome at all. Whatever brought us here might not have foreseen the children's journey into the desert. What if our abductors tried to rectify this mistake by getting rid of them?

"So, where is this place?" Aiesha is running out of patience.

"Azon was paranoid," Sky responds. "He wouldn't tell any of us where the dome was, fearing that we'd leave without him."

"Then why are you even telling us this?" Aiesha fires back.

"You're not listening!" Sky throws her hands into the air.

"What is it, Skylor?" I ask.

She folds her arms before her. "I may not know where the dome is, but I know how to find it. The Neuros finally cracked Project Exit."

CHAPTER 33

Texas, Johnsen's farm: Ten minutes before abduction

"Why aren't you playing outside?"

"They're standing too close today," the little boy whispers.

"What are you talking about?"

"The men in the forest, they're standing too close."

With sudden alertness, his mother briskly makes her way to the window.

"I don't see any people."

"They're there. Just behind the first row of trees."

She gazes into the shadows dubiously. "What do they look like? What colour are their faces?"

"They don't have faces."

An uncanny silence fills the room. Without warning, she storms across the carpet and grabs the child by his arm. "You never listen when I tell you to do something!"

"I'm too scared to go outside, Mommy!"

"I'm sick of your made-up stories; just wait till your father gets home!"

The child struggles against the pulling force, but she tightens her grip.

"Please! Mommy, don't make me!"

She drags the now screaming child across the carpet. Confused by the racket, a little girl comes running out through the hallway. Frightened by the entire ordeal, she starts to sob.

"Stop throwing a tantrum, Matthew, you're upsetting Talaya!"

She finally reaches the front door and yanks the boy outside. Fed up with the racket, she scoops up the tormented girl and drops her outside too. The door slams shut with a loud thud. A distinctive click follows as the lock is turned. Muffled screaming and banging emanate from the other side of the door.

Then suddenly, it stops.

CHAPTER 34

Small hands clench the sturdy bucket, pushing it against the force of the flowing river. The bottom of the girl's blue dress lightly touches the water's surface as her arms wrap around the dripping wooden vessel. Quivering underneath its weight, about a quarter of the liquid spills out as she lifts it from the water. Too short to balance the burden, she compromises by squeezing it tightly against her hips and slowly begins her struggle through the camp.

The girl makes her way to the Adjustment Shack and then around the Lodge, taking the flattest path. She passes the Cave and steadily trudges along the thick desert sand, finally approaching the boy on his knees. He carefully rubs the dirt from a seed's surface and places it in a shallow hole. After sprinkling the pit with a potent, green substance, he covers it with sand. The girl carries the bucket to him and dutifully places it next to his side.

Pure, white symbols cover their right arms. Within the body of the marks, translucent rings connect and intertwine. Twinkling light reflects off the centres of the intersecting circular shapes; like the whites of watchful eyes that refuse to look away.

"Thanks, Talaya," Matthew says, taking it from her. He lifts the heavy bucket and pours the river water onto a row of newly planted seeds. Talaya crouches on her knees to get a better view of the crops. She likes the way the water vanishes into the sand.

"I think we've planted enough for today. Go back to the river and I'll finish up here," he says. She pushes herself off the ground and starts to walk back across the desert terrain. Matthew feels around in his bag for any remaining seeds. His fingers come across a stray, pointy one. He must have missed it before. He clasps the seed and lays it down on the ground. Picking up his shovel, he begins to dig another hole.

Almost having reached the acquired depth, he is forced to stop when he hits a strange object. Matthew pokes around it, but it seems to be stretching out indefinitely. Its bright orange surface has a scaly, reflective layer covering it. Curious, he takes his shovel and jabs it into the target.

With a sudden jerk, it disappears. The entire desert begins to rumble, the ground threatening to tear open beneath him. He looks up in the direction of the camp and sees Talaya still walking back. He quickly jumps to his feet and starts to run. "Talaya!" he screams, trying to catch up with her. "Run!"

She turns around, freezing instantly. The very ground is lifting and falling, as if the desert has turned into a sea of waves. By now, Matthew has dropped the shovel and is running as fast as he can. The sand is moving underneath his feet, but he dares not look down. He reaches Talaya and grabs her by the arm, pulling her alongside him as they flee for camp.

CHAPTER 35

Cold ground presses against the side of my face. Everything happened so fast. I lift myself up and look around. Both Skylor and Aiesha are still on the ground, curled up in protective positions and bracing for the impact.

It came out of nowhere. A monstrous earthquake, sweeping everyone off their feet. It hasn't stopped yet. I can make out faint screaming in the distance. It's coming from the plantation at the edge of camp.

The Adjustment Shack sways from side to side, threatening to crumble at any moment. I grab Aiesha by her arms and kick open the door. After several panicked tugs, I've dragged her outside, placing her a safe distance from the unstable structure. I run back inside and do the same with Skylor, leaving her next to Aiesha.

I begin to stumble towards the noise, but the shaking gets worse as I get closer, causing me to lose my balance every few steps. All around the camp, Marks are sprawled out across the ground. A single confrontation with the unknown has reverted these warriors back to their true forms—scared kids who don't know what to do.

With immense struggle, I finally arrive at the border where the campgrounds meet the warm desert sand. My stomach drops when I witness the horrifying scene playing out in front of me. Geysers of sand shoot up into the air, whilst other parts of the planet's surface sink, only to shift back again moments later. My heart nearly stops beating when I spot the two small figures in the middle of all the chaos. It's Matthew and Talaya.

Without a second thought, I sprint into the sea of shifting sand, moving as fast as my legs can carry me. Left and right, large patches disappear and reappear again in explosive bursts. I concentrate on the path before me and keep the rest in my peripheral vision. When I reach the two Whites, Matthew lets go of Talaya's hand and hauls her up to me. "Take her!" he shouts, his voice quavering. "Please!"

I pull the young girl into my grasp, tightly embracing her. Then I turn around and run back with every ounce of energy I've got left in me. Talaya pushes her face into my heaving chest, too afraid to look down at the wild dunes. A sudden patch of sand disappears in front of me, forcing me to leap over the crater and skid across the scorching surface of desert terrain, grazing open both of my knees. I haul myself back up and continue with the same speed until I finally reach denser soil near the campgrounds. I gently place the traumatised girl onto her feet, and turn around, fearing the worst.

Relieved, I spot Matthew only a short distance away. He dodges the ruptures and bolts towards us in a zigzag formation. When the rumbling begins to cease, he slows down to catch his breath.

"It's okay!" he happily exclaims. "I think it stopped!"

For a brief moment I have some hope left in me. After all the loss and misfortune, something good is finally coming our way—a mere story that we can laugh at around the campfire tonight. What happens next, however, is something that will haunt me for the rest of my life. It will play off in my head every night before I go to sleep. Like a broken record.

I see an innocent ten-year-old boy standing in the distance, a feeling of relief setting on him for the first time in a very long while. And then, just like that, he is gone. The ground underneath Matthew's feet disappears, and he does too.

Sucking up everything in its path, the opening of a giant jaw appears. The body follows, stretching straight up into the sky, like a giant oak tree sprouting from the ground. Orange pointed scales cover its entire tube-shaped form, reflecting the suns' rays into my eyes. But I refuse to look away.

The desert worm with no eyes faces us, showing off the rows of dagger-like teeth that stretch into the back of its throat. Its body reaches into the clouds, rising like a skyscraper until it arches over and plummets head-first into the sand, burrowing deep into the ground from which it came. Its tail disappears, and everything turns quiet as if it were never here.

For a few seconds, I stare into the distance, wondering if anything I just witnessed was real. If I had imagined it all. But then I look down and become aware of the little hand that I'm still holding in mine.

My shock is instantly replaced with hate. Hate for the beings that brought us here and left us alone to die. Hate for the Marks who carelessly placed the Whites in harm's way, allowing this atrocity to occur. And finally, hate for myself and what I will do when I find those who are responsible.

CHAPTER 36

The entire camp is in chaos. Elementals who felt the impact from far away come running out of the forest like mice fleeing a burning field. Water from the overflowing river floods the grounds, leaking into every nook and cranny. A steady stream of liquid creeps its way towards the ash-filled fireplace, gradually engulfing the pit and washing away everything in its path.

I walk amongst the wreckage, clutching Talaya in my arms. She hasn't uttered a single word since her older brother's demise, yet her trembling body speaks more than words ever could. Skylor and Aiesha are still where they were before, but the Adjustment Shack isn't. The earthquake caused the river to overflow and everything standing in its way has been washed away.

"What happened?" Sky asks me, her eyes anxiously pinned on the little girl.

"Something came out of the sand and kill—" I look down at the girl, then quickly correct myself. "The worm *took* Matthew."

Skylor tries to hide the tears, but her sniffling gives her away. "Talaya, are you okay?" She looks over to the girl who buries her face deeper into my chest. "I'm so sorry," Skylor's voice finally breaks.

Aiesha barely manages to hide the evident pain in her expression.

"I'll take her to the Lodge," Skylor offers. "I can't believe it's still standing."

"No," I stop her. She looks confused. "The camp needs you to lead. Now more than ever. Aiesha can take her."

Aiesha takes the little girl from my arms. Skylor doesn't protest. Instead, she looks even more distraught than before. When Aiesha and Talaya are out of earshot, Skylor lets go of what's left of her strong stance and allows the tears to freely flow down her face.

"It's my fault," she says, distant. "I'm the one who stationed them there. I just wanted to keep them safe." I look at the once fearsome leader who is now breaking down before my eyes. I try to remain angry at her deceit, but no matter how hard I try, all I see is a scared, remorseful girl.

"Did you know about the desert worms?" I demand.

"Not at all," she cries. "Azon didn't bother to tell us!"

"Then you couldn't possibly have known," I try to console her.

"Are you going to tell the camp about me?" she suddenly asks.

The thought hasn't occurred to me until now. Nobody is going to react remotely well. There might even be anarchy. "Not yet," I decide.

She looks mildly surprised at my decision.

"Let's first focus on controlling the chaos."

Within seconds, Rusty comes running towards us, blood and tears streaming down her face. "They're gone," she stammers, almost incoherent between rapid breaths. "All of them," she cries, clearly disorientated.

Skylor quickly steps forward and grabs her arms, steadying and holding her in place.

"I… I made it out," Rusty says, desperately attempting to communicate.

"I'm going to need you to calm down," Skylor says slowly. "Start from the beginning."

"The Cave," Rusty mumbles whilst more tears escape her eyes. "Everything started shaking, it collapsed." She begins to hyperventilate. "They're all dead."

"I think you have a concussion." Skylor searches for an open wound by carefully trailing her fingers along Rusty's soaked hairline.

Rusty cries out in pain.

"I need to close this up," Sky says, "or it will get infected." She proceeds in the direction of the Adjustment Shack but quickly realises her mistake. She turns around and contemplates the earthquake's implications for a few seconds, then speaks. "I'll get the Elementals to gather the necessary materials so I can sanitize the wound. Until then, we'll have to stop the bleeding." She gives me a nod, then leads Rusty away to the Lodge.

Without wasting a moment to think, I run over to the Cave to see if there is anyone left inside. Only upon arrival do I realise the true horror of it. The earthquake has triggered a landslide, which caused the Cave to collapse in on itself. Where there was once an entrance, there is now nothing but immovable boulders and debris. Germ stands before it, shouting frantically in the hope of receiving a response.

Like the overflowing river, a solid stream of dark liquid slowly seeps out from beneath the cave rocks. With sinister twists and turns, it gradually pools around his feet, staining the sand crimson.

CHAPTER 37

Two days have passed since the catastrophe struck, and activity around the camp is stagnant. Those who are injured now lie in the Lodge, receiving care from the last two remaining Neuros—Skylor and Rusty. Germ helps them where he can. He hasn't been the same since the Cave collapsed. Nobody is. Most of the Elementals have ceased their patrols and refuse to go on their shifts, whilst the Apex have abandoned hunting entirely. They won't go into the forest, and nobody is willing to try and persuade them.

At the fire pit, I crouch down among the dust and dirt. With swift motions, I wipe away the jumble of rocks and replace them with a dry layer of leaves. Using a flat stone and a borrowed knife, I scrape the edge of the blade against a piece of flint. The rapid, repetitive movements heat the surface and quickly create a stray spark. Within seconds a few more follow, causing the leaves to smoulder and catch fire. I add tinder on top of the first layer, then blow into the glowing embers, watching with satisfaction as the flames grow in size. The campfire ignites in a magnificent blaze of light.

I look up at the darkened and defeated faces surrounding me. The light illuminates their weariness and the grief-stricken shadows under their eyes. I clear my voice and address the group.

"We've called you all together to discuss a serious matter."

I turn to Sky, who seems far away even though she is standing right beside me. Reluctant to participate in the conversation, she wipes away at the oily strands of hair covering her eyes and beckons the group to listen.

"I haven't been completely honest with you," she begins hesitantly. "A long time ago, I ran into the forest, chasing after a delirious new drop. Within minutes I was lost. I survived for weeks on my own, before returning as a hero in your eyes." She exhales a built-up sigh.

"I lied. I didn't survive on my own. After several days of wandering through the wild, I stumbled on another camp filled with Marks."

Her words are met with enraged outcries from the group.

"But they're not like us," she says hurriedly. "Their leader was corrupt and extremely dangerous, he—" she looks around at the resentful faces, the trust lost from their gazes. "He had a black mark."

She tried to divert the attention away from herself and it worked excellently. Now, everyone has grown quiet and is staring at me. They had enough reason to be wary of me before. Skylor has merely gone ahead and added the final nail in the coffin.

"What are you doing?" I ask her, feeling angry and betrayed.

She doesn't answer me. I look at the crowd again, their expressions now suspicious and cynical.

"The point is," I begin again. "That Black Mark believed there is a way off this planet. A way back home."

This sparks interest in a few, but definitely not all of them.

Skeith is the first one to speak out.

"Did Skylor tell you this?" he asks.

"She did," I respond hesitantly.

He continues to stare at her with disdain. The Elemental are excellent judges of character and, having been fooled by such an elaborate lie, wouldn't sit right with them. What little trust they had in Skylor is now gone. I doubt she'll ever get it back.

"At this point Skylor will say *anything* to save her skin. Why should we believe anything that comes from her mouth?" he says.

I agree with Skeith but saying it out loud will not solve anything right now.

"It doesn't matter whether you believe her. We need to start hunting again, and more importantly, we need to reinstitute patrols."

Some of the Marks nod their heads, the hunger clearly getting to them.

This time, it's Kyle's turn to respond.

"You can forget it!" he stands up. "Survival of the fittest, I've always said. No wonder all the Neuros are extinct."

Germ flinches as the words touch a wound still too tender. A few Elementals shoot disapproving glares at Kyle, but nobody is prepared to stand up against him.

"Skylor and Rusty are still here. They're not dead," I reply starkly.

"Not yet," he says with a threatening undertone. He stands and ushers the other Apex to follow. The rest of the Marks disperse and the meeting is closed.

I jog after Sky, who is already on her way to the Lodge. Judging by her speed, it's clear she's trying to avoid me. "Hey!" I shout at her. "What was that all about?"

She continues to walk. "I'm sorry, John. I panicked."

"That isn't good enough." I won't allow the topic to slide. "You made it seem like my mark means corruption," I snarl at her.

"Can you prove that it doesn't?" she retorts.

This hurts me more than it should, especially coming from Skylor. "How can you say that?"

"For all we know, it could be. Marks of a feather flock together."

I decide to retaliate. "You're just biased because of your mistakes, Skylor."

This causes her to stop in her tracks. "Perhaps. Or maybe you just haven't had the opportunity to show your true colours yet."

"You can't truly believe that! I risked my life to save Talaya."

She raises her eyebrows condescendingly. "To me, it looks like you were trying to play hero. As if you wanted to prove your worth to the camp."

Unbelievable. I study her closely, astonished at how her personality has changed from a victim to the accuser within seconds. "What about Germ? When Kyle attacked him, I intervened."

"Yet you allowed the Shrieker to almost kill Kyle. You didn't intervene then, did you?"

This leaves me at a loss for words. With nothing left to say, Sky alters her path and walks towards the river. I stare after her, my mind still racing.

I'm not a bad person.

I walk down to the Lodge where the injured still lie in their beds. A bandage fashioned from leaves and twine is tightly wrapped around Rusty's head, but she is already back on her feet and seeming a lot better.

Talaya is sitting on the edge of Matthew's empty bed. I gently place my hand on her shoulder. "How are you feeling, Talaya?"

Expressionless, she remains staring at the wall.

"She hasn't said a word after the accident," Rusty responds.

"She wasn't exactly yammering away before the accident," Germ says.

Rusty jabs him in the ribs with her elbow.

"What? It's true!" he cries.

"I'm so sorry about the cave," I tell Rusty and Germ. Their faces sink.

"We were on the verge of a breakthrough," Rusty shakes her head. "We lost everything."

"And everyone," Germ adds. "Those Neuros were the closest I ever came to finding my own kind on this planet. Nobody knows what it's like to be me."

I pat him on the back. "You're not alone. I found someone else like you."

"You're pulling my leg. This isn't the time for jokes, John!"

"I'm not joking, Jeremy. I met another Pink Mark at the other camp."

Germ's face lights up. "Really? What was he like? Or was it a she? You know what, it doesn't matter, just tell me if they were good at anything."

"It was a boy—" I begin, but Germ cuts me off.

"I knew it! So, what was his talent? Was he really witty and funny? Or maybe extremely charismatic and well-liked?"

"He was just like you," I laugh. "He knew a lot of things."

"I know a lot of things!" Germ jumps up and down. "What's his name?"

"They called him Jester, but I think he mentioned his name was Roderick." I decide to leave out the part concerning Jester's constant humiliation and impending punishment.

"Did you hear that, Elizabeth? He has a nickname, too!" Germ squeals.

She punches him in the arm. "Don't call me that."

"Alright, Elizabeth."

Rusty scowls. "Well, I'm glad for you, Germ, I really am," she says. "Maybe you should bugger off to that other camp and find your Pink boyfriend. While you're at it, the two of you can even take over our research." She tosses a pile of bandages onto the bed and prepares to storm off. "After all, what's better than a cave full of hardworking Neuros? Two Pink know-it-alls of course!"

"I didn't forget about you, Rusty," I interject.

She looks taken aback. "Who, me?"

"I felt bad for taking so long to give you my phone. Like you said, the battery was probably drained by the time you received it."

"It was," she admits. "But your hardware was all that really mattered."

"I still want to make it up to you though." The two phones in my shoes press uncomfortably against my toes. I'm surprised that no one has noticed my awkward limp yet. I can only hope that they still work after all this time. I bend down and untie my laces.

"Oh, John," Rusty says sarcastically. "You really don't have to. I already have shoes." Her expression changes when I bring the phones into view. My fingers play with the buttons until both devices turn on. I give a long sigh of relief. "The other camp was hoarding the stuff. I doubt they'll miss these."

Rusty takes the two phones and inspects them closely. "They're almost fully charged," she marvels. She allows herself a few more seconds to bask in the light of the glowing rectangular screens, before switching them off to preserve the batteries. Rusty looks at me with a newfound respect in her eyes. "If you ever need anything, you know where to find me," she says.

I nod, grateful for the offer. Glancing over my shoulder, I steal a second glimpse at Talaya. She hasn't yet moved since I entered the building. Even though the little girl is surrounded by people and is out of any immediate danger, she seems scared.

"Will you guys mind if I talk to her alone for a few seconds?" I ask.

"If you think it will help," Rusty says. She ushers Germ out of the Lodge for some fresh air.

I sit down on the bed opposite Talaya, but she doesn't acknowledge my presence. Instead, her eyes dart to the entrance of the Lodge. I get up and close the door, but when I return, she continues to peer over at it.

"You don't have to be scared," I suggest. Attempting to crack a joke, I say, "Nothing can hurt you now. If anything tries, I'll feed them to Beetroot."

She doesn't respond. I decide to try a different approach. "Do you like stories?"

The suggestion sparks a bit of light in her glassy eyes. I didn't expect her to answer, but I don't need her to. When Carter was young and Dad's absence had only just begun to take a toll on him, I would sneak into his room at night and tell him stories about the imaginary worlds that were beyond our reach. Some of them contained horrific monsters and fantastical treasures; others were filled with wandering spacemen and determined lone rangers. I created a world that was more pleasant than the real one, in which people were happy, and didn't die.

"Once upon a time, there was a small boy and girl from a faraway world. They weren't like the other children at their school, because they were special. They could see things that were invisible to others and hear things that no one else could hear. One day, a witch came along and noticed the little boy and girl. She saw the wonderful things they could do and became very jealous. So, one night, when they were both sleeping, she broke into their house and sneaked into their rooms. With her magic wand, she constructed a pallet of white paint made from the strongest materials she could find—like the claws of a polar bear and the teeth of a lion. Drawing the prettiest patterns she could think of, the witch put a sleeping spell on them."

Talaya looks enthralled, totally captivated by my words. It's working.

"Together, the boy and girl now lived in a dreamland they could not escape from, no matter how hard they tried. Sometimes, the witch would even send them nightmares, but the children were not able to tell that none of it was real. One day, the boy found a way to escape the dream, and finally woke up. This came at a great cost, because he left the little girl behind. He didn't mean to, but everything happened so fast. And now he can't come back."

"Where is he?" Talaya asks softly.

"He woke up," I gently assure her. "Every night, he crouches beside the sleeping girl's bed, holding her hand and waiting for her to wake up, too. One day, she will. Then they'll be together again."

The small girl exhales a breath of air. She takes a while to process this information. After a few seconds, she curls up inside herself again, only to take a quick glimpse at the door every few breaths. She still seems scared, and struggles to force her gaze to the ground. I peer at her bare feet and notice some scratches in the wall where the wood meets the floor. Kneeling down to get a better look, I discover that the carvings were made purposely, most likely with a sharp river rock. In the centre of the drawing, the two small, crudely drawn stick people stand alongside each other, holding hands. The right figure is an exact duplicate of the left, except for two curled lines flowing down from each side of its head, resembling a girl's hair. In the background, hundreds of stick people surround the two figures, all of them at least double the height of the children. It reminds me of something you would find in a mental asylum, or in the hospital room of a patient with severe PTSD. At first I assume that the others are supposed to represent the older Marks, but then I notice a finer detail that is almost hidden beneath the incessant scratches. I trail my fingers along the curved outlines of the little children, and then do the same with the masses of grown figures. Something is definitely missing, and I doubt that it was left out by accident. The two children look forward, their eyes fixed before them. Their noses consist of even simpler constructions, and the mouths are expressionless horizontal lines. The heads of the other figures surrounding them, however, are totally blank. They don't have faces.

"What are you afraid of?" I urge a bit more, hoping that she will open up to me. I put my hand on the edge of her shoulder and squeeze it lightly. "Talaya, please tell me. I can only help if you let me."

To my surprise, she lifts her face out of her palms and whispers something incoherently. I drop to my knees beside her, turning my head at an angle for a better chance to hear.

"What did you say?"

She whispers again, this time slowly and clearly. "They can hear us."

Talaya lifts her head and glances at the door again, but this time she doesn't take her eyes away. I carefully follow her gaze and realise that she is not staring at the door at all, but at the dark corner beside it. I jump up from the bed and dash to the doorway, where an uncanny coldness greets me.

The ill-lit corner is empty, yet the hairs on my neck still rise. I shouldn't be afraid of the shadows before me. I'm too old to fear the dark, or things that go bump in the night. I wonder what would happen if I closed my eyes and reached out before me. Would my fingers graze the wooden wall, or come to a sudden stop against something else entirely?

I look back at Talaya, who is staring at me. She looks terrified.

CHAPTER 38

"Extradimensional beings," Germ clamours away. "I knew it!"

"What do you mean?" I ask.

"Think about it. If we had no ears, we wouldn't know that sound existed. If we had no eyes, we wouldn't be aware of colours. What if there are entire dimensions invisible to us because we don't have the necessary organs to detect them?" Germ looks ecstatic, like someone who has spent a lifetime on research only to finally stumble upon the necessary proof to confirm his theory. "These aliens are not from a planet as we perceive it, but from a reality that cannot be observed with the five senses."

"We don't know that Germ, it could just be some sort of imaginary friend," I suggest.

He snorts. "Imaginary friends are neither imaginary, nor friends. It's no coincidence that children her age are especially more susceptible to seeing these *friends*."

I don't really know what to make of this information. Even if I did, it wouldn't help our predicament. Nonetheless, I don't like the idea of invisible beings following me around camp. If Germ's theory has any truth to it, then Talaya has every right to be afraid. Something in the Lodge is watching us.

"Where are you going?" Germ asks as I distance myself from him.

"I'm going to get us some food."

"That sounds great!" he shouts after me. "Get some Rodback, will you?"

"I'll try," I assure him, though I have no idea what Rodback actually looks like when it's still breathing.

Ever since the Apex decided to stop hunting, they've been making themselves scarce to avoid their responsibilities. Kyle remains in the Lodge and sleeps most of the day. His arm hasn't fully recovered, not that it ever will, and the pain keeps him up at night. He tirelessly moans in his sleep, refusing to quiet down. Many of the Apex have since bullied weaker Marks at the other end of the Lodge into swapping beds with them. There has been a definite shift in loyalty pertaining to his leadership. While Kyle's strength weakens, so does his sway over the Apex.

My visit to the other camp has given me a new appreciation of the norm here. It also made me realise how easily that norm can be broken. Whether we like it or not, the Reds are capable of overtaking an entire camp if they wish to do so. Kyle has always been a loose cannon, but at least he listened to Skylor. Now that her influence is fading, he might become desperate enough to try something foolish. I need to step in before that happens.

At my request, Aiesha has been keeping an eye on the Apex. She followed them around the camp borders and informed me of the location of their hideouts. Determined and alone, I scale over the collapsed Cave and into the mountains that loom just above the river. The sound of rushing water trails off into the narrow gorge as I cross the uneven surface of the ridge. I look out over the desert that stretches into the horizon and spot the same glimmer of water I noticed on my first day.

When I find the group of Apex, they act on the defensive, clearly not expecting to run into other Marks this far out.

"What do you want?" one of them snaps.

"I want what everyone wants," I respond with my hands in the air. "To eat."

They eye me up and down, most likely trying to decide if they can, or should, take me on. The Apex hardly seem their old selves. Most of them look tired and malnourished. Their muscles have begun to waste away, as they haven't been making use of them for quite some time. They seem lost without Kyle's authority.

I push the matter further. "You're not going to achieve anything by hiding out here all day. If anything, the entire camp is going to starve and so will you.

This triggers the reaction I was expecting. "Don't you think we know that? It's not like we're holding out on the others. We're not hunting at all," a Red Mark shouts.

"Ever since your pet bit Kyle, we've been short on strength."

Finally, some truth. It's not that they're acting out or purposely being defiant. They're simply too weak to go into the forest and too proud to admit it.

"If you're lacking strength, I can help you," I suggest.

They laugh mockingly, but then realise that I'm serious. Talking amongst each other, the Reds begin to consider my proposal in a different light. One of them stands up and walks closer. Ginger hair covers the top of his head in wild, frizzy curls. Tiny brown freckles sprout across his chin, making their way past his ears and around his eyes in cloudy swirls like that of a racoon. The boy is hardly a shadow compared to Kyle, but he seems too self-assured to care. His almond brown eyes flick across the terrain behind me, searching for any surface or object that could hide a person and compromise the privacy of our exchange.

"My name is Erik," he announces. "Do you know why we are called the Apex?"

"No," I admit.

"It's short for 'apex predator'," he proclaims, crossing his arms before him. "Warriors like us once conquered the Earth, dominating every species who dared to stand in our way. We've been torn from that world and dropped into a new one, but our task has not changed." He tries to make himself seem taller than he really is by shifting his weight from his heels to the base of his toes. Leaning forward, he still doesn't manage to match my height. He compromises by staring squarely into my chin. "We have not even grown to our full potential," he says as if to prove a tacit point, "yet we're already slaughtering the inhabitants of this planet and feasting off of their flesh." The others grunt in unison, encouraging him to continue.

"So how?" he states bluntly. "How can *you* help us?"

I look at his fatigued figure, the bones in his ribs threatening to pierce through his skin. I'm amused at his stubbornness. He is willing to die before admitting defeat. They all are. That's why they've been hiding away all this time. They're too ashamed to reveal themselves to the rest of the camp as weak and starving. Pride will be the end of the Apex, unless I can help it.

I think back to what Azon told me at the other camp. He boasted that the Reds prided themselves on their power. He subdued the Apex by taking it away from them and persuading them that they never had any to begin with.

I survey the feeble bodies that are sprawled out on the ground and decide to do something that might get me killed. I laugh. It begins as a snigger, barely audible, but works its way up to a full-on cackle. I laugh until tears leave my eyes and I'm struggling to catch my breath.

The boy doesn't know what to make of this. His face contracts.

"Are you kidding me?" I finally manage to say between pants. "Do you truly believe that you are at the top of this food chain? That might have been the case on Earth, but certainly not here. Do you want to know why?" I stop laughing and my expression becomes very serious. "Because a bunch of beings literally abducted you and dropped you on another planet. Like ants." I stomp my feet on the ground to illustrate a point. "They are fully in control. We're just pawns in their sick game, and unless we find a way off this planet and out of their destructive grasps, you will never be worthy of your name."

The boy's eyes narrow. "Did you come here to mock us?" he asks accusingly.

I shake my head. "I came here because I'm not planning on staying in this camp much longer." I give it to him straight. "When the time comes, I'm going to need everyone to work together and be at full strength." I peer down at his concave stomach and add, "Or at least fully fed."

He shifts his gaze from my chin to my eyes, trying to determine if my concerns are in fact genuine. It might be due to the Apex's lack of leadership, or simply because they're too weak to subdue me, but the boy eventually concedes and no one stops him.

"You're going to need a weapon," Erik says.

"I already have one," I grin.

Beetroot followed me as I trekked up the hill, stalking me all the way to the Reds' hideout. Although the Apex have no way of detecting her presence, I've learned to spot the recognisable glimmer by now. Her camouflage is as adaptable as that of an octopus, morphing to imitate rocks and twigs amongst the sand. The cloaking mechanism is most effective when she's moving, but if standing still, a stray shadow or gust of wind might give her away.

"Here girl," I mouth the words. Beetroot emerges next to me, turning back to her neutral colour: pitch black.

Erik jumps backwards, surprised by her materialisation. He quickly regains his composure but refuses to take his sight off the Shrieker.

From there on out, Beetroot and I lead the Apex into the depths of the jungle. Aiesha referred me to an area where three-horned, gazelle-like creatures graze in an open meadow. The majestic Rodbacks like to prance around and feed on luscious shrubs. They breed frivolously and in abundance, with many young fawns playfully cantering around their mothers. Although the herd itself is harmless, they are almost impossible to hunt. Situated in the middle of a field where the plants are only knee-high, they are able to see everything that approaches from any angle. This territory has a distinct disadvantage for them, though. Out in the open, there is no protection from the predators that scour the skies above.

Every so often, a Ptera will descend onto the herd, causing a few of the Rodbacks to scamper away from the others and into the forest where the Apex can pick them off. That's if other predators don't get to them first. I have a similar plan in mind.

We tread quietly around the area, picking out the weakest targets in the herd. When satisfied with our choices, we spread out and create distance between each other. I venture off from the Apex and lead Beetroot around to the opposite side of the field. Returning on my own, I wait a few minutes before giving a silent signal to the others. As they prepare for the incoming charge, I release a loud cry into the air. The herd of Rodback freezes in place, scouring the meadow for intruders.

Before they can pick a direction to dash away, Beetroot barges out of the forest. Having hunted just moments before, she ignores the bewildered creatures and runs towards me like she was trained to do. Luckily for us, the Rodback don't know that.

In a wild stampede, the herd gallops right into our trap. The moment they enter the dark concealment of the woods, the Apex jump out from the trees and take down the chosen few, knocking them to the ground. A stray arrow glides through the air and whisks past my head, hitting a lone stag that managed to dodge the initial attack. The large creature crashes into the ground, the shaft of the arrow sticking out between its antlers. The rest of the squirming animals don't put up much of a fight, and within minutes they're pinned on their backs with hooves in the air.

The Apex cheer in celebration of a successful hunt. They raise their red marks into the air like rowdy waves in a sea of blood. We lay the carcasses next to each other. Erik points to the biggest stag with the wooden shaft sticking out of his head. Two girls walk forward and begin to skin the buck with small knives purposely crafted for this task. The sharpened stones are swiftly pressed underneath the Rodback's rugged skin. Skilled hands carefully guide the tools across the animal's gut until the hide can be peeled off. After they have pulled the loosened skin from the body and folded it into a wet heap, the others cut up the remains and distribute the weight equally amongst each other.

On our way back, the Apex can't stop talking. This isn't all bad, because they scare away most of the predators that are lurking near the camp perimeters. Most. There's a reason the creatures we eat are mostly monstrous. The ones that aren't scared enough to flee the noise, are drawn to it. We are ambushed by prowling Reptants soon after the hunt. Most of them retreat when Beetroot approaches, but two refuse to give up the chase and repeatedly try to attack the younger Marks in the group—which ironically includes Erik. When Beetroot is finished dealing with them, we gladly add their scaly flesh to the rest of our pile and press onwards.

Our arrival at camp is a sight for sore eyes. Before we can even begin to prepare the raw meat, the Elementals chop down some trees to add to the fire. Once the wood is in abundance, we feverishly stoke the campfire, adding shreds of meat as the flames grow higher. A trail of smoke rises into the air, its delightful aroma spreading throughout the camp and luring every Mark in the vicinity. By the time the final sun begins to set on the horizon, Marks of all colours have come together to join in on the feast.

I sit up straight and glance around at all the faces. Skylor and Talaya aren't here. Neither is Kyle. The Apex do not seem to care either way. Erik pushes his way through the outskirts of the group and past eating children who are too busy assuaging their hunger to care. He sits down next to me and drops a pile of tanned material into my lap. The course texture clings to my skin, but it provides some comfort, nevertheless.

"As a token for your service," he says, pleased with himself.

Germ gasps at the sight of the animal hide. "It might be bigger than Kyle's!" he exclaims.

Erik snorts. "Might? It's a whopper. You'll be able to cover two beds with it."

285

"Thank you," I say, not very enthusiastically. It's a kind gesture, but certainly not one that comes without complications.

"It's nothing compared to Beetroot's mane, though," Germ boasts. "Her fur is softer than silk."

Erik grunts in response to the comment. "We considered skinning your pet a few times. Dared each other to, in fact."

Germ's eyes widen.

"The Red Mark who went through with it could keep the rainbow pelt."

Germ looks like he is about to be sick. Erik is clearly teasing him, but I think we both know that his statements are genuine. Germ scraps the remainder of his food into the pit and leaves the conversation, clutching his stomach.

"Where is Kyle?" I wonder aloud.

Erik's response is quick and definite. "Kyle would rather have let us all starve than hunt with you. He even said so himself. Therefore, he's forbidden from joining us tonight."

I contemplate this. Kyle relied on the Apex for food, but now they aren't willing to give him so much as a pitiful scrap. Even though he is dead weight at this point, the thought of letting him starve doesn't sit comfortably with me. I haven't yet forgotten Skylor's harsh words.

Corrupted.

In no shape or form is this a good trait to have. In fact, it's the opposite of good. It's downright evil. Azon made this very clear. And to go as far as to insinuate that my sole existence on this planet is defined by a mark that means corruption is terrifying.

I am not a bad person.

286

I excuse myself from the group, taking my food and blanket with me. As I walk away, I try to recollect the events that led up to my abduction. What did I do before it? When I arrived at school that morning, Daniel and Sam bombarded me with questions, but I shrugged them off. Then… *I remember.* Carter was in trouble. I attacked some boy and hurt him badly. I don't even know if he's okay. He might not be. Carter was so scared. He wanted me to stop, but I couldn't. A cold numbness spreads across my face as I recollect other events.

I allowed a Shrieker to nearly kill Kyle.

My shoulders stiffen.

I caused a new drop to die.

I enter the Lodge and stop before Kyle's bed. He's awake, listening to the laughter outside. I take the remainder of my meal and place it at his feet. He stares up at me but doesn't say anything. Kyle sees the large animal hide around my shoulders, and immediately realises its implication. He has been replaced.

I don't think I'm a bad person.

CHAPTER 39

Patrols have recommenced and are in full force. The cooperation between the Apex and Elementals has progressed smoothly, and both sides are now open for negotiation. Hunting has not yet resumed, because it hasn't been necessary. Given all the food that is still untouched from the night before, we're attempting to preserve it rather than allowing it to rot. Meanwhile, the Apex are once again safeguarding the borders of the camp to prevent predators from entering our territory.

I wash the remainder of the rocks in the river and carry them back to the fireplace. The loads aren't as heavy as they were before. After the earthquake, most people began to wash their own plates after they'd eaten. The plantation, however, has been abandoned. The desert is now a forbidden zone.

I go back to the Lodge to check up on Talaya. Perhaps I can get her to leave Matthew's bed and nibble on some leftover food next to the warm fire. Once inside, I'm pleased to see that the injured have diminished significantly. Kyle is the only one who still lies underneath his covers. I reach Matthew's old bed, but it's cold and empty. Talaya isn't in her own bed, either. I walk the entire length of the Lodge and back, but I can't find her.

"Germ, have you seen Talaya?"

He scans the different beds then shakes his head.

I look around for Skylor, intending to ask her, but she's nowhere to be seen either. "How about Sky?" I ask Germ.

He takes his time to think. "I haven't seen her or Talaya since yesterday."

"At the feast?"

"No, before that. They never came to the feast."

I don't like this one bit. I contemplate waking Aiesha but decide against it. She needs her sleep now that she's back on night shifts. My mind races as I shift through their possible whereabouts.

They're not at the fire or in the Lodge. There is neither a Cave nor an Adjustment Shack to hide in anymore. There is only the river, from which I just came, as well as the abandoned plantation. I set off on a hurried pace towards the base of the mountain and work my way towards the desert. The seeds of worry bloom into a massive hedge of weeds.

They're not there, either.

Alarmed, I walk back to the campfire, gathering my thoughts.

"John," a voice interrupts the quarrels in my head. I look around to face Skeith. He's supposed to be out on the day shift.

"Is something wrong?" I ask him, already knowing the answer.

"You'll want to see this," he says in a grave tone.

I follow him past the boundaries of camp and into the forest. We do not need to travel far before I spot the girl leaning against the overgrown tree. It's Skylor.

Several thick vines hold her twitching body firmly in place. A foamy discharge seeps out of the corners of her mouth and slowly trickles over her swollen, blue lips. Her glazed over eyes face the moistened ground, as if still searching for a way to escape the tree's deathly entanglement. At first I think it's my imagination, but then I see it happen again. The vines are moving, slowly wrapping themselves tighter around her body like a nest of snakes.

"It's a strangler," Skeith says coldly. "It waits for prey to rest underneath its branches, then the vines trap and smother the animal, so it can feed off the carcass's nutrients."

"Sky sat here?" I ask incredulously.

"Skylor wouldn't have touched the tree on her own accord. She knows what will happen if it detects warmth." Skeith shakes his head.

"What are you trying to tell me?"

"Someone knocked her unconscious and purposely put her underneath a strangler to make it look like an accident."

My fears are coming true, but in a more sinister form than I'd anticipated.

Erik appears behind me, holding a bucket of boiling water. Skeith nods and allows him to move past us. "This is the only way to release her," he explains. "The tree is sensitive to heat and needs to be overwhelmed by it."

Together, they carefully pour the water against the tree's sleek bark. The vines immediately loosen their grip on

Skylor and retract into the low-hanging branches. I drop to the ground beside Skylor and push the tip of my index finger against her neck.

With relief, I pull away after registering a faint, rapid pulse. My reassurance is cut short when her body goes into full-blown convulsions.

"She's having a seizure," Skeith says.

"Will she be okay?" I ask, jumping to my feet.

"I don't know."

None of us have the skills to help her. Skylor is usually the one who deals with medical emergencies.

I turn to Erik, who isn't sure what to do, either. "Take her to Rusty in the Lodge. If anyone knows what to do, it will be another Neuro."

Erik nods and heaves Skylor over his shoulder before bolting back to camp. I inspect the ground where Skylor was lying, and then search around the base of the tree. "Where's Talaya?" I finally ask.

Skeith frowns. "We didn't know she was missing," he responds.

This sends off another alarm in my head. Whoever did this to Skylor could have harmed Talaya as well. "I think I know who is responsible," I say.

Together, we bound back to camp and barge into the Lodge. I go straight toward Kyle's bed. "Where's Talaya?" I demand.

Kyle laughs. "What are you talking about?"

With a temper much quicker than mine, Skeith takes the blunt tip of his spear and pins Kyle to the bed by his throat. "He's not going to ask you again," Skeith threatens.

"I don't know!" Kyle squirms under the increasing weight of the weapon.

"You threatened them, remember? Survival of the fittest." I take the cold spear into my own hands and push it even deeper into his neck, making him choke. "What kind of a coward would harm a six-year-old girl?"

I suddenly remember what Skylor said about my mark, but I don't care.

"You three were the only ones in the Lodge last night. Only you know what happened, and the fact that you're choosing to play dumb says more than I need to know."

"I was asleep!" Kyle screams. "I swear! Skylor gave me something strong for the pain that knocked me out good. I didn't see anything."

"You're lying," I grow angry.

"I've had enough of your crap," Skeith says menacingly. He takes the back of his spear and lifts it up all the way past his shoulder, threatening to impale Kyle. "Your words say one thing, yet your body reveals another." For a fleeting moment, Skeith twists his head like a snake assessing its prey. "Is your throat itching?" he hisses. "Is that why you insist on scratching it like someone plagued with a rash?"

Kyle pulls his arm away from his neck and self-consciously tucks it underneath his pelt.

"Exactly what I thought. You have the audacity to call yourself an Apex, yet you can't even look me in the eyes. I think it's time I showed you who the real king of this jungle is." Skeith leans forward like a provoked animal, his eyes hovering over Kyle's exposed neck.

"N-no! Wait!" Kyle stammers. "What if it was the other camp?"

This catches my attention.

"Enough of your lies," Skeith snarls.

"Let him speak." I prompt Skeith to lower his spear, which he does begrudgingly. "What makes you think that?" I ask Kyle, who seems grateful for the reprieve.

"Skylor couldn't stop bitching abou—" Skeith knocks the wind from his stomach. Kyle wheezes for a few seconds and rolls onto his side. As he recovers, he begins again, slowly considering his words. "She couldn't stop complaining about the other camp and this guy named Azon. Skylor kept saying that Talaya was our only hope off this planet, and that they would eventually try to take her from us."

Every fibre in my being wants to believe that he's lying, but there must be some truth to this. Kyle couldn't possibly have known of Azon's existence if Sky hadn't told him. Germ and Aiesha both join me by the bedside.

"Are you implying that Azon came into the Lodge and took Talaya?" Aiesha frowns.

"I don't know. I was sleeping, remember?"

I frown. Images of the tournament flash in my head. I hear the crowd shouting *Homo homini lupus* as Talaya runs from the enraged Reptant. "If this is really true, then we need to act fast."

"You're telling me," Kyle yawns.

"The risk is too big not to call his bluff," Aiesha says. "We need to travel to the other camp. If necessary, we might even have to infiltrate the building to retrieve her."

The two Elementals stand alert. Their assertive faces reveal an awareness of what is to come.

"I'm entrusting you two with this task," I inform them earnestly. "If Azon has Talaya, there is no telling what he might do to her..." my voice trails off.

"Don't worry, John," Aiesha reassures me with a strained smile. She's trying to conceal the true danger of the journey ahead. "We'll be quick."

I trust in her abilities, but the scars peeking out from underneath her torn clothes make me want to grab onto her and not let go. "Please be careful," I say instead.

She grasps my shoulder. "If you're fast, it's just a twenty-five second sprint."

Skeith observes our interaction and doesn't seem too pleased. Ever since Aiesha took me into the forest with her, he's shown a disliking for me. He's clearly fond of her, but the feeling isn't reciprocated.

"What if Kyle's lying?" he asks.

I look at Kyle and then at Germ, whose face hasn't yet healed completely. "What do you think is an appropriate punishment?" I ask him. Germ's response comes quickly and nonchalantly. "Well, the Romans believed in *lex talionis*—an eye for an eye."

"I like the Romans," Skeith says.

CHAPTER 40

*T*he old building creaks between the howling gales of wind. Crooked walls made of wooden boards provide little resistance against the unforgiving gusts of air. Rows of shuttered windows enclose darkened rooms filled with sleeping bodies. Wakefulness lacks from the atmosphere in all but one.

Two feet stick out from underneath the sagging bed, a single shoe covering the left. They shift momentarily, a mixture of frustration and excitement coursing through the terse body that is attached to them. If one of the nuns walks in on her now, there will be fiery hell to pay.

The teenage girl picks up the oily wrench, continuing her work. It's funny. Usually, she'd spend hours upon hours fantasising about leaving this wretched place. Simply filling her bag—not that there was much to pack—and running away to a place far beyond its reach. Many did. Usually, their disappearances would go unnoticed for a day or two. Then, an impersonal notice would appear in the newspaper, and a week later a colourless black and white head and shoulders shot with the heading MISSING would be pinned to the lampposts at the corners of crowded streets. The process seemed more like an outdated farewell ritual than anything else, seeing that none of the missing children ever returned.

Those who left the orphanage were secretly envied by the rest. Those who were left behind merely assumed that the children who had vanished did so purposely. No one ever considered the less savoury possibilities. Why would they? The imagination of a young mind was the only tool they had to escape the morbid truths of their reality. A child would never purposely fantasise about getting lost or killed... or abducted.

The girl quickly screws another bolt into the tainted piece of metal. In less than a week, she'll turn sixteen, and then she will be forced to leave the children's home. Some who exhibit good behaviour are allowed to stay until adulthood. Not her. The nuns who run the place despise her very existence. A walking sin, they call her. Besides, it would make no difference if she lived on the street. Adoption days were avoided like the plague, and she'd rather spend them in the scrapyard where she could play with old pieces of car parts and other miscellaneous metal. There was a time in her life when she abided by everyone's expectations and attended every visit. After several sessions of rejection, she made the decision never to go again. At least then she could tell herself that she was alone by choice. Not because she wasn't wanted.

She carefully connects the minute solar panel to the rechargeable lithium-ion battery. With calculated precision, the circular, sapphire glass is placed above the plastic hands and positioned onto the dial ring. As she finally closes the case body with a click, the metallic springs move to life and the arms begin to rotate clockwise.

With satisfaction, she straps the cold watch onto her wrist and exhales a breath of built-up air. Now she'll be able to count every second left in this damned place. Afterwards, she'll make a life for herself somewhere better—somewhere like the scrapyard. In the scrapyard, between things thrown away, nothing from the material world matters. At least there, everything has a function. Every piece, no matter how small or rusty, has to fit.

"Elizabeth?"

Without making so much as a noise, a nun has appeared in her doorway. The girl covers the contraption with a piece of cloth and leaps into her bed. With a graceless rush, she covers herself with the sheet and pretends to be asleep.

The unyielding woman enters the room and inspects the girl. She gasps.

"Is that a bruise on your arm?"

CHAPTER 41

I nervously walk across the campgrounds. They should have been back by now. What is taking them so long? I circle the Lodge a third time and pace towards the campfire. What if something happened to them? If Kyle is telling the truth, then it means that Azon knows where we are. It means they might be watching us right now. I shudder at the thought of Aiesha being ambushed. If they held her captive, she wouldn't be treated well. She'd begin to look like the inmates of the other camp—starving and tortured.

Captivity is no place for an Elemental. Especially not Aiesha. I circle the lodge again and peer inside this time. Erik and a group of Apex surround Kyle's bed, standing on guard, almost too eager to keep him confined. Skylor is still not moving. Her body is laced with abrasions and contusions where the vines wrapped around her. It looks as if someone took a leather belt and whipped her repeatedly.

"John, sit down. You're exhausting yourself."

I look at Rusty. Her head wounds have healed completely, but her hair is now shaved off. I remember how people back on Earth had to cut away their hair if they had a brain operation. That way the wounds could be treated more easily.

"How are we going to leave this planet if we can't even keep the children safe in our own camp?"

"I guess we won't leave then," she says jokingly.

"Don't you want to go home?"

She takes a while to consider my question. "Earth is overrated." Rusty peers over at Skylor's lifeless body and sits down next to her. With a gentle touch, she lifts Sky's limp wrist and presses the cold, swollen palm against her face. "That planet basically consists out of dirt, water and food. We've got all of that here too."

"What about family?" I prod. "Don't you have people back home who are missing you? People who're wondering where you are?"

"Not really. I'm an orphan," she states bluntly.

I instantly regret talking about family. "I'm sorry. I didn't know."

"It's fine." Rusty adjusts Sky's pillow and measures her pulse by placing her fingers against the smooth curve of her neck.

I try to change the subject. "How's her heartbeat?"

"Erratic," she replies, worried. She takes a piece of cloth from the bucket on the floor and gently wipes the sweat off Skylor's forehead.

"Seven hundred and twenty-one days, five hours, twenty-two minutes," Rusty says under her breath.

"What?" I lean closer.

"It's the exact amount of time I've spent on this planet. Or at least the amount of time from the precise moment I took the solar cell out of the Cave's watch a few days ago."

"Why so precise?" I ask her. Maybe it's just some sort of obsession she uses to cope. Most of us have our methods. Skylor arranged her bowls and herbs. I preferred jogging.

"I want to know when I'm going to die," Rusty says, and laughs when I wince. "Haven't you noticed yet?" she asks. "They don't exactly announce it to new drops, but it should be fairly obvious by now."

"I don't know what you're talking about," I say.

She sways her head as if to mourn my ignorance without stating that I'm not a Neuro. "On Damnatus, nobody lives a day past eighteen."

I flash her a look of doubt.

"Have you seen any adults walking around lately?" she asks sarcastically.

"No," I admit.

"Weird, isn't it?" she says. "I have two theories. One shows mere correlation, and the second proves causation—which would be very bad for all of us."

"What are these theories?" I ask.

"The first—and less likely—assumes that the abductions only started happening a few years ago. It would mean that the children here simply haven't had enough time to grow up yet. Therefore, it's just a coincidence."

"The second?" I ask, her expression making me nervous.

"Children aren't allowed to grow up."

"Like Neverland?"

This causes her to smirk. Not with happiness, but rather a nihilistic grin. "Sure," she humours me. "But instead of Peter Pan, you're a lost boy. A very lost boy. Instead of ceasing to age upon arrival on this planet, you grow like any other kid would. The only twist is that you will forever stay just that. A kid. When you reach the age of majority, you'll mysteriously disappear. That is if you're lucky. Normally there's nothing mysterious about it. Whether you're trampled by a herd of Rodbacks, eaten by a wandering Reptant, or simply choke on some poisoned fruit, you'll never live a day past eighteen. Even the most experienced Elementals have entered the forest the day before their eighteenth birthdays, and simply never returned."

I suddenly feel the need to calculate my own age. On the day I was taken, I had barely grazed sixteen. Rusty seems to read my thoughts and interrupts them with an answer that penetrates my spine like a freezing dagger.

"You've been here for a year, John."

"That's not possible," I laugh away my doubt. "I loosely counted the weeks and I'm certain that no more than a few have passed."

Rusty looks sad to be the bearer of bad news. She isn't going to allow me to linger in my own fantasies. Then again, I don't expect anything less from her. "The days here are much longer," she explains. "They roughly consist of twenty-eight hours, give or take a few minutes. It might feel like a few weeks have passed, but it's been a lot longer in Earth days. Not only that, but you're not taking the length of the journey into account. By studying the watches and phones of all the new drops, we have determined that the trip from Earth to Damnatus lasts at least a month, if not more."

I'm left speechless by the Neuro's flawless calculations. There's hardly a point in trying to disprove them.

"Why do you think I kept my watch untouched and pinned to the Cave's wall?" she asks with a sense of pride. "Someone had to keep count of Earth's real time."

"I don't have long then," I realise.

"You'll be fine," she brushes it off. "In less than a week, I'll turn eighteen."

"What?" I choke. She stated it so casually.

"Someone needs to stay behind and break the curse," she jokes.

"You of all people should want to get away from here right now," I suggest.

"On Earth, I'm doomed in a different way. I'll rather take my chances out here."

After a period of silence, Rusty speaks again. "This is the only family I've ever known, John." She looks down at Skylor, caressing her cheek with a light touch. "It might not seem like much, but it's more than I could ever ask for."

For the first time, I notice a special bond between the two of them. "I understand," I finally realise.

"Do you?" she asks sceptically.

I release a sigh, knowing all too well what it's like to feel unwanted. "My dad abandoned us when I was just a kid. He didn't bother to say goodbye or even leave a measly note. He just vanished." I pull away from her stare, suddenly feeling overcome with emotions. "So, to answer your question, yes. I know how you feel. More importantly, it means that I know how they feel. My mom and brother. I promised myself that I would protect them and never walk out on them like my father did. I will gladly risk my life to save other families from going through the same suffering we went through. And that means bringing these children back to their real homes."

Rusty stares at me, her eyes redder than they were a moment ago. "Then you'll have to move fast, because there's only one way off this planet."

"What do you mean?"

"Skylor called it Project Exit. It's not just about finding a door and turning a handle. It's more complicated than that. For some reason, you cannot enter the dome alone. At least one representative of each colour Mark has to accompany you. They are the keys to the door. Azon is cheating though, because on his first try he left all the Whites and Neuros behind to die. He's stealing a second chance he doesn't deserve."

"Why are you telling me all of this?" I ask Rusty, who is sharing all of the secrets that Skylor chose to keep from me.

"You're a good person, John."

Her statement surprises me. The words that left her mouth so earnestly are in sharp contrast to those of the unconscious figure on the bed.

"Skylor was never the same after meeting Azon. She feared that you might also leave us behind if you knew the truth. I can tell that you're worried about Talaya, but she's safe. After Azon's first attempt at the Exit, he realised his mistake and rushed back to camp. He retrieved a White body and tried to enter the dome a second time. Needless to say, it doesn't work on the dead."

I shudder at the thought of Azon travelling through the desert with a little corpse hanging over his shoulder. "Even if he has no choice but to keep Talaya alive, we don't know where to go. Searching for the dome could take us months."

"That's where you're wrong," Rusty says with a conspiratorial smile. She reaches into her back pocket and pulls out a small, rectangular device. Besides the detachable compartment at the back, the only visible component is a plastic screen with flashing symbols. She turns it around to reveal an outstretched antenna.

"I was able to save it before the Cave collapsed. Combined with my watch's solar panel, your satellite phone possessed the last components we needed for it to work. Those batteries you retrieved were the icing on top of the cake. We now have the power for Project Exit."

"What is it?" I gawk at the complex device.

"This piece of technology operates a lot like a radio receiver. Instead of converting waves to a readable format, it merely picks them up and points us to their origin. There's definitely something out there. We just need to follow the frequencies." Rusty peers over my shoulder, and her expression hardens. "It seems we were just in time, too."

Aiesha and Skeith enter the Lodge, exhausted. "They're gone," Aiesha states. "We searched the entire camp for traces of Talaya but came up empty. Wherever they went, she went with them."

I suddenly have a grotesque realisation. Azon is going to leave Damnatus without us. I look at Sky, who remains motionless and unable to give orders. When I turn back, it's clear that everyone is looking at me instead. They're waiting for instructions.

"Tell everyone to gather their belongings. We're leaving camp tomorrow."

"Shouldn't we go immediately?" Skeith says. "We're already a day behind the others."

"No," I answer without hesitation. "We're waiting until the Elementals are back from their shifts."

"If we lose too much time, none of us will make it back home," he argues.

"We're *not* leaving them behind," I say firmly. "We'll need to prepare throughout the rest of the day, regardless. We leave in the morning."

Skeith doesn't look pleased with my decision and walks off. I turn to the remaining Red Marks in the Lodge. "Gather everyone in the camp. I have a plan."

The Apex leave the Lodge with Aiesha and Rusty. Germ remains behind. "What's wrong?" I ask him.

"I don't know if I want to go, John. I never fitted in back on Earth. Here I have a purpose."

"You're being too hard on yourself, Germ."

"Oh, it doesn't take a Neuro to see it! For crying out loud, my mark is Pink! I won't last a day outside of this camp, so there's no point in even trying."

I can hear that he's on the verge of bursting into tears. "That's not true. You're one of the nicest people I've ever met. You'll have a purpose when we get back, because you'll still be my best friend."

He wipes a finger underneath his glasses, pushing away a tear.

"And it will be a rainy day on Damnatus before I leave a friend behind to die. Besides, it's hard to kill a Germ."

He takes his glasses off and rubs the foggy lenses with the edge of his shirt and he sniffs, "You had me at friend, no need to embarrass yourself any further, Johnny."

I laugh and give Jeremy a tight hug. "You almost got me tearing up there."

"What, scared you'd miss your old pal, Germ?"

"Nah, I would have asked Rusty to knock you out if I had to. I just didn't want to carry you all the way."

We both laugh.

It feels good to experience hope for a change. After all that has happened and everything we've been through, we're going to have to do all we can to stay positive. We sure as hell are going to need it where we're heading.

CHAPTER 42

"We need to cross the desert," I announce to the group.

"Are you crazy?" Skeith objects. "Pteras can scoop us up like mice in an open field. And what am I forgetting? Oh yes, the four-hundred-metre-long demon-worm resting right beneath the surface."

Aiesha interjects. "Okay, but what do we know about snakes and worms in general? They tend to rely on the Sun's heat to keep a high body temperature and will usually lie just beneath the surface where it is warmest. In the night, when the surface loses its heat, they burrow deep into the earth where it is warmer. Therefore, they shouldn't be able to sense our movements at night or in the early morning."

I look over to Germ, who confirms this with a quick nod of his head.

"Any other objections?" I clear the air. "None? Alright Apex, I'm going to need you to start hunting and not stop until the Elementals have returned from their day shifts. If we want this to work, we're going to need as much meat as possible to lure the Pteras away from the desert." I take a last glimpse at the group in front of me. "We'll meet at the campfire at sundown."

"What will you be doing until then?" Aiesha asks me.

"I have some business to take care of," I try to sound as vague as possible.

"I'll come with you," she offers.

"I need to do this alone," I stop her. She isn't sure what to make of this, but I cannot afford to tell her anything else. She'll try to stop me if I do. "Keep an eye on Sky for me," I say.

She hesitates, but finally gives a reluctant nod and makes her way to the Lodge.

Before I leave the camp, Kyle approaches me. He looks tired and malnourished. "I told you, it wasn't me."

"You saw them take her and did nothing," I say with disgust in my voice.

"I was asleep," he argues.

"I don't believe you. It wouldn't be the first time you turned a blind eye."

"I didn't come here to fight. I wanted to give you this." Kyle extends his arm, offering me his only knife.

"No," I protest.

"Just take it," he insists, forcing the weapon into my palm. "See it as a symbol of my gratitude for the other day's meal. Hopefully you won't need to use it."

Kyle walks off to the Lodge, humming a suspiciously upbeat tune. I stick the knife's handle into my shoe until the cold blade grazes my ankle. With a quick shout and a few seconds' wait, I grab onto Beetroot's mane and sling myself onto her back.

* * *

I hold on tight while the Shrieker's instincts take over, letting her take full control of our journey. Within minutes we've passed the Clearing, and after that, the infamous waterhole. She rushes past trees and bushes while clumps of fur trail behind her like the breadcrumbs from a forgotten fairy tale. As I had hoped, we soon near the ledge. Like a trained dog, Beetroot jumps over it.

The Ashfalt lies before us in its magnificent wake. My suspicions were entirely correct. Newton's 4th law of motion: If left alone, a Shrieker will always find its way back home.

"I know you're here!" I shout into the dry air of the empty plains. I stride forward, kicking the black ash aside as I do so. "There's no need to hide!" I cautiously take a seat on the burned down land and stare out into the distance.

Beetroot lies next to me as I remain motionless for the next half hour.

A subtle breeze whisks traces of ash onto my face and hair. The burnt smell of death still has a tight hold on the Ashfalt. It won't allow anyone to forget what happened here.

Beginning to feel that I've wasted my time, I push myself off the ground to go back. Before I mount Beetroot, a subtle movement in the sand catches my attention. Like a sculpture being formed out of clay in front of my very eyes, a figure slowly emerges, heaps of ash falling from its body. Without hesitating, the girl walks closer, her skin black with soot. The skin around her abdomen pulls tight around her protruding ribcage and her jaw forms a white line where it meets the elevated cheekbones. Hypnotised, I watch as the girl creeps closer. She comes to a stop several feet before me. Ceasing all movement, she waits.

"Why did you give me the golden plate?" I finally ask.

She doesn't answer.

"We found a way to leave this place, but we won't be able to do it alone. I need your help."

She continues to stare at me, expressionless, like a wild animal trapped in a zoo enclosure. I'm starting to wonder if she can understand me at all.

"You don't have to live like this. We can go back to Earth. To your family."

She continues to hold eye contact, but then breaks it to look at my mark. Hers is covered in ash, just like the rest of her body. It's practically invisible except for the faint outlining. She finally takes her eyes off mine and turns around to walk away. I reach out to touch her, but Beetroot snarls and bares her teeth at me. A warning.

I begin to lose hope, but then the girl stops in her tracks. With the graceful posture of an acrobat, she arches her shoulders back and howls into the void. For a moment, the colourless plains remain still and untouched, as if merely another element in some art exhibition's painting. But then it comes to life.

In a wave of dust and obsidian, a hundred shaded figures rise from the ashes. Like phantoms emerging from an all but lifeless planet. No marks are visible, yet this absence seems to be the very thing that unites them. Indistinguishable from one another, they move forward as one, following me back to camp.

Germ was wrong about one thing, though. The Feral still speak. Just not in the language of man.

CHAPTER 43

I awaken in the cold dead of night, looking into Aiesha's emerald green eyes. This time she's not hovering over me, but beside me in bed, sharing the generous amount of warmth that the leathery hide provides. Her hair falls across her face in silky black streaks, grazing my shoulder with a reassuring touch. I shift my weight on the hammock and allow her agile body to mould into mine. Together, we gaze up at the unknown cosmos, listening to the unfamiliar sounds that toil away outside.

Accommodating the Feral at camp was somewhat of an adjustment. They refused to sleep in the Lodge—in fact, they refused to sleep at all—and lay on the ground beside the campfire for the remainder of the afternoon, suspiciously eyeing the Marks as they walked past.

Strangely enough, the Feral seemed to know their way around our camp. Before I could introduce the group to any of the other Marks, some had already wandered off to the river for a swig of water. When they returned, patches of sooty ash that previously covered the lower halves of their faces had washed away. Upon closer inspection, we noticed that many of them had scaly, red rashes spreading from the corners of their mouths, all the way down to the bottom of their chins.

Malnutrition, Aiesha had said. Whatever they were eating down at the Ashfalt might have been enough to keep them alive, but it has not been sufficient to prevent a serious vitamin deficiency. We could only assume that the rest of their bodies bore similar bumps and malformations, because they were quick to cover up any bare skin with more soot that they scraped from the fireplace. The muddy masks that are indistinguishable from one another are used as tools to hide their identities. This practice is in sharp contrast to that of our own Marks. Our Elementals used markings to divide themselves into different hierarchy statuses. The Feral used them to abandon theirs entirely.

In bed, I turn to face Aiesha. She seems embarrassed at first but relaxes when she notices my reassuring gaze.

"It's unusually cold tonight," she says as an excuse for climbing in bed with me.

"Not anymore," I flash her a warm smile.

"I thought you wouldn't mind the company."

"I don't."

We spend the last couple of moments in each other's embrace. She twirls tangled bits of hair behind my ear, while I track her quickening heartbeat and the warm, damp breaths against the skin of my neck. I close my eyes and prepare myself for the journey that awaits us. If I could, I'd capture this fleeting moment of happiness and bask within it for the rest of eternity. I'd like to believe that if given the choice, she would too. If only it were that simple.

"Are you awake?" Aiesha rocks the hammock, causing it to sway from side to side.

"Yes," I answer unwillingly.

"Then it's time to go." She tears herself from my grasp, pulling the Rodback hide with her. An airy breeze rolls into the Lodge.

"I know."

As I trudge along the rows of beds, I make sure to wake every Mark that I pass. Among the anxious bodies, several unwilling moans accompany my prod as I pass them, but they comply nevertheless and follow me down the dark aisle. The Feral await us outside. I acknowledge their presence and head for the fire with the intention of extinguishing it, but then decide against it.

We now know that we are not the only Marks to have walked the surface of Damnatus. More will follow long after we have gone. For all we know, a new drop might arrive before the suns rise in the morning. At least the light could lead the child to safety and shelter. Perhaps he or she might even choose to keep the fire alive, allowing many more Marks to follow its beacon. Instead of smothering the flames, I walk to the edge of the forest and carefully select an armful of the finest branches in sight. Dragging the heavy bundle towards the hearth, I feed the wood to the growing flames. Satisfied with the progress, I finally turn around and head into the desert, the different ranks of Marks following behind me.

Barren terrain stretches out as far as the eye can see. We are about to cross an ocean of sand, and our hope is not to be pulled into its yawning depths. Uncomfortably aware of

the passing time, we slowly walk past the withered plantation and into the cold night.

The first barrier between the camp and the unknown
are the Elementals, who form a systematic, protective arc.
Following close behind are the Neuros and the Feral in a
closely quartered group. The Apex make up the final line
of defence, each person bearing a weapon and armed with
protective gear. Leading in front at the very centre, Beetroot
and I tread alongside each other. Still unconscious, Sky
hangs limply on the creature's back and needs to be read-
justed every few minutes to prevent her from falling off.

I peer over to Aiesha. Just like the other Elementals, she
concentrates on the sand beneath her. She looks nervous;
unsure of our decision. This motivates me to walk faster.
Running is not an option, as we don't know how deep the
vibrations will penetrate the earth, nor how deep the worms
are resting.

After a few hours of walking, we have not yet felt any
movements from beneath. Unfortunately, we haven't seen
any fruitful land either. The desert seems to grow larger the
farther we travel into its depths. If the suns come out and
shed their light upon the sand, heating its surface, we might
meet the same atrocious death Matthew had the unlikely
fortune of incurring.

The sky starts to emit a dusky glow. The night has almost
passed when one of the Elementals alerts the group to stop.
I make my way towards the edge of their arc, and bend
down to see what the Green Mark is referring to. A small
sprout of tender shrubbery sticks through the sand. "There

will be more of these," he says. I thank him and head back to the centre as I urge the group to move again. I tell Aiesha about the shrub so she can explain its significance.

"It means we're heading towards water," she says enthusiastically.

I want to believe this but force myself to remain sceptical. "How can we be sure?"

"If we're heading towards water, there will be a lot more shrubs to follow."

And so they do. Every few minutes an excited shout indicates that another person in the front line has stumbled upon some shrubbery. The white sand becomes scarce, instead changing to a darker, browner soil. This suggests that the ground has become too thick to slither through from beneath, but I urge the group to keep their steady pace and not slow down. We can't be sure of anything out here.

A strange scent replaces the stark desert air. The flora grows tall and more unwieldy as the light encompasses the shadowy horizon. Germ's rapid breathing catches up to me. "Hey Johnny, how are things looking?" Morning light flickers off the beads of sweat running down his forehead.

"We're making progress," I assure him.

"Great," he manages to say between pants, then hesitantly adds, "Rusty and I were wondering if we could stop for a few minutes."

"It's not safe yet," I say. "We need to go farther."

"That's the thing. We're not like the Apex and Elementals. We *really* need a break."

316

I look back at the Feral, who are clearly struggling to keep up. We can't stop now, or we'll place the whole group in danger. The suns are already encircling the sky above, shining down and heating the planet's soil beneath us. In addition to worrying about what lies below, I repetitively turn my gaze to the skies above. Out here in the open we can easily be picked off by Pteras, unless my plan works. The Apex travelled to the Dengar terrain and laced the borders of forest with more meat than the Pteras can even hope to consume in a day. Hopefully they only attack to hunt, and not for pleasure. If so, there will be no need to follow us.

A whizzing sound comes clear up ahead. It sends a jump in my step. "Do you hear that?" I ask Germ with a hint of excitement.

"I can't hear anything at this point. I'm probably going to collapse now," he laughs nervously.

"I hear it too," Aiesha says.

We finish hiking the uphill stretch of land and utter joyous cries of relief. Before us, a stupendous lake stretches across the desert. I look left and right. No ends are visible on either side, but it is possible to see where the water meets land on the opposite shore.

I finally stop the group to rest and send two Elementals to scout the edges of the lake, one in each direction. The rest of us sit down and make way for the Apex, who finally trample along, carrying two roasted Rodbacks on their shoulders.

"Where is the rest of the meat?" Aiesha asks.

"It's all part of the plan," I smile at her. "We constructed three piles of flesh and spread it out across the edge of the

Dengar. The goal is to keep the Pteras occupied and spare us some time."

"Will it work?"

"Have you seen a Ptera?" I wink at her.

It takes some time for the two Elementals to return. "We have surveyed both directions of the lake and couldn't find an end," Skeith says.

"How long do you suspect it would take to walk around then?"

"I'd say at least a couple of days, give or take."

I frown. "We don't have a couple of days."

If Sky was telling the truth, then catching up with the other group is our only chance off this planet. Even if we had time to spare, our food wouldn't last that long.

"What are you saying?" Skeith asks.

"We're going to have to cross the lake."

At first, they doubtfully exchange glances at each other, but after grasping the seriousness of my proposal, they seem to consider it more carefully.

"It's not impossible," Skeith says.

The other Elemental scans the waters, then converts his attention to the masses of children. He crinkles his nose indecisively and adds, "We won't be able to take any food across."

I make up my mind. "If the other group came this way, then their food would not have lasted either. This is the only way."

"We're going to risk everyone's lives on the words of a traitor?" Skeith says angrily.

"Every day we stay on this planet is a day too long. We aren't risking our lives; we're trying to save them."

I look at Aiesha, who is standing by my side. "Tell everyone to eat as much as they can. Afterwards, we're crossing the lake."

I walk over to Sky, who has begun to shift around, but has not yet woken up. Someone is going to have to carry her across. I would have asked Kyle to do it, but he's hardly able to carry his own weight, much less someone else's. It will have to be a member of the Apex. Someone who wants to prove something and doesn't mind risking his life to do it. Erik.

As everyone rips into their food, I wander a bit farther down the hill. I can hardly remember what isolation feels like. Leaning on some flattened foliage, I peer out over the blue lake, surveying its vastness. A gentle breeze tugs at the water's edges, pushing it onto the grey shore. The lake distorts my reflection, making me seem much taller and more grown up than I remember being. The texture of my skin is rough and dark, having been kissed by the suns' unforgiving touch. I lightly graze my fingers over the curve of my upper lip, where black stubble has begun to sprout. My blue eyes are still the same, but the stare is different. There's something in it that was not there before.

"Hey Johnny." Germ takes a seat next to me and hands me a piece of Rodback. He chews into his then says, "I didn't want to correct you in front of everyone, but you're not supposed to swim directly after eating a meal."

I look at Germ incredulously and am suddenly reminded of the first day he showed me around camp, right after offering me some Rodback. I smile and give him a friendly pat on the back.

"You're not supposed to abduct children and leave them on a prehistoric, monster-infested planet either, but here we are."

CHAPTER 44

*T*he open road stretches ahead into the horizon. The radio drones in the background, filling the empty silence. Music starts to play. More Than a Feeling, *by Boston.*

"My song!" the girl in the passenger seat leans forward and turns the volume knob all the way up. Music bursts out of the car and onto the empty plains.

The young driver turns to look at her, and she at him.

"Eyes on the road," she says in a tense tone.

He smirks and continues to stare at her, teasingly. He lifts his right hand from the steering wheel, followed by the left, and uses them to blow an invisible kiss through the air.

"Kyle, stop it, we're going to crash!"

He leans forward and gives her a quick peck on the cheek, then turns his eyes back to the road.

She looks at him from the side, and frowns at the red mark on his upper arm. "I still can't believe you got a tattoo without telling me first." She turns to the road again and crosses her arms.

"I've told you a million times, I have no idea how it got there."

"You're lying," she dismisses him.

"No, I'm serious. I just woke up with it."

She continues to frown and turns even farther to the side, now looking out of the window.

"Babe, I'm telling the truth. Why would I even get a tattoo like this? It looks like hieroglyphs scribbled in red ink, for fuck's sake!"

She dismisses him and hums along to the song.

The car steadily drifts over into the other lane. She ignores it at first, unwilling to give him more attention—but then a large vehicle becomes visible in the distance.

A delivery truck.

"Stop it, it's not funny anymore!" she screams.

His face, now beaded with sweat, turns a dark shade of red. "It's not me! I'm not doing this!"

Kyle tries to force the wheel to the left, but it doesn't budge. Panicking, he repeatedly steps down on the brake pedal, but the car only gains more momentum. The truck's speed remains unchanged. A thunderous honk echoes their way, drowning out the radio.

Kyle looks at her, helplessness tainting his tears. With nothing to do but wait for an unjust fate, they embrace each other tightly. The impact is brutal, shattering every window and sending the car swerving across the road. Black smoke escapes the wreckage and stains the skies above.

Disorientated, yet alive, a middle-aged, leathery driver runs across the road. He peers into the passenger seat window and sees the mangled body of a teenage girl. Bewildered, he leans into the vehicle and attempts to obtain a better view of the driver's side. The seat behind the wheel is empty, its seatbelt still plugged in.

The radio fades out, its final notes carrying a dying melody into the unknown.

CHAPTER 45

Except for the splashes of water against skin, Kyle's nervous humming is the only sound that echoes across the still lake. The smell of rotting moss floats on the surface like a wandering spirit unable to find its final resting place. I carefully wade into the clear, iridescent chasm. My heart beats slower as the initial shock of the ice-cold water kicks in. I turn around to meet Beetroot's gaze. She shifts uncomfortably around on the shore, uncertain what to do.

"Come, Beetroot!" I scream at her.

She releases a howl that trails more on the edge of a wail. She seems scared of the water. I suddenly realise that she might not know how to swim. This thought unsettles me.

"Jump, girl!"

This time, a clear tone of desperation taints my voice. She instinctively picks up on this and in response, produces a high-pitched shriek; one that can only be recognised as the trademark of a Shrieker. For a brief moment everyone stops to turn around and look at the troubled beast. With the situation remaining stagnant, they quickly move on and continue to swim. Having no other option, I slowly follow their lead and begin to paddle away. Beetroot releases a final whimper in protest, then darts forward and leaps into the water.

To my surprise, she swims reasonably well and is able to keep her head above water as she follows behind us. Satisfied with her progress, I turn around and concentrate on propelling myself forward with constant thrusts. Within moments, the lake's muddy bottom disappears, dropping down deeper into murky darkness.

I notice that far below some patches are much darker than others. Instinctively, I try to avoid these spots and adjust my route accordingly. This becomes more difficult as the journey progresses, as they seem to be increasing. As we steadily near the centre of the lake, these patches move and morph together to form a larger area that cannot be bypassed. With no other choice, we swim over it. The water drastically drops in temperature as we swim above the shadowy depths. My heart beats in my chest like a frightened child banging against a hollow cupboard. Judging by its size, I'd guess that a massive crater is beneath us, stretching down all the way into the planet's crust.

I look over my shoulder and spot Kyle, clearly struggling to keep up with the rest of the group. I can visibly make out his abrupt kicking movements as he tries to compensate for his injured arm. His shoulder hasn't healed entirely, forcing him to fight twice as hard to keep afloat.

Having reached the midway point, I call to the group and urge them to wait. Most seem happy to oblige. Their tired breaths bounce off the water's surface and dissolve into the misty atmosphere. Beetroot doesn't obey my command, and paddles onward towards dry land.

An eerie silence ensues, accompanied by the peaceful water lapping along the far edges of the lake. I mindlessly stare into the darkness beneath, wondering how deep it goes. Water that was dark blue a few minutes ago now looks like black ink. I look around at all the wet faces, most gripped with unease. Satisfied with the length of our break, I turn back to our goal and ready myself to give the "okay" signal, but something stops me from doing it.

I'm almost certain that an object brushed up against me. I try to dismiss it as underwater foliage, but just as I start to move again, I hear a faint splash behind me. This time I'm sure it happened. I quickly turn around and thoroughly scan the waters. Then a shiver shoots through my spine.

Kyle's gone.

I struggle to gather breath as my body freezes in place. Something hard bumps against my leg, and air shoots into my lungs.

"Get out of the water!" the words escape my mouth as a terrified yell. The group immediately starts to surge forward, but not fast enough. A sharp, high-pitched scream emanates from somewhere at the front, but is quickly silenced as the girl disappears under the water. Panic rips through the waters like a wave.

Kicking rapidly and without coordination, I propel myself through the dense waters, occasionally surfacing to gasp for air. My throat burns as I swallow mouthfuls of sour liquid and have to force back a choke. All around me creatures move like stray currents, dragging children down.

Something big strikes my upper body. I respond frantically by hitting it repeatedly until it sinks down into the shadows.

This altercation happens numerous times until I finally find myself scrambling to my feet, realising that I've reached the shore. I crawl to safety, only to turn around and watch helplessly as the remaining few struggle to land. Flinching involuntarily every time someone gets pulled into the deep, the body of water soon becomes no more than a spectral grave. With the last few climbing out, I notice a misshapen bundle moving towards us.

Erik is desperately trying to catch up but is dragged down by Sky's weight. Still too far to be helped out of the water, we sit in silent fear, watching tensely. For a brief moment, it seems like he is letting go of her body in order to save himself—but then a swift tug from below reveals otherwise. Sky vanishes beneath the surface.

Ragged and torn, I look out over the waters, unable to process the scene that is playing out before me. This is my fault. My legs cramp up and my breathing intensifies.

No. She is not dead.

Whether my face is wet because of the water, the tears, or both, I wipe it off and haul myself up.

Not yet.

A familiar hand grabs onto mine from behind, but I break loose from its grasp and launch myself into the lake.

Blinded by darkness, I swim downwards in the direction that Sky sank. I manage to grab onto her and drag upwards. To my horror, she isn't sinking, but is being pulled. I suddenly remember the metal blade that is strapped to my leg.

I pull it out of my shoe's heel and repeatedly jab it into the darkness. Sky's body suddenly becomes lighter.

Unwilling to let go of the knife, I use my free arm to alter our direction and swim upwards. Just as the remainder of my breath depletes, we emerge above the surface. Many Marks wait at the edge and grab onto Sky as I push her cold body ashore.

Some gather closer to help me out as well, but before any of them has managed to secure a proper grip around my forearm, a sharp pain shoots through my leg and I'm yanked back under. The distressed faces above become blurry and malformed. As the light fades, I pull at the murky claws that are wedged in my leg. I manage to remove some of them from my flesh but grit my teeth together when they re-enter my leg even deeper than before.

Needle-like daggers force their way under my skin and clutch onto my leg from within. I kick away from the creature, but they stay firmly attached.

As my body sinks deeper, a sort of peacefulness begins to overpower my fears. I finally let go of the creature's claws, and my arms go limp. The air leaves my lungs and is quickly replaced by water.

CHAPTER 46

My sight is blurry. The first thing that penetrates my vision is the slanted figure hovering over me. I'm not breathing willingly, yet periodically, warm air flows into my lungs. I quickly become aware of a growing pressure in my chest. A surge of vomit erupts from my stomach and my body contracts, forcing the black water out of my throat.

The figure becomes visible within the suns' glaring rays. She moves out of the way, allowing me some space to breathe. Aiesha watches me with attentive eyes. She brought me back.

"I thought we lost you," she says with a sigh of relief.

As my breathing settles and my eyes begin to focus, I roll onto my side and scan the faces surrounding me. Less than half of the group remains. I stare at the lake in denial, scanning the surface for any signs of life. "Where is everyone?"

"They didn't make it," Aiesha says.

A few metres away, Skeith's loud panting pulls my attention to him. He lies on his back, his chest heaving. His shirt is ripped away and a dark stream of blood stains his abdomen.

"He went after you," Aiesha says. "You were gone so long—" her voice trails off, but she pulls herself together. "We thought you both drowned."

"He saved me?" I ask. Skeith never seemed to like me before.

"Elementals are excellent judges of character. Although he doesn't show it, he must have seen something in you."

I bend over and bury my head in my arms. "We shouldn't have crossed the lake. We should have walked around," I mutter.

"Don't be so hard on yourself," she says in comfort. "If we walked around, we could have starved and even more would have died."

"If we hadn't come, nobody would have died."

"No, John." Aiesha forces me to sit up straight and look her in the eyes. "Eventually, we all would have perished."

She helps me to my feet and leads me through the crowd. Most of the casualties were Feral. They were too weak and malnourished to make it across. Those who survived have already covered their bodies in dust and sand, unwilling to display their marks publicly. I'm pleased to spot Germ and Rusty beside each other, both safe and unharmed.

I walk back to Skeith and offer him an extended hand. "Will you be able to walk?" I ask with concern.

"Yes," he says between laboured breaths.

"Are you sure? Beetroot can carry you."

"I'm fine," he insists.

I glance around at the tired bodies but can't seem to distinguish Sky from the crowd.

"I'm back," a familiar voice pushes past me and kneels next to Skeith. "I wasn't able to get my hands on much, but this should be enough to do the trick." Skylor tears a plant's stem in half and pushes out the yellow liquid. It seems to provide some relief for Skeith. "We'll just have to stick a few leaves on to protect the exposed parts for now."

I look down at my bleeding leg, but it doesn't seem as important as Skeith's injury. Before I'm able to ask any questions, Sky turns around and faces me. "I woke up wet with a mouth full of lake water," she says. "But at least I woke up."

She bends forward and takes my hand. "Thanks, John. I owe you an apology."

"No need. Find Rusty and wish her a happy birthday. She'll appreciate it more coming from you."

The idea brings a smile to her face.

"I'm going to survey the area," I inform the others.

"I'll come with," Aiesha offers.

We leave the group to regain their strength and wander off into the hills of ferns and rocks. The creatures here are meek and scarce. They scuffle away when approached, and burrow deep into the ground. I pull out the device from my pocket and inspect the blinking lights. It hasn't stopped since we crossed the lake. We're getting close.

"How do you think it will look?"

"The dome?" Aiesha asks.

"Yes," I say.

"Well, if I had to guess, we'd be looking for a hatch that leads inside."

"Or maybe we need to be searching for a portal. Who knows, we might even be beamed back to Earth today."

She looks at me with a grin, but she isn't sure if I'm joking. I laugh. If only it was that easy.

"I wonder if we'll find out what my mark means," I think aloud.

"It's really bothering you, isn't it?" she asks.

"Yeah," I sigh.

I've never really cared much about other people's opinions, but somehow, this is different. Whether I like it or not, this mark is a part of me. It has influenced my actions and decisions more than I would like to admit. Deep down, I know that once its meaning is revealed, it will expose a part of me that I haven't been able to access before. My true self.

We turn a corner that leads to an open meadow. In the centre, a giant dome expands into the sky. Light bends around it and bounces off in silver rays. All this time, the exit has been right here.

Stupefied, I sit down between the flowering vegetation and take my time to absorb the image.

Aiesha lowers herself next to me. "You know, John," she begins. "Each mark has distinct, detectable traits. When faced with problems, Apex engage directly. Neuros analyse, then interact. We Elementals observe from a distance. We watch our prey carefully and study its patterns and behaviour. By doing this, I know what it is going to do before it knows it. I am in control." She seems troubled. "Even the plants here have distinct personalities... but not you, John. You have remained stoic, which infuriates me, because that makes you unpredictable. Even if you wanted to, you wouldn't possibly be able to fit into any other category, because you aren't prone to latch onto a specific, predisposed way of thinking. They always fall back on their ways, and it makes them predictable. It makes them weak." She takes her eyes off the dome and turns her gaze to me. "Maybe that is what your mark means. Nothing. It doesn't mean anything. It's simply void of colour." She studies me, still trying to read my thoughts. "See, even now I can't tell what you're thinking."

I'm thinking about the way the rays of light play around her untainted skin, and how her breath always smells like wild mint and berries. I'm looking at the way her dark, wet hair falls across her shoulders, the dampness still clinging to the fabric of her shirt, accentuating her engraved scars. Her bright green eyes are always moving, searching for clues that will unmask the concealed secrets within mine. Most importantly, I'm admiring the fact that she never complains about her duties or acts like a victim, even though she has every reason to be upset at her fate. It is she who decided to take on the duty of provider and pioneer on this distant, faraway planet. Then again, the unknown was all but unfamiliar in her world.

I lean closer, meeting her lips in a kiss.

She doesn't pull away.

CHAPTER 47

The group approaches the dome with similar confounded reactions. It's almost too good to be true. We slowly move towards the suspicious structure but remain on the lookout for Azon and his followers.

The building stands out in the middle of nowhere. I scan the fields for any signs of life but come up empty. A pang of fear slowly begins to encroach on my thoughts. What if the other Marks already went through? I would have failed everyone here.

I begin to work through all the possible scenarios in my head. Without Talaya, we can't enter the dome. Our only option would then be to travel back to camp in hope that another White might someday be dropped in the Clearing. I wince at the thought.

Standing beside me, Aiesha looks at me with empathy. "It's possible that they haven't arrived yet," she suggests. "They might have travelled around the lake instead of through it."

I look at her doubtfully. They knew we would follow them and would subsequently have come here by the quickest means available.

Skylor interjects. "John, maybe we should search for the entrance."

"I thought you said we only get one chance to enter?"

"Yes," she nods her head in agreement. "That is what Azon said, but we should check for ourselves."

I agree, and so we begin to circle the large dome-like structure. I pick up a chipped piece of stone and use it to scrape the wall's surface as we travel around it. The dome's foreign texture chisels away at the rock until nothing is left to hold. I hoped to track our progress, but not so much as a dent is left in the gleaming material.

It doesn't take long before we spot it—a door, simply standing there in the side of the dome. Almost mockingly. We call the group together before approaching it. It doesn't appear to be a regular door. The rectangular outline in the metal surface suggests that it might be able to slide open. An image of a hand is indented into the metal, like an impression left in wet cement. The tip of each finger is topped with a glassy stone of a different, crystalline colour. Red, Green, Blue, White and Pink. The palm of the hand is covered with an impenetrable black, the only colour that does not allow light to travel through it.

I hesitate, then lean forward and press my hand against the door. It slides a few centimetres into the hand-shaped impression and stops only once my wrist is firmly lodged within the metal. The glassy globes feel cold against the tip of my fingers.

"A negative hand," Germ whispers in awe.

Below it is a small protruding black box that rests barely a metre above the ground. It's so low that even a toddler could reach it.

Sky inspects the device. "A biometric scanner. I thought as much," she declares, tilting her head to the side to examine it from a different angle. She takes a calculated step closer and pushes her hand against its surface. When nothing happens, Sky hesitantly pulls back.

"I think you're supposed to use your mark," Germ suggests. She considers this for a moment, then manoeuvres herself into a squatting position. With a shaky motion, she cautiously presses her blue mark against its dark, flat surface.

To everyone's surprise, a line of parallel red lights beam out of the scanner and playfully skim the skin on her arm. After covering every intrinsic detail of the sapphire symbol, the beams retract. We wait in suspense, but nothing happens. The door remains shut.

"John," a deeper, more urgent voice drones behind me. I turn around to face a disheartened Skeith, who directs my gaze to the top of a hill roughly fifty metres away. I'm torn, as feelings of fear and hope accumulate inside of me.

Azon and his group are standing on an elevated strip of land, looking down on us from across the distance. They seem to have been waiting in silence, only now choosing to make their presence known. My stare drifts across the menacing faces in the other group, stopping only when I land on what I'm looking for.

They've got Talaya.

CHAPTER 48

"Where are the rest of them?" Sky says, alert.

Aiesha focuses on the group, roughly scanning them. "I don't think there are any others," she answers. "Look, some of them are injured."

She's right. The individuals who remain appear haggard and grim. They've lost a lot of people.

"They went through the lake too," I conclude.

In their rush, they must have made the same fatal mistake we did. Yet, for some reason, they haven't gone through the exit yet.

Sky answers the question on everyone's mind. "They don't have any Neuros left. They can't leave."

She's right. None of Azon's Neuros made it across the lake. The kind, Blue girl from the hall is missing. In her place stands Jester, his hands tied with a pink scarf. The rest of his body is now properly clothed to protect his skin from the suns' harmful rays and other elements. I shift my focus to Talaya, who is anxiously peering back at us. She doesn't seem to be hurt and stands alone in front of the group of strangers. Holding on to her is the same person I saw back at the foreign camp. The Black Mark.

Azon's arms are crossed like that of a parent who is about to tell off a child.

"Good morning, John! I see you've met my wife."

I frown and turn around to look at my group. The Feral girl steps forward and joins my side, her body still covered with dirt. She gazes at Azon with a fiery hatred that cannot be quenched.

"Hello, dear Claudia. The mud suits you!"

My eyes widen. I reach out and slowly wipe the mud from her arm. I pull away when the jet-black mark appears. All this time, there's been another Black Mark in our group, and we didn't even know. She didn't want us to.

"Listen carefully! This is what's going to happen," Azon shouts across the empty plain. "You're going to give us one of your Blues, and little Speechless here won't get hurt." He lifts Talaya up by the shoulders for all of us to see.

"It doesn't have to be like this!" I shout back at him. "We can all go in. Nobody has to die!"

He laughs cynically. "You're naïve, John. That's the reason every single one of you will die." Regal in posture, Azon pinches his index finger and thumb together and brings it to his mouth before letting out a long whistle. For a moment nothing happens, yet the opposing group glances around nervously. A Shrieker's cry fills the air—but it doesn't come from Beetroot.

Beetroot's reaction is similar to mine, but instead of retreating, she takes several uneasy steps forward and begins to growl. I attempt to pull myself onto her back, but she shrugs me off. The group begins to panic. Beetroot hunches over me and wraps me inside of her protective brace. She stands firm as a statue, shielding me from view. I tug onto her mane and attempt to pull myself out of her hold, but she refuses to release me. Alert, the Feral girl steps forward, her body still covered with dirt. With a single shout, she commands the other ashen figures to congregate behind Beetroot. They obey, like a trained army ready for war.

Following her lead, Erik takes charge of the Apex, steering them into a line behind the Feral. They raise their weapons and release a battle cry that stretches across the plain and reaches the other group who, except for Azon, are standing around uncertainly. Aiesha nods at Skeith, who signals orders to the other Elementals. Like a pride of lions, they creep closer to the other Marks, and raise their spears. Skylor grabs Rusty's arm and pulls her away from the group. Together, the two Neuros back towards the unopened door. Germ quickly joins them; his panicked breathing audible all the way from the front line.

Azon whistles a second time and moves aside as the ferocious beast breaks away from the crowd. Another Shrieker is heading straight for us, his fur changing colour from one second to the next. One moment, it's a dusty yellow that seems to melt into the sand beneath it, and the next instant it matches a muddy, grey-stained boulder that has broken loose from the hill and is rolling towards us. If you looked from afar, the creature might have been indistinguishable from a rampant sandstorm.

With a sudden jerk, Beetroot turns yellow like the sand beneath us and instinctively charges ahead, leaving me behind. Both Shriekers increase their speed until their morphing coats become no more than a blur. In a spectacular display of claws and teeth, they ferociously clash on the battlefield. The army of Marks behind me lower their weapons momentarily. Sky pushes her way through them and addresses me.

"John, they might not be distracted for long. We need to get Talaya."

A quick glimpse of Sky's expression tells me everything I need to know. Beetroot is smaller than the other Shrieker. Chances are she only has a few minutes to keep him off before he overwhelms her. After that, he'll target us, picking everyone off one by one, without anything to stand in his way.

The Feral leader approaches me for orders.

"Claudia," I say, watching as her eyes betray the slightest flash of humanity. "That little girl has a white mark. We need her alive at all costs."

The Feral girl surveys Azon's group and nods at my directions.

"Don't come back without Talaya," I order the rest of the Marks. With that being said, the Feral charge into battle. The Apex and Elementals raise their weapons and follow directly behind them.

Skylor readies herself for battle, tying her hair into a tight ponytail. Rusty helps her to adjust the elastic hair band and gathers all of the remaining black knots into a braid. "John, guard the door. Don't let them take Talaya in there without the rest of us," she warns.

"You can't go," I protest. "You and Rusty are the only Neuros left."

"You still haven't learned to think like a Neuro," Skylor smiles weakly. "They won't kill us, because they need a Blue Mark to get through the exit as well."

"Then I'm staying behind with John," Aiesha quickly intervenes, not about to take no for an answer.

Sky looks at her, then at me.

"He'll need help fending off other Marks," Aiesha tells her.

"I want to stay, too," Germ chirps. "We only have one of me, right?"

Leaving no further time to waste, Sky nods decisively and takes Rusty's hand before storming off after the others.

The Shriekers' distressed cries echo across the field, setting the tone for the rest of the battle. Chaos ensues as the groups clash on the front. Marks begin to plunge to the ground, taking the first blows. Azon's fighters might be fewer than ours, but they certainly aren't weak. Their Apex are robust and resolute, and the Elementals are not far behind in terms of physical strength. Where they lack in power, they make up for it in carefully crafted weapons consisting of sharpened bones and rocks. Azon has prepared for war.

"John, you should try your mark," Germ suggests. For some reason the thought hadn't occurred to me. I slightly bend my knees and push my mark against the cold surface of the scanner. Just like Sky's first attempt, beams of light shoot out of the device and move across the black symbol. The electric current grows in strength until it suddenly stops and the beams retract. The door releases a groan and slides open.

"It worked!" Germ gawks into the passageway. Almost immediately after the first door opens, a second one is sealed shut. An identical scanner sits on the metal wall. I quickly walk forward and press my mark against the second device, but this time it doesn't work. "It's not opening!" I scream.

"What do you mean?" Aiesha shouts back from outside the dome, keeping her sight pinned on the fight in case anyone decides to target the exit. I furiously swipe my arm against the device but stop when I hear movement from behind me.

I turn around to see the first door sliding shut. It's going to trap me inside. I hurl myself out of the passage as the door seals closed behind me. This isn't working. Our time is running out quickly, and Beetroot is already injured. She uses the bigger Shrieker's weight against him, dodging most of his slower attacks. He struggles to grab hold of her, but finally manages to pin her to the ground, biting into one of her hind legs. Another howl erupts across the battlefield.

I open the first door again by holding my arm against the scanner; only this time, I keep it there. "Germ, try the second scanner!" He dutifully runs into the passage and holds his mark against the wall. We watch with amazement as it opens. A third door awaits us. With a sudden epiphany, I realise what is needed to get in. One of each Mark needs to be scanned. They are the keys.

I don't need to tell Aiesha what to do. She's already at the third entrance, watching as it opens. Before I can stop him, Germ joins her at the fourth door down the hallway. Even though his arm left the second scanner, the doors stay open.

This is very strange. For some reason, only I am required to stay at my door.

Germ and Aiesha hesitate when they arrive at the fourth door. Something appears to be covering the ground. I remember a similar scene near the Clearing. The remnants of the previous drops are scattered across the floor. These are the Marks Skylor was talking about; Azon's followers who never returned back to camp. This is how they died.

Aiesha shouts a warning from inside the passage, but it's too late, as a hard blow to the head knocks me to the ground. The doors immediately slam shut behind me, trapping both of them inside. One of Azon's Apex, bloody and bruised, hauls me up and pushes me against the scanner. He presses his face against mine, taking deep, rapid breaths. Glistening droplets of sweat cling to his brows. Instead of hitting me again, something unexpected happens.

"Please," he says. "Keep them open." He places me back on my feet and brushes the dust off my clothes. "Don't close the doors," he begs.

Confused, I turn around to witness a scene of horror. Darkness engulfs the battlefield as the sky turns black, swarming with predators. Shadows encircle us, growing larger with each passing second. They start out as abstract shapes, but quickly become more defined and distinct. The Pteras draw closer, their webbed talons poised in anticipation. Crooked beaks snap open and closed in a display of frantic bloodlust. With wings spread overhead, they glide down with ease.

A surge of panic rips through me. I dreaded this possibility so much that I even took precautions for it. The Apex laced the entire Dengar terrain with fresh meat from their hunts to keep the Pteras filled and distracted. Somehow, the Pteras managed to fly the entire distance in time. The commotion at the lake, along with all the bodies, must have led them to our location.

The first of the creatures arrives at the scene, flashing its teeth in a feverish grin. Unlike the beaks of earthly winged animals, the outline of its jaw is ribbed with a row of sharp, gnawing knobs. I shudder at the thought of what my crunching bones would sound like once lodged inside its inescapable hold. As the Marks begin to scream, the Pteras join in with mocking shouts that overpower their cries for help.

The flying creatures outnumber us two to one. At a moment's notice, everyone has simultaneously stopped fighting and began to run towards the dome. The first victim to fall prey to a sly attack from above is a Feral boy. At least three times his size, the creature grabs hold of the boy's arms and effortlessly lifts him off the ground. They ascend into the sky at a frightening speed and soar past the other Pteras, who are flocking down to the open plains. When the Ptera in question has reached an altitude of significant height, it stops its ascent.

I peer up at the sky, struggling to make out what's happening. The Ptera adjusts his grip on the boy, who seems to be desperately grabbing onto the bird's neck. For a moment they hover in place. Then, it releases its hold and drops the boy to his death.

He lands next to me, his bones shattering on impact. Blood seeps out of a cracked skull. Bulging red eyes stare up at me. The Ptera swoops down to feed on its kill, but the Red Mark reacts violently and jumps in front of me. Blocking me from harm's way, he bolts forward, lunging into the bird's extended legs.

Not reacting fast enough, the Ptera's disproportionate weight causes it to trip and topple over next to the Feral boy. Before the bird can regain its balance, the enraged Apex climbs on top of its leathery chest and sticks a dagger into its neck. The Ptera screeches and jerks its head to the side. The Apex knocks its beak to the ground, then drags the dagger all the way down to its chest, peeling open the bird's throat.

Covered in gore, the Apex turns to me once again. He peers over at the slain Feral boy and then at the door, as if to indicate a self-explanatory point. I nod. For a third time, I firmly place my arm against the scanner and watch as the door slides open. The Apex runs in and opens the second door without any prompting. He must have done it before. Germ and Aiesha suddenly appear behind it, but the boy leaves them unharmed. After a minimal exchange of words, Germ opens the third door and Aiesha the fourth, leading them to the fifth. This time, a large heap of decaying bodies blocks the entryway. A sickening sight.

I stare down the gloomy hallway, now twenty metres in length. It doesn't make sense. Even if Azon was missing a

Mark long ago, they could simply have turned around and gone back. The doors only close if the Black Mark lifts his arm… then it hits me. Azon must have feared that the other Marks would find a way to leave without him. He didn't want them to return to camp knowing the secrets of the exit or of its whereabouts.

Azon purposely closed the doors. He trapped them inside to die.

The Pteras have all flocked down to the plains below. They begin to pick off the weaker Marks, clutching on to their bodies with eager talons and raising them into the air, just as the dead one did with the Feral boy. Having no choice but to join forces, the Marks of both groups merge together to fend off the birds. In the distance, another Ptera slams against the ground before it's impaled by a spear.

The Marks desperately try to run for the exit, but other Pteras swiftly take the place of their fallen companions. As they pierce their talons into the children's defenceless bodies, I realise that we're not going to make it. Azon isn't going to be able to protect Talaya for much longer. Bodies are pulled into the sky towards the forming grey clouds. Marks fiercely punch and stab at the birds, but the sky is an environment that proves impossible to compete in. As another Ptera reaches the bulging clouds, it releases a terrified Mark and watches as the flailing body makes contact with the dense soil beneath. Before the others are able to reach the same height, something unexpected happens. A drop of liquid rolls down my temple and splashes onto the ground. It begins to rain.

The drizzle soon turns into a downpour, and buckets of water hit the steamy sand. The dust and dirt wash off the Feral, streams of tainted black liquid draining into the earth. The Feral boy at my feet slowly turns a pale white, and a green mark is revealed on his outstretched arm.

The Pteras drop from the sky, their wings heavy with rain. Those who are strong enough to withstand the pressure swerve to the ground and drop the Marks before flying away. Even the Pteras seem surprised at this unnatural weather, as thunderous lightning bolts frighten the creatures out of the sky.

The fallen Pteras are unable to take flight again, and trample around on their rigid legs, using their bent wings as crutches to manoeuvre forward. They slowly make their way across the field and attack the Shriekers. The bigger beast puts up a fight, but Beetroot remains motionless on the ground. The other Pteras peck away at the marked bodies who are not able to get up and run.

As the surviving Marks reach the dome, they bolt through the passage one by one. Frantically piling up at the end of it, they quickly begin to behave like cornered animals. Skylor is among the few who return, but Rusty isn't.

Skylor is the only Neuro to have survived.

The crowd lets her through, treating her like royalty. She scans her blue mark, and the door opens. For what feels like an eternity, the filled hallway waits in silence. Two camps of children, close enough to brush shoulders, bear a few fleeting seconds of peace. They push up against the sixth door. Sealed.

The last two Marks arrive at the exit. Azon moves slowly, limping and pulling Talaya behind him. He holds a knife to her throat. "Only one Black can enter," he says, coughing up blood.

"We can both go," I tell him.

He responds with a vehement laugh. "Are you daft? Each group only has one Black. Only a Black can open the dome. See what I'm getting at here? You're not going in." When I refuse to respond, he smirks even more aggressively. "I'll kill her, then none of us leaves this forsaken planet."

"Okay," I concede. "Just don't hurt her."

I carefully move to the side, tightly keeping my arm pinned against the wall. Moving it even slightly could result in the doors closing, trapping everyone inside. Azon pushes Talaya into the hallway and allows her to walk ahead on her own. He then turns to me and presses the knife to my neck. "Just to make sure," he whispers, twisting the knife into my skin. "You won't let it close on your friends, will you?" he says teasingly. "I can't kill you yet, but you'll bleed out eventual—"

Azon rips through the air as he is slung backwards and lashed into the dirt. Beetroot towers over him, pinning his body to the ground with strenuous force. Her fur is soaked in blood and her legs sway weakly beneath her weight. She makes eye contact with me and sees the dark stream of blood flowing down my neck. Although no words are exchanged through that glance, we both understand each other perfectly. Enraged, Beetroot shrieks into the air, then leans down and bites Azon in the neck.

He cries in terror. "I didn't ask to be here. I just want to go home!"

"You left innocent children behind these doors to die!" I shout back at him.

"I did it for the group," he pleads.

I peer down the hallway and look as Talaya lifts her white mark to open the final door. The others follow her, vanishing into the darkness. I turn back to Azon.

"They *were* the group!" I shout in anger, releasing my arm from the contraption and bolting down the hallway. The doors instantly begin to move, but at a slower pace than before. At the fifth door, I bump my shoulder, and at the sixth, I spiral to the ground. As the metal doors close behind me, they cut off all outside noise. Azon's muffled screams disappear.

CHAPTER 49

For several moments, I am trapped in complete darkness. Intricate mechanisms begin to click into place like the rusty gears of an old clock. The movements do not generate much noise, but the vibrations that go along with them pound against my head, threatening to knock me over. A white light flickers on, illuminating the rest of the empty hallway. There are no more doors, except for the opening at the end of the passage.

I carefully step inside, and a metal barrier closes behind me. Another light reveals a massive chamber. The energy seems to be emanating from the walls themselves. No other doors leave the room, resulting in a dead end. The other Marks aren't here. No traces indicate that they ever were.

"Congratulations, Black One," an automated voice echoes through the air. I swing around to find its source, but the voice is coming from all around me. "Many have tried to leave this world, yet most have failed the test."

"You've been testing us?" I ask in disbelief.

"No, John," the voice corrects me. "We've been testing *you*."

I hesitate. "Why me?" I shout at the bodiless voice. "What does my mark mean?"

The marks suddenly appear on a big projection. Characters flicker across the wall's concave surface in single lines, running down in a row.

"A generation of young specimens were selected from your planet based on the traits they displayed. Your assignment was to unify your group and lead them to salvation. You're a leader, John."

I stare at the wall and begin to read the words in awe.

Red signifies physical strength, offering protection for the journey.

Green signifies mastery of the elements. These individuals are able to study the land and its creatures and can provide navigation along the way.

Blue possesses intellectual prowess and can specialise in a variety of trades that prove useful to research.

Pink represents the bearer of knowledge. Often mistaken for intelligence, this individual provides information to those wise enough to listen.

White represents the ultimate test. These are the innocent. They offer no inherent value to the group, yet their survival determines its very future.

The groups who find their way to this place, but neglect to care for their most vulnerable members, will find themselves unable to enter.

A leader without compassion is not worth saving.

I stand in silence, my eyes still glued to the wall before me. The words remain unchanged, their unambiguous truths beaming out from the surface.

"If this was all some kind of test, then why didn't you tell us?" I grow angry. "You left us alone on this planet to suffer and fend for ourselves. We weren't given a purpose. Only pointless suffering. We could have reached this place much quicker, if we had known."

"Is it not clear to you by now?" the voice drones on. "In order to be tested, you cannot know the existence of a test at all. The Black One who came before you was destined to fail the test, yet he almost breached this building after acquiring hidden knowledge of its contents."

"What did their deaths achieve?" I demand to know.

"More than you can possibly fathom."

"But why was I tested? Please, just tell me."

"You come from a broken world, Child of Earth. This assessment was put in place to find a suitable leader for a new civilisation. One who does not fear power or disregard the weak. You will be the first of many to lead the habitation of a new world. Beyond this room, a new life awaits you, free of pain, corruption and suffering."

My thoughts begin to flutter around in circles as I consider the possibilities that are being laid out in front of me. A new world. A chance to start over and do things right the first time. With a snap of my fingers, I could authorise it. Growing excited at the idea of a society of my own creation, a lingering feeling begins to pull my mind in a different direction. I remember my mom and brother, and the millions of innocent people who are back on Earth.

"What about the people left on Earth? Are you just giving up on them?" I shout.

"We have no choice," the voice answers in vagueness.

"No, you can't!" I realise the true implications of this. "Please, give us another chance. We can make them change their ways. You said so yourself—I'm a leader. So let me go back and lead. Let me prove to you that there is still hope!"

There is silence. A door opens at the far side of the dome. A figure enters, and the door automatically shuts behind him. At first he looks unrecognisable, but as he slowly nears, the reality of it all sets in and tears start to burn my eyes.

"Dad?"

The old man doesn't respond with words, but rather with a smile. His hair has lost its colour, and now looks infused with burnt charcoal. As he moves forward, his gait is hindered by old age. Forgetting everything else, I run to him and embrace him. I remembered him to be very tall, but now I tower above his head.

"You finally found me," he smiles.

"You've been here all this time?" I ask in disbelief.

He nods gracefully. "John, come with me."

"Where?"

"To our new home."

I don't understand. None of this makes sense. All those years ago, he was merely abducted like me? My gaze hunts for any features that might seem off about him. He's wearing an old, black jacket—the same one I last saw him in. Various wrinkles embroider the pale skin atop his forehead and below his dark, vacant eyes. He looks unharmed.

"What about Mom and Carter?" I ask hesitantly.

"It's too late for them," he replies with a comfortable ease that chills me. "We can create a new home," he continues. "A better one."

I look into his eyes. The same blue marbles I grew up looking into.

"You want me to leave them behind?" I take a step back, still analysing him carefully. "Like you left us?"

"They'll understand, John. It's for the greater good."

I begin to grow distant from the man standing before me. I might recognise my father, but I certainly don't know him. Not anymore, at least. I take another uneasy step back.

"Whose greater good?" I ask him. "Surely not theirs, or any other person back on Earth."

I suddenly wonder if he has a mark. What colour would it be? If he is inside the exit, then it means he had to complete the tasks as well. Somehow, he managed to survive for four long years on this remorseless planet.

"I'm going back." I make up my mind.

"Are you sure, John?" His expression remains unchanged.

"I've never been more sure of anything in my life."

He solemnly stares at me, not blinking or breathing. I'm not waiting for his approval—I don't need it anymore—but some kind of reaction would be suitable. Strange noises begin to escape his pursed lips. He shivers like someone who has just returned from an excavation in the Arctic. Soon he's shaking uncontrollably. It's as if he were previously attached to some kind of operating switch, and someone just pressed the 'off' button.

In a fit, he collapses to the ground. Convulsions rip through his body until his movements cease entirely. A final pall of grey smoke escapes his mouth and evaporates. Slowly creeping forward, I stare into the expressionless eyes that have now grown entirely black.

I bend down next to the cold mass, carefully pulling up the sleeve of his jacket until his entire right arm is visible. He doesn't have a mark.

"Was that another one of your tests?" I confront the voice, growing livid. "This isn't my father. What have you done to him?"

All is silent again, until the automated voice whirs back to life.

"Are you certain of this choice?" it asks.

"Yes," I answer firmly.

"You would choose death over life?"

"I'm not worthy of life if I leave them behind to die."

"It's been decided," it declares with sudden authority and a formidable tone of decisiveness that was absent before. "You will be given a final chance at reversing the effects of those who came before you. Time is limited to save your world from the ignorance of its inhabitants. Be warned, John. Bring this message to the world. Mankind will soon be plunged into an age of darkness, for the Sun will turn black and your moon will disappear behind the smoke of warfare and destruction. Earthquakes will move every mountain and island, and stars will appear to fall from the sky. Famine and plague will riddle the bodies of your children, causing them to cry out in pain. Your oceans and rivers will run red with the blood of man and beast alike."

The voice pauses then utters a final warning.

"We will come with the clouds."

CHAPTER 50

Many thoughts scramble through my mind whilst I exit the chamber. How will I be able to lead humanity out of the dying state it is in? Will knowing what I know now give me some sort of advantage? Most importantly, if my help was urgently needed to populate a new planet, why were they so easily persuaded to allow me to return to Earth? It's like that was their plan from the very beginning. To send me back.

I slowly walk on into a different hall. This one looks like the assembly room back at my school, only much bigger and filled with rows of yellow holograms instead of plastic chairs. Thousands of them are stacked behind each other in compact rows. Together, they emit a luminous glow that grows in strength as I near.

The apparitions move in place while vitals and other holographic ciphers flash beside them. Their marks are on the same projection, positioned in the middle. My pace quickens as the distressed faces flash by. Holograms of boys and girls run alongside each other, their heartbeats rampant and irregular. In every tenth row, an isolated Black becomes visible amongst the other Marks. They are far and few between. White toddlers who are barely able to walk, and likely much younger than Talaya, appear even more sparsely. Very rarely, a hologram will suddenly go dark, then simply disappear completely. In a matter of seconds, the area will shimmer with a static charge before a new face takes its place. I feel a strange connection to these children. A sense of obligation and duty. Even though it would be impossible to return, the urge to go back to the treacherous outside world progressively intensifies.

I don't want to leave them behind.

I try to force my gaze away from the dull-eyed, staring phantoms, but stop moving when one in particular grabs my attention. I walk over to the lonely figure and come to a halt before it. Slowly, I stretch out my arm and wave my hand. Then, I raise my other arm above my head and move it through the air as well. The life-size hologram waves back.

It's me.

No. I refuse to believe it. These holograms can't possibly be all of the children who are still left.

A golden ECG monitors the activity of my heart, tracing it in a crooked line that curves at every rise and fall. With each beat, an electrical pulse shoots through my chest and travels to my mark, which in return flickers with the resonating energy coursing through my veins. Beneath it, a display of various statistics and numbers flash perplexingly. The only figures I recognise are my blood's oxygen levels steadily increasing, as well as my body's temperature slowly dropping.

Mesmerised, my eyes remain on the other, alien digits. A flickering number sits in a separate section above all the rest.

22

The other holograms don't show a number at all. I stray away from my astral reflection and continue to wander between the static children until I stumble upon another Black Mark. She too has a number displayed above her head.

43

I stare at her vitals, trying to determine the correlation between them and the number. Unlike mine, her heartbeat is extremely fast and her oxygen concentration very low. She isn't standing still, either. Her hologram is running in place from something only she has the misfortune of seeing. She sways to the side and leaps through the air like someone pursued by a pack of wild dogs. Suddenly, the number above her head spasms, then morphs into *42*.

Hypnotised, I stare at the new number. Something has changed. The ciphers surrounding her block skyrocket through the ceiling and show no sign of slowing down. The Black Mark is in a lot of distress. She's struggling to maintain control over whatever situation she is in out there. With a snap of the fingers, the number changes again.

41

Again.

40

Again.

39

Then it stops. Her running ceases and her vitals begin to recover back to normal. The girl drops to the ground and buries her face in her arms. I want to reach out and console her, but I know this attempt would be pointless.

I turn my back on the girl and move farther down the aisle. Seeking out the Black Marks specifically now, I read the digits above their heads as I pass. Some numbers are as little as zero, whilst others surpass hundreds.

Reaching the door at the end of the hall, I turn the knob and stumble through the opening. The small, compact chamber seems to be some sort of waiting room. The leaden floor is slightly elevated at the far end and appears to lead to another exit that is not yet visible.

Aiesha runs up to me and grabs me in her arms. "You're safe," she says with a sigh of relief. The entire group is here, huddled in the corner. They're not sure where to go next. I count the heads of the survivors. There are twenty-two.

Most of the Marks have abandoned their weapons entirely, and the crafted tools now lie scattered across the room. The Feral have begun to wipe the remaining ash from their skin, revealing the marks on their arms. They now stand completely naked amongst the rest, some even beginning to converse nervously in their native tongues. The Feral leader is absent from the group, along with countless others.

Germ joins us, with Jester following shortly behind. "Look who I found!" Germ announces.

"John!" Jester throws himself onto me, dispensing with the formalities he'd previously restricted himself to. "You did it! You saved us from that dictator."

"I know what your marks mean," I finally tell them.

"What?" Germ's eyes widen in wonder.

"Bearer of knowledge," I reveal to him, stretching the words with a sort of mystical emphasis.

"The aliens said that?" he inquires, for once not too sure of the answer.

I nod. "But you already knew that, didn't you?"

Germ smiles, then buries his face into Jester as tears roll down his cheeks. I look over his shoulder to peer at Skylor, who has Talaya clasped tightly in her arms. Skylor's expression doesn't seem like that of someone who has just been saved. Instead, you'd think that her journey was far from over. She seems alone and lost without Rusty by her side. Whether she's trembling with excitement or as a result of the stressful events that played out a few moments ago is uncertain.

"Are we going to wake up now?" Talaya asks, her voice louder than it's ever been before.

I hesitate. The young girl seems excited, the life finally having returned to her eyes. I never thought we would get this far. Especially not her, I realise ashamedly. All fairytales have to come to an end. It's just part of growing up. But she's far from grown, and right now she doesn't need to come to terms with this reality.

"Not yet," I tell her. "But sooner than you think."

She carefully considers this and then nods in acceptance. After all, waiting is merely a prerequisite for something that is bound to take place eventually.

"What's going to happen to us?" Aiesha asks, her fingers wrapped inside of mine.

I look across the rows of faces staring back at me. I know that we are far from finished. The difficult part is yet to come, but they don't need to hear that. Not yet.

The room full of children waits for guidance. An answer. I straighten up and hide the growing fear and uncertainty behind a smile.

"We're going home."

A cheer erupts throughout the group as Marks of all colours begin to embrace each other. The room is engulfed by a golden gloom that blinds us almost instantly. A hand reaches out to grab me, but the fingers slip away and disappear along with everything else in a haze of light.

I don't know what comes after this, or if I'll remember what happened before. All of the atrocities that took place. The lives lost. Tomorrow I might see my mother sitting on my bed, waiting to tell me that I've been missing for an entire year. I'll be confused, with no memory of what happened. Only a well-placed sign might wake me from my slumber. A scar left behind. A mark.

They say it's common for abductees to forget their experiences almost completely upon return. Usually, all that remains is a lingering feeling of wanting to change the world for the better.

Perhaps that feeling is enough.

EPILOGUE

DF Malan High: One year before the abduction

"*A*re there any further questions concerning the upcoming biology finals?"

"Sir Steyn?"

"Yes, John."

"What is the most effective way of tracing a species' population growth?"

"Or, in most cases its decline," the teacher responds, "but nonetheless a relevant question. When scientists want to study a specific species, there are several ways of approaching the task at hand. One of the most popular approaches, and my personal favourite, is something we like to call the mark-and-search method. It involves removing a select few individuals from their environment and marking them separately, or in groups. This way, it is possible to distinguish them from the rest of the population. It is also common practice to conduct several tests to alter the individual's behaviour or physical workings before returning them to their original environment. Now, keep in mind that it is not always preferable to interfere with nature, but if the need arises to save a species from its own extinction, we are often left with no choice."

ACKNOWLEDGEMENTS

Thank you to my mother, who supported me
every step of the way.
My sister, who dragged me out of the house for fresh air.
Herman Steyn, my high school biology teacher, who
taught me the mark-and-search method.
Matthew, my esports caster in crime. A great
source of encouragement.
Jay, a dear friend. Today is my turn to publish, but
tomorrow is yours.
Jimmy, who saw my potential.
Hansel Pereira, who made the book's magical cover.
My online community: The Pack.
And lastly, my father. Gone, but never forgotten.

Printed in Great Britain
by Amazon